Interim
in the
Desert

INTERIM
in the
DESERT

>>>>>>

Stories by

Roland Sodowsky

Afterword by

Robert Flynn

Texas Christian University Press
Fort Worth

Library of Congress Cataloging-in-Publication Data

Sodowsky, Roland.
    Interim in the desert : stories / by Roland Sodowsky.
        p.   cm.
    ISBN 0-87565-079-1 : $19.95
    I. Title.
    PS3569.O377I68   1990
    813'.54—dc20
                                                                    90-50198
                                                                         CIP

The following stories were published previously:
"Duty and the Civic Beast," *Stone Drum*, Spring 1986.
"Tearing the House Down," *Pax: An International Journal of Art, Science, and Philosophy*, Winter 1985–86
"Orielle Bastemeyer, Where Are You?" *Cimarron Review*, Fall 1979.
"Nineswander's Fence," *Kansas Quarterly*, Summer 1989.
"World War II," *Concho River Review*, Fall 1990.
"Knoxless," *Cross Timbers Review*, Summer 1990.

Designed by Whitehead & Whitehead

Contents

For Willard and Pauline Sodowsky
and for
Christi, Stet, and Hondo

Interim in the Desert

I | »
KNOXless

I WAS five years old when my grandmother told me about the time she was locked in the toilet at the Knox store.

"Your dad had to make them take the door off," she said. "You remember that."

Her voice had a distant, warbling quality, as if it were indeed reverberating from behind a locked door, and I had no trouble imagining her trapped in the little orange-painted room with its frosted glass window high overhead. Her dying a few weeks later made the story even more prophetic and ominous, for she had seldom spoken to me. In fact, I don't think she ever told me anything else.

When I was older and my best friend Benny Grant was working at Knox's, I wondered why she had told me that story. As she related it, there was no question at any point while she shouted and banged on the door, which was less than ten feet from the cash register, and while my father helped remove the door—the grumbling pump attendant said there was nothing wrong with the lock—that the incident could have been funny. What was her dire warning? The button on the lock in a greasy restroom, I understood, barely suggested the evil she was hinting of. Even the room in which she had been caught, that upended orange coffin, was, I thought later when Benny worked at Knox's, only the symptom of a trap within a trap, and my grandmother did not know but felt the subtlety of the evil it represented.

She told me the story in the back seat of our Ford while

we were parked at the gas pump behind Knox's. I was afraid of the anger in her blue, watery eyes, and, as I listened to her then, I also feared for the most important event in my life, our Saturday trip to town. I used that toilet myself most Saturdays while my father bought gas, and when he paid at the counter Mr. Moser, the owner, included a bag of peppermints for me with my father's change.

Knox's was the last in a series of immeasurably pleasant stops in town. They included Martin's Grocery, where, if the butcher was in a good humor, I might be given a wiener; the bank, which gave away chewing gum; Armbruster's Feed Store, which had a salted peanut machine; Hallren's Creamery, where my father sold our cream, the employees all wore white, and there were exotic smells and continuous loud, satisfying clangs. Other farm families were making the same rounds, of course, including our neighbors, so at each of these stops there was a good chance I might see Benny, who was two years older than I and the fourth of the Grants' six children.

I was alert to anything that might jeopardize our trips to town, and a toilet with a treacherous lock might be just such a danger. Each Saturday came after what seemed like years of waiting, and I was perpetually afraid that the next one might not come at all. On some Saturdays, in fact, we stayed home. Every trip was uncertain until we were actually on the road. Only my mother and I really wanted to go. My father said there was too much work to do, my mother would only buy some useless nonsense in the five and ten or Cohlmia's Drygoods, the amount of cream we had to sell wouldn't pay for the gas to town. My grandmother recited a history of the scoundrels in town, the savings and loan that took my grandfather's money and went broke, the car with the ruined transmission that Ross Motor Company sold my uncle. My mother argued and I pleaded. It was touch and go.

The real name of the Knox store was "KNOXless," but we ignored the "less" part. Although the store faced Main Street and had a large orange and blue sign, it displayed little merchandise other than stacked buckets of grease and oil. Most of the business was done at the pumps in the rear, which customers reached through the alley. Probably the farmers went there to buy their dollar's worth of gas and a gallon of kerosene not because Knox's was cheaper but to avoid the newer cars that filled up under the fancy Cities Service and Sinclair signs on Main Street.

My grandmother was buried next to my grandfather under the bent cedars in Hilltop Cemetery. I saw that we went to town as often as ever—more often after she died—in spite of her experience at Knox's, so I forgot about her story until Benny went to work there. Mr. Moser at the Knox store died too—three years after my grandmother. The store was closed for two years, and the farmers had to buy their fuel on Main Street. Then Dale Brower leased it and opened it up again.

The year after my grandmother's death I started school, to my delight, for then I could see Benny every day. We weren't in the same classroom, but the Grant children got off at the next-to-last bus stop and I was last, so I could sit with Benny the length of the long, tedious route and give voice to the thousand ideas that teemed in my head whenever I saw him.

When I was eight I convinced my parents I was old enough to walk the two miles to the Grant house, and then I went there at least twice a week in the summer, probably to the disgust of Ord Grant, Benny's father, a small, grim man who tried to keep his children—there were seven by then—busy every daylight hour.

Ord raised turkeys in a pen large as a baseball diamond. The fence towered far above my head. The turkeys made endless noise and required endless work: feeding, watering, culling, dusting for one parasite or another, watching,

guarding. They escaped from the pen and had to be
caught. Some got sick and died, and others hanged themselves in the mesh of the fence. We seldom worried about
predators on our farm, but snakes, skunks, owls, eagles,
raccoons, coyotes, and bobcats were always a threat to the
Grants. All the Grant children performed, angrily, I
thought, tasks around the pen. Wanda, who was nearest
my age, seemed to me to be unrelated parts of stick-like
limbs, stringy hair, and sullenness that continually emerged
from the mesquites with another bucket of water for the
turkeys. As I talked and followed Benny, he showed me
where a coyote had dug under the fence, a bobcat had
climbed over, or traps set on the top of the posts had been
sprung. Once, when I arrived just after breakfast and while
the turkeys made an even more deafening row than usual, I
watched Ord shoot an enormous owl that had alighted on
a trap during the night. As the turkeys strutted about, their
round, fearful eyes followed me constantly. For the slightest reason—a dove veering overhead, a grasshopper with
the bad luck to land in the pen—they ran screaming to or
from things. I thought they were well suited to feed owls
and coyotes, and good for not much else.

In spite of Benny's many chores, we sometimes slipped
off to go fishing, and by the time I was nine Benny and I
had become fishermen. At first, using cane poles and grasshoppers, we fished for perch. Then Benny's grandfather,
who lived on the river and caught channel catfish, gave
him an old rod and reel, and I claimed a rod with a broken
tip that my uncle Gene, the one who had bought the car
with the bad transmission, had left at our house. We—
Benny, I should say, for he caught most of them—
discovered the joys of catching bass on artificial lures. We
became purists and forgot about perch. Ord Grant, I think,
let Benny go fishing with me because he could supply a
meal at the Grant table, where the family ate in two shifts.
Benny caught fish always, everywhere. I knew the ponds as

well as he, knew the mesquite stumps, drowned cedars, and dark walls of moss the bass lurked around and in, but they ignored my offerings and waited for Benny. I stood beside him, cast my lure in the same place at the same time as he did and reeled it in at the same speed, empty, while a bass leaped and struggled on his line.

I was never jealous of Benny as he filled his stringer, for he could always do things—important things—better than I. Although we were about the same height and weight, he was far stronger. He milked cows with a steady rhythm that layered the foam thickly in the bucket. In a race he quickly left me behind. On the school bus, in the game played across the aisle that we called slap-hands, he was so fast and devious that the tops of my hands were often still beet red and stinging after I had walked from the bus to our house. I never thought that the difference in our ages had anything to do with our abilities. I regarded even my intense Saturday browsing in the town library and the comic book racks at Jensen's Bookstore, places which did not interest Benny, as further evidence of his superiority.

Since I couldn't catch fish, I became an expert on lures. Our mailbox overflowed with fishing catalogs. Benny might catch a bass with a Hawaiian Wiggler, but I knew all the Wiggler models and their weights, their rubber skirt lengths and colors, and their trailer hook sizes, knew which came closest to being truly weedless, whether they floated or ran deep or shallow, and how the retrieval speed affected them. The names of the plugs—Silver Minnows, Finnish Minnows, Miracle Minnows, Wounded Minnows, Crippled Shad and Speed Shad, Hula Poppers and Jitterbugs, Mepps and Abu Spinners—rolled richly from my tongue when I chattered about them to Benny. I knew the sizes of their treble hooks and self-swivels, knew which had caught record bass in Florida and Georgia.

Being an expert didn't mean that I, or Benny, owned many lures. They were expensive by our standards, and by

our parents' too. If I was ever jealous of Benny, it was
when, at one of the ponds, he stumbled upon a new—
new!—Hawaiian Wiggler No. 3, its bright red and white
skirt intact, that some trespassing fisherman had lost. We
hoarded our money to buy plugs. If we snagged one on a
branch in a pond, we risked our lives to retrieve it.

So when Dale Brower reopened the Knox store and put
in a long counter of rods, reels, and most importantly,
lures, Knox's became the focal point of our lives—even
more so for Benny than me, because I couldn't give up the
library or Jensen's Bookstore. Every Saturday, thumbs
hooked in the pockets of our jeans, we inspected the rows
of cellophane-lidded boxes to see what lures had been
added or sold. Again and again we debated the merits of
gold, green, and red-and-white River Runts. I had read
that, all things being equal, bass preferred a red-and-white
lure over anything else, and I fervently believed this, although I had never caught a bass on one. Once we
watched blankly while a tourist selected, as casually as if
they were turnips, a dozen plugs, and Dale Brower ban-
tered pleasantly in his deep voice as he rang them up at the
cash register. Occasionally, when we had saved enough, we
picked out a Bomber or Flatfish or Whopper Stopper that
we had chosen and changed our minds about for weeks,
and bought it.

All the farmers knew Dale Brower. He looked more like
a preacher than a farmer, I thought—gaunt but handsome,
with fiery eyes and thick black hair—and indeed he sometimes preached in the rural churches. But he had been a
farmer too until the greenbugs, no respecters of looks, took
his wheat crop. He became a Bible salesman then.

He sold one to my parents one hot Sunday afternoon in
August. "Praise God!" he said as soon as the screen door
closed behind him. "Praise God!" He raised his right hand
until his fingers touched the low ceiling of our kitchen.

Then he dropped to one knee and prayed, and my parents bowed their heads.

They were hopelessly trapped from the moment he entered the house. At least, peering through the screen door from the porch, it seemed so to me as I watched them at the kitchen table, saw the eagerness and misery on my parents' faces as Dale bullied them with his unanswerable arguments—his bad luck on the farm, his status as a neighbor, God and their duty to Him, the undeniable need of our household for the magnificent Bible, solid as a block of granite, on the table before them, and their good luck that he had shown up to sell it to them. It wasn't an ordinary Bible, the kind people carried to church on Sundays; we had one of those. It was a huge Holy Family Tree, Lineage, and Historical Record Bible, with full-page color illustrations, maps, charts, concordance, commentaries, a dictionary, prayers and meditations for every day of the year, Easter dates to the year 2000, lists of miracles and strange and interesting facts, gilt-edged pages, bookmark ribbons of red and blue silk, and a thick section of terribly official pages for the recording of births, baptisms, marriages, military service, and deaths. It was leather bound, with—when ours arrived in the mail six weeks later—our name in gold on the cover.

The buying of the Bible unsettled my parents, I thought, as nothing ever had before. It cost forty dollars, and doubtless that much again in the monthly payment plan they agreed to. When it came they unwrapped it, set it on the kitchen table, and regarded it warily.

"I don't know where to put it," my mother said. "There isn't any place right for it in the front room."

My father put his hat on and turned toward the door. "Then we'll have to buy a good table for it. And a house good enough for the table."

"I didn't say buy it," my mother said.

"You didn't say not to."

"Neither did you."

Finally my mother removed their wedding photograph and some trinkets from a small table in the front room and put the Bible there. I could feel a tightness in the house for weeks afterwards, and it returned each month when my father removed one of the payment coupons from the book Dale Brower had left behind. And I noted that my parents, who both read the Bible regularly, continued to use the small, worn one they kept on the dresser in the bedroom.

The Grants didn't buy a Bible. "Ord didn't even let Dale get out of the car," Benny said. All the Grant children referred to Ord by his name or said "He" or "Him" in a way that couldn't mean anyone else. When they spoke to him directly, they didn't call him anything.

"What did he say to Dale?" I asked. I wanted to know. When Dale had been at the table with my parents, it had seemed to me that everything he said was irrefutable. Not *right*, but irrefutable if I had been my parents sitting at that table.

"He said, 'If it don't kill bobcats or feed turkeys you just as well get on down the road.' Then he went back to the turkey pen," Benny answered. I nodded. It occurred to me then—I had always known but never thought about it— that the Grants didn't go to church, and therefore would be immune to Bible salesmen. There wasn't a Bible in their house; I was sure of that. Ord's answer made sense, just as turkeys and atheism made sense. Their noise and the stupidity and perpetual terror in their staring eyes were godless, no doubt about that, and, Sunday or no Sunday, they had to be fed and watered. It was my parents' misfortune to be believers, and therefore easy prey to Dale Brower.

They were still making payments on the Bible when we heard that he had reopened the Knox store. My father said, "We know where he got the money to do that." My mother didn't answer. The winter after they bought the Bible there wasn't enough cream to sell, and we didn't go to town for weeks at a time. My father brought seed wheat from the granary which my mother cooked and we ate for cereal. I thought my parents wouldn't trade with Dale, but within a few weeks, after they had been to the bank, creamery, feed store, and grocery, they began pulling up to the pump in the alley behind Knox's just as if Mr. Moser hadn't died. I couldn't understand their lack of principle; Dale Brower had taken them—my father practically said so, and my mother's silence amounted to the same thing— yet here they were, back for more, as if an old habit were more important than their pride. I was ashamed of them.

My own interest, and presence, in the new Knox's I had no trouble justifying: there wasn't a comparable counter of fishing lures anywhere else in town, so I had no choice. But I still disliked Dale. I counted out my dollar and thirty-five cents to him grudgingly, knowing that, although I needed the Hawaiian Wiggler far more than my parents had needed the Bible gathering dust in our front room, I had nevertheless been cornered by Dale, as they had been, and separated from my money.

It was not long after the Knox store reopened that changes began happening between me and Benny, or I should say happening to Benny that changed his behavior toward me. They started when he was in the eighth grade and got worse when he went into high school. His voice deepened, he broke out with pimples, and suddenly—sud- den to me; one day we simply weren't the same height anymore—he was several inches taller than I. Now we sat together until Virgil Scholtiss and A. J. Barnes got on, and then he moved to the back of the bus with them and they whispered, snickered, elbowed each other, and grunted barnyard noises the rest of the way to school. In the eve- nings the pattern was reversed. All this was not easy for me; at first I could not comprehend it when, in the evenings, I found Benny's legs braced across the seat in the universal "Don't sit here" signal of school bus language. I argued; then I gave up and adapted.

Benny learned to masturbate, and he reported his score each morning: "Fire one," "Twins," or sometimes "Triplets." It was pointless to me, but I pretended interest because he was interested. He worried about his pimples. I thought I wouldn't have any, because my cousin hadn't. We still fished together, but often when I walked over to the Grant farm, even when we had agreed to meet, I was told that Benny had gone off with Virgil on his motor scooter, fishing, or A. J. and his father had picked Benny up in the Barnes' pickup.

When we did go fishing, I saw that Benny had accumulated in his tackle box twice as many of the plugs, the good ones, that we had eyed and wished for, and I couldn't buy.

"Ord's paying me to trap around the turkey pens," he explained. Ord had built a second turkey pen that spring, even larger than the first, and something, coyotes or more likely wild dogs, had gotten in and killed thirty young turkeys.

"How much does he pay you?" I asked.

"Dollar for skunks and possums. Five dollars for anything else." Benny grinned. The week before, he said, he had trapped a possum near the creek. "I sneaked it up to the pens and shot it, and Ord paid me for it."

But one Saturday when I was studying the lures at Knox's and Benny was there with Virgil Scholtiss and A. J. Barnes I discovered another reason why Benny had more plugs than I. The three of them had been talking and joking with Dale Brower before they came over to the fishing tackle display. Dale had put in some shelves for car accessories—rear-view mirrors, steering-wheel knobs and covers, pistol-grip spotlights and the like—and floor-to-ceiling racks of tires. He had a special on tires, and there were several other people in the store. A town boy, Gary Frazier, was working out back at the pumps while Dale ran the cash register and waited on customers inside.

"There's a new Lazy Ike," I said to Benny, edging between him and A. J. Barnes. "Did you see it? And a Paul Bunyan Sixty-Six—"

"Beat it," A. J. whispered. His elbow hit me in the ribs.

"What?"

"Beat it," he said again. His pointed nose and face were so close to mine I could see the Clearasil on his forehead.

I doubled my fists. Virgil was as big as a man, but A. J. was thin and, even in the cowboy boots he wobbled around in, shorter than Benny. He was a bully when he could be, and I thoroughly disliked him, especially since Benny had started changing.

Benny said, "Go on. I'll talk to you later."

I started to protest but stopped when he pushed me away. He was looking over Virgil's shoulder in the direction of Dale, who was with a customer at the tire racks. Virgil half-turned from the counter, as if to hide Benny and A. J. I backed off then, stubbornly, pretending to look at some mud flaps with reflectors on them and then at a counter of mufflers and chromed ends for exhaust pipes. Finally I left the store. I crossed the street, went inside the post office, and watched through the window. I was still mad.

The three of them came out a few minutes later. They stopped in front of the windows at the dime store and at Cohlmia's Drygoods. A. J., who was walking between Benny and Virgil, kept glancing back at Knox's. They crossed the street and walked more quickly down the next block. When they disappeared around the corner, I waited a little longer, then went back to Knox's. The Lazy Ike was gone, the Paul Bunyan Sixty-Six, and, I was pretty sure, a Tadpolly. I knew they had taken the lures, but for a moment, recalling their thumbs hooked as usual in the front pockets of their tight jeans, I couldn't understand how. Then I remembered A. J.'s cowboy boots, the tops of them. The boxes would fit there neatly.

I never said anything to Benny about that. I worried about him getting caught and at the same time hoped that Virgil and A. J. would be. That same Saturday night, however, I looked at the massive unopened Bible in our front room and felt a satisfaction in their stealing from Dale Brower. He deserved it, for he too was a kind of thief, a worse kind. It was complicated; Dale and his family had to eat, I understood that. But so did we, and somewhere in there right and wrong were mixed up with need and weakness and bullying and God. It was like a puzzle, not with missing pieces, but too many.

Benny understood, I was sure, that I knew. On Monday we sat together as usual on the bus, and it wasn't anything he said that told me he knew, but the way he talked, a way that meant, "We'll talk about this, but really about this." It was a tone I had heard him use with Virgil and A. J., and had thought it sounded mean, but now it included me, and I liked it. He talked of sprung traps at the turkey pens, of touching girls' breasts accidentally and intentionally, of the senior boys' conquests in the back seats of cars. I basked in his tone and was part of, I thought, the hard wisdom in his eyes, until Virgil and A. J. climbed on the bus.

It seemed to me that things had turned around as Benny and I got older, that I knew less and talked less and he more and more, and now I thought this made sense, that I should learn from him. I had begun to feel stirrings myself like Benny's; sitting with a girl on the bus, which had never occurred to me before, now interested me. Surprisingly, some of them liked the idea too, and the braced-leg "Don't sit here" signal, or moving the leg suddenly, which meant an invitation, took on a complexity I hadn't imagined before. Even Wanda Grant had become whole, rounded, lively-eyed, and beckoning. I had pimples too, despite my cousin. And I was also, finally, beginning to catch bass; I hadn't told Benny yet, but I was learning.

Three weeks after Benny, Virgil, and A. J. stole the plugs at Knox's, Benny got a Saturday job there. Gary Frazier was to help Dale inside, and Benny was in charge at the gas pumps.

"If I'm not busy at the pumps, I'm supposed to help in here," Benny told me. I was standing at the fishing tackle counter. The Lazy Ike had been replaced, and there was a new jointed L&S Panfish Master, brown with bright yellow stripes. I had been reading about it; it floated at rest and dove when it was pulled. The jointed body gave it a double-action wriggle. I knew it would catch bass.

"How come he gave you a job?" I asked.

Benny grinned the way he had when he'd told me about pulling the possum trick on Ord. "Every time we came in here, I'd hit him up about it. Last Saturday he said okay."

It was like, I thought, turning a young coyote loose in one of Ord's turkey pens. I looked at the little room in the corner at the back of the store and remembered, for the first time in years, my grandmother's warning. Dale had repainted the restroom, using what must have been the original can of orange paint. I wondered if Knox's was the trap, or Benny was, or both were; if the trap had a trap in it.

I started telling Benny what I had read about the Panfish Master, but Virgil and A. J. came in then, so I left.

"Why did Dale Brower hire Benny?" I asked at supper that night. "Why didn't he hire a town boy?"

"Dale's from out here," my mother said. "Maybe he wanted to hire someone he knows."

I said, "I don't know why people out here trade with him anyway, after he gypped them with those Bibles. Us too."

My mother said mildly, "Oh, were they a gyp?"

"Gyp or not, that's where we trade," my father said.

"It's better to be gypped by someone you know?"

He frowned at me and tapped the table. "It's better to know when you're talking too much."

The following Saturday Virgil Scholtiss and A. J. Barnes were sitting on the fenders of A. J.'s dad's pickup in front of Knox's when I went in. I didn't speak to them because they usually ignored me, but as I passed through the door, A. J. said, "*He* can go in, the little son of a bitch."

Benny saw me but didn't speak. Gary Frazier was at the cash register, and Dale was showing mud tires to a farmer. The Panfish Master was still there, but I had spent my money on used comic books at Jensen's. There hadn't been enough to buy it anyway. I checked the rest of the counter. Shimmy Wrigglers in three colors had been added, and there were two new Daredevles.

I thought Dale had probably kicked Virgil and A. J. out because they were hanging around Benny when he was supposed to be working. I didn't want that to happen to me, so I left soon.

As I walked out, A. J. said, "What'd you get?"

"Nothing."

"Nothing? You went in, didn't you?"

"Just looked." I felt stupid.

"Just looked." A. J. mimicked me in a high nasal voice. "We ought to turn him upside-down and shake him out."

"Ought to." Virgil nodded.

"Ought to tell Brower he's stealing plugs."

"Ought to," Virgil said. I walked away quickly.

The next week I looked around for Virgil and A. J. before I went in but saw no sign of them. Benny was dusting shelves. He came over to the fishing counter quickly when he saw me.

"Some guys this morning said that's the hottest plug on the lake." He pointed at the Panfish Master. "You ought to get it."

"I'm broke," I said.

Benny looked toward the back. Gary Frazier was pecking at the adding machine by the cash register, and Dale was standing beside him talking on the telephone. Benny said, "You ought to get it anyway."

"What?"

"Take it anyway."

He glanced at the back again, then reached over and unfastened a middle button on my shirt. He said in a low voice, "Just slip it in there and button it."

"I'm scared to."

Dale laughed loudly, hung up the phone, and began talking to Gary. Benny said, "Dale's going to help me reset the counter on the pump. Just stick it in your shirt. Look at something else a little bit, and leave."

"What about Gary?" I asked.

"He never leaves the cash register. Go on, *do it*."

"All right," I said, and slid the box inside my shirt.

Benny and Dale went out the back door together. Gary was still running the adding machine. I was very scared. The painted eyes of the plugs on the counter reminded me of the staring turkeys in the Grants' pens, and again I remembered my grandmother and her warning. Thinking of excuses I could make up to Benny, I took the box out and put it back in its place on the counter, hoping that would ease the thumping in my chest. I rebuttoned my shirt and moved over to pretend to look at a rack of seat cushions.

"So long," I called to Gary as I went out the front door, and then I stopped. Dale was blocking my way.

His hand closed over my wrist. "Thou shalt not steal. That's the eighth commandment. Don't you know that, young man?" He smiled broadly. I was puzzled for a moment until I realized that he had come around the building. Then I was frightened.

"I didn't steal anything," I said.

"The eighth commandment. Your folks should have taught you that." He tightened his grip on my wrist. Two farmers, one of them a huge man in striped overalls and a red flannel shirt, stopped with their children to watch us, and across the street I saw Virgil and A. J. under the post office awning.

Dale said, "Now I'm going to give you a chance to be honest and redeem yourself. Will you take that chance?"

"I didn't steal anything," I repeated.

"All right," He glanced around, still smiling, at the little group that had formed. "Let's say you didn't. Then let's say you tell me what this is." He slapped my stomach with his free hand, then again. His smile faded, and he slapped me once more. He jerked my tucked shirt from my jeans, pulling off one of the buttons, and raised it.

The big farmer stepped toward us and waggled his finger at Dale. "That's enough. You can't undress him." He chuckled and spat tobacco in the gutter. "Look like you caught the wrong boy."

"I got the right one," Dale said. He turned and shouted into the store, "Gary!" But Gary had come to the door and was standing right in front of him. I looked into the store too, but not for Gary.

"L&S Panfish Master. You see if it isn't gone," Dale said. He still held my wrist while we waited.

"It's right here," Gary called.

The farmer waggled his finger at my wrist, and Dale released me. "Well, I was sure—" Dale began. I wasn't listening to him. I was still peering toward the back of the store, beginning to blubber. Then my parents pushed into the circle, and I heard my mother's sharp, angry questions and an unfamiliar tone, placating and hopeless, in Dale's voice. And I thought how big my father's fists looked as he tried to push past the farmer in the striped overalls, who gently blocked the door as Dale retreated inside.

What happened that Saturday probably had nothing to do with Dale's bankruptcy a few months later, although I liked to think that it had. My parents stopped trading there, of course, not that their dollar or dollar and a half a week made any difference.

But that was all later and meant little to me. On the bus that Monday morning I thought about my grandmother's ominous words again. I had nearly been trapped in Knox's, would have been if I weren't so scared; if, one part of me thought, I weren't weaker than Benny in still another way. Dale had fired Benny, so Benny had been trapped, but Dale too had been caught. I remembered reading about Chinese boxes; it was a little like them, except these boxes had names like trust and betrayal and accusation, and sometimes they fit inside, sometimes outside each other, you were never sure.

I was thinking about these things when Benny got on. As I had expected, he passed on toward the back of the bus without looking at me. The worst part was that if he had pointed at my leg braced across the seat and said, "Move it," I would have done so, joyfully.

2 » World War II

I FIRST became aware of the second World War because of two workhorses, Pal, a bay gelding, and Nellie, a black mare, that my father used to plow the fields on our farm in Comanche Valley. There is a photograph in our family album, taken by my father with his Kodak, of me in overalls on Pal's broad back, looking small and frightened.

One day we had a Ford tractor, and the horses were gone. I was told they had been sent to a glue factory.

"What for?" I asked.

"For the war," my father said.

"What's the war?"

I don't remember his answer, or whether I thought the horses would survive the glue factory. But it was clear that the war, which could replace two enormous, fat-rumped horses with a sleek gray tractor—the greatest change in my life up to then—was not to be taken lightly.

That must have been in 1943. Perhaps selling the horses brought the war home to my parents and made them think that my father's turn for the draft was nearing, and that they should not rely on one sickly boy to perpetuate themselves. Or maybe the price of wheat went up that year. At any rate my mother gave birth to my brother, Ted, in June 1944.

By then I had heard of the Germans and the Japanese.

The sharp monosyllable *Jap* stuck with me, as *German*—
which I confused with *germ*—did not.

One hot day the summer Ted was born, my father gave
me the corn knife and told me to cut the pigweeds around
the one tree, a demoralized cedar, in our yard.

"The chiggers will get all over me," I protested. "It's too
hot."

"Play like the weeds are Japs," he said. "Cut the weeds
and kill the Japs."

Before I tired of the game, I had left weed stobs to dry
hard as iron not only around the tree but along the path
all the way to the henhouse.

I was spanked once because of the war. One afternoon
that same summer Mrs. Bastrop came with her daughter,
Carla, to visit my mother. I was six then, ready to start
school, and already something of a big mouth. Carla was
the same age, but she was larger than I. I told her about
the Japs.

"They kill people with corn knives," I said. "They're
mean men and they kill little girls."

"Where are they?" she asked, looking around.

"In Kansas." I knew about Kansas because we had gone
there to my uncle's farm for Thanksgiving.

"Where's that?"

I pointed up the hill where the road disappeared. "Over
there. They're coming to chop off your arms and legs with
a corn knife."

She ran screaming into the house, and my mother
spanked me with the butter paddle.

My father was never drafted. Later, after my clash with
Carla Bastrop and when Tommy Baker lived on the Clark
place, I was disappointed that he had not been one of
those who came home with empty ammo boxes, bayonets,
and mortar shells made into ashtrays.

Comanche Valley had its heroes from the war. Jack Major had been on the Normandy beach on D-Day. He had a

white cross-stitched scar that ran from his ear to the tip of his chin. The day after he came home he rode a horse up into the hills, roped a two-year-old steer, tangled his leg in the rope, and couldn't get loose from either the steer or his horse. His father rescued him several hours later.

Alfred Hadl had been in the Second Armored Division. His tank was hit by a mortar shell, and he was trapped inside for twenty-four hours. He was a tall, red-faced, thick-shouldered man with large hands, a heavy jaw, and angry eyes. He seldom spoke, and I thought people were afraid of him; I was, for certain. When he and Jack Major came to the high school basketball games, they smelled strongly of whiskey. And there were others like Tommy Baker whose experiences, or ordeals, I had not heard of.

Alfred Hadl eventually married Ida Gladden, the high school history teacher. The year before she married Alfred, Ida roomed with a widow on a farm, and she rode the school bus with us. Some of the children—girls as well as boys—corrupted "Gladden" to "Goblin" and screamed "Miss Goblin! Miss Goblin!" at her each evening on the bus. I fell in love with her, a little, that year. She was not pretty, and probably not as young as her long-toothed smile made her seem. She never became angry at the children, at least that anyone could see, but she must have hated the teasing, for it was cruel, and the children meant it so. When she married Alfred I was puzzled twice over: puzzled because his height and size and the anger in his eyes were frightening to me, and he seemed remote and powerful, full of knowledge gained at some terrible cost; puzzled because Ida Gladden—Ida Hadl—seemed wholly unaware of his anger and remoteness.

I fought with Carla Bastrop at the Hadl's wedding. The children in Comanche Valley were perpetually at war. I remember recesses at school in terms of arm-twisting, gouging thumbs, and desperately angry wrestling on ground that grew only sandburs. As the runt of my age

group and the loudest, I was often a target. In the church-
yard after the wedding, Carla, who was a head taller,
cornered me with two of her friends and stuck her white,
splotchily chapped face in mine.

"Your dad's a CO."

"He is not." I didn't know what a CO was; probably
she didn't either.

"CO! CO!"

"He's not!"

They tore my shirt and bloodied my nose before we were
separated. On the way home my mother said CO stood for
"conscientious objector" and explained what it meant.

"Are you?" I asked my father.

"No."

"Dad was just too old to be drafted," my mother said.

Carla called me "CO" once at school the next week, but
a teacher heard her, and that was the end of that. From
then on I was on the alert; I believed my mother, but our
honor—courage, virility, ferocity, whatever—had been im-
pugned. It fell upon me to defend us.

Our school was small and poor. Our books were ancient; it was not unusual to find our mother's or father's
name among the many others scribbled inside the tattered
covers. In the age of the atomic bomb, we read about the
Spartan phalanx, the Macedonian long spear, and the Roman short sword.

When I was eleven I translated this reading into a sizable
undertaking during the vacation Bible school picnic on Comanche Creek. A sandy bend on the creek was overgrown
with giant sunflower stalks from the previous year, and I
saw that they would make perfect spears. I organized all
the children, sixty or seventy of them, into two armies,
appointed an opposing general, and we maneuvered, am-
bushed, killed, maimed, took prisoners: we made war.
When the teachers finally broke it up, they banned me from
Bible school. I didn't care, for I had found my vocation.

If I had my doubts about that notion, they were dis-spelled that fall by Tommy Baker. In him I found a hero, from my point of view more than a war hero: he brought the war to me.

The Bakers bought the Clark place that summer and moved into the old house half a mile south of us. It was near the corner where I met the school bus. When wheat-sowing was over in October, an extra pickup was often parked besides Tommy's when I got off the bus after school. I could see the men, the two older Keeler brothers, Frosty Tucker, and sometimes others, squatting with Tommy under the sparse cedars in front of the house.

I was drawn to this circle of men in their ragged, dirty blue jeans or overalls, their denim jumpers and red-checked caps and battered workshoes, these men with their ciga-rette papers, Bull Durham sacks, and guttural laughs and their sticks eternally tracing something, nothing, in the fine dust at their feet, as nothing had ever drawn me before. Each day as I left the bus corner I passed more slowly and bent my route closer to them, until I stood outside the cir-cle under the cedars listening, and finally I squatted too, not quite in the circle, not quite out. They never—Tommy Baker or any of the others—acknowledged my presence with words, yet, I felt, they accepted it with their silence.

"We all took care of Mattigan," Tommy would say. He was a small, compact man with a long, rectangular face. When he talked a knot of muscle worked at the hinge of his jaw, shadows played along a furrow in each cheek, and his lips pulled apart from clean straight teeth in a skewed grin. I remember that grin as being very important to me— to the circle of men, to us. It included us in what I came to understand as the iron mirth of maleness, and war.

"Mattigan was an old Arkansas hillbilly, always whit-tling on a whistle or something like that. He wanted to kill a Jap more than anybody you ever saw. He'd beg Sarge to let him go out on patrols, and here was the rest of us hop-

ing to God we didn't get picked. Sarge would say, 'Mattigan, you old fart, your joints creak so loud you'd get us all
killed.'

"One day we captured four Japs. That evening Sarge had
us take those Japs over behind a little knoll from our pe-
rimeter, and he told Mattigan to guard them for the night.
Old Mattigan looked at him, and he said, 'Sarge, I'll watch
them like they was my own babies.'"

Tommy paused to glance around the circle. There was a
hard edge in his voice that we all—I and the others in the
circle—responded to. It felt good, hearing him. His one-
sided grin had a ruefulness in it; it said, This was bad, you
could kill, you could die; that's how it was, and we were
there. It said we were hard too; it said we knew there
wasn't much difference between living and not living, and
we weren't worried about it. It invited us to join Tommy
there in some nameless place in the Pacific, and we
accepted.

"About midnight comes pow! pow! pow!—a whole slew
of shots behind that knoll—and we heard Mattigan yell.
We grabbed our rifles and ran over there, and there he was
leaning against a tree stump cutting a plug of tobacco.
Grinning like a skunk in a henhouse. The Japs were all
dead, just where we'd left them. Mattigan told the Sarge,
'Them sons of bitches tried to escape, Sarge; I hollered, but
they just kept a-running.'"

Tommy struck a match on a brass button on his overalls
and re-lit the stub of his cigarette. "They were still tied up
tighter'n sausages. He shot his whole clip into them."

Tommy laughed then, and the men around the circle
laughed too in low, grudging tones, glancing up at him
from the cross-hatched lines they had drawn with their
sticks.

I soon gave up trying to imitate that edge in Tommy's
voice and his rueful grin. What I really wanted was the

fatalism behind the voice and the grin, what I conceived of as a kind of invulnerability. You could be made to fear, you could be killed, but you couldn't be made to give up that hard laughter. It was beyond flesh and bullets.

"Once a shell about buried Sarge in his foxhole," Tommy told us. "He ran over and jumped in a hole with Joe Slape. Joe was an old farm boy from Missouri. He turned white-headed first week he was with us. Sarge jumped in and hunkered down with him, and then he sniffed the air and hollered, 'Joe, I believe you've crapped your pants.' Old Joe said, 'Yep, and I'm going to do it again, unless you want to crawl out of this hole and do it for me.'"

The Keeler brothers and the others who listened to Tommy were in their early twenties then, too young by a year or so to have been drafted before the end of the war. I thought that might be why they listened so intently— knowing how close they had come to being taken from Comanche Valley and set down in the deadly places Tommy talked about. But there was something else, too. Frosty Tucker, his head cocked and his teeth caught over his lower lip, listened to Tommy in good-natured idiocy; while in the Keeler brothers I recognized even then a proto-ness in their ridged brows and flat foreheads, their long, chinless heads. And that was good to me, too: the simple-ness, the responses to Tommy's stories that were no more than man-animal grunts.

That fall and the next spring when it was again warm enough to squat under the cedars, while his two little girls chased each other in and out of the trees and ignored us as we ignored them, Tommy Baker more than made me yearn to be in dangerous places, to fight and defend and suffer with other men. He filled me with the certainty that I would do these things. I began to grow, finally, that win-ter, to catch up with my classmates; I understood that growth as part of what I learned from Tommy, part of a grim pressing forward in my life. I would be a soldier; there would be war.

Tommy often repeated himself. That was all right: I re-told his stories with him, my lips moving silently.

"The American soldier is the meanest son of a bitch on earth," he told us. "The meanest man I ever saw was a little guy from Chicago name of Levitt."

Tommy had been arranging rows of blue cedar berries in the dust as he talked. "Damnedest thing Levitt did once. He got a coil of copper wire and lined up a bunch of Jap heads on the ground. Then he wired them all together, like this—" Tommy pointed at the cedar berries—"and he gave them orders: 'Left face!' he'd say, and turn them left; 'Right face!' and he'd turn them right. He did it all day long."

In April the greenbugs ate Tommy Baker's wheat and everyone else's in Comanche Valley. That summer Tommy got a job at Boeing in Seattle, leased out his land, and the Bakers moved away. I never saw Tommy again.

I became Ida Hadl's best student before I was ever in her classes. As a sixth and seventh grader I read all I could find about the Napoleonic wars, the Civil War, the Great War, World War II. I read all of Ernie Pyle's books and found, I thought, in Bill Mauldin's Willy and Joe cartoons confir-mation of the truths I had heard from Tommy Baker.

I went to Ida Hadl with my questions: how could Napo-leon, much less Hitler, not have prepared better for the Russian winters? Why wasn't World War II also a trench war? Which was the best helmet?—the British inverted sau-cer, the German deep tortoise shell? She didn't have the answers, but she helped me look for them.

When I went to their house, Alfred Hadl listened but seldom spoke. Occasionally something we said amused him, and his rumbling laughter startled me. The anger I used to sense in him had abated, I thought. I became more at ease around him, although his size—he was not fat; he towered over everyone, massive and solid—still manifested to me some knowledge, some powerfulness beyond other men's, maybe even Tommy Baker's. These men, Tommy Baker and Alfred Hadl, whom I had never seen together, became inseparable in my mind during my teenage years. One had told me everything about war, and, I thought, fear: how to face it, to laugh at it, and to love it. The other, Alfred Hadl, had told me nothing, not one word, yet his silence was important to me; I felt that I had learned as much, almost, from it as from Tommy Baker's stories.

When I became Ida's student in fact, I was a nuisance with my questions and with my impatience at peacetime history. The history of the world was the history of war. I rejoiced when the Korean War started; the timing was perfect, and when I was needed most I would be ready. I grieved when it ended before I was old enough to go.

By my sophomore year I had decided that my way to war was through West Point. My grades were good. I had already won the county history prize twice, and an essay I had written about infantrymen's weapons took second in a state American Legion contest. I bombarded our representative with letters, sent him clippings, and got Ida Hadl and my other teachers to write him. I received nothing but form letters in reply, so after graduation I enrolled at the teacher's college in Bixton, which still had an ROTC unit then. I signed up for the Army ROTC basic courses, and I tried out for and won a place on the drill team. I managed to spend much of my time in my ROTC uniform, which I recognized as World War II surplus.

At the end of the first semester I took my finals and came home to Comanche Valley, and, when Christmas was over, I paid a visit to the Hadls.

After Ida and I—with Alfred listening—had talked at the kitchen table for half an hour, she brought out a jug of red wine. We speculated about what West Point would have been like, and I told them about ROTC—the Tuesday formations, classes taught by graying non-coms, drill team practice at sunup. Remembering the anger I used to sense in him, I was uncomfortably aware of Alfred listening. I wondered what he thought of my playing soldier—what it must appear to him I was describing. I wanted to ask him about the war, wanted to say, "Could you tell me about the tank?" Instead I said to Ida, "Once I was going to write a paper for you about the medals Comanche Valley veterans had brought home. I wonder how many there were in Comanche Valley."

She replied, "You wouldn't have found out about it, but Alfred has a Bronze Star in a shoebox somewhere."

"Where it belongs," Alfred said, his tone closing the subject.

"I must've been a pain in the neck to you in school," I said later, when the jug was nearly empty and Alfred, although he was still drinking, seemed to be nodding off.

"Your feuding with Carla Bastrop was a nuisance. I never knew whether you were fighting or flirting." Ida frowned. "I worried about your fascination with war."

I said, "That started with Tommy Baker. Do you remember when he lived in the Clark house? I used to sit out there under the cedars listening to his war stories. I suppose he was in the Philippines, or the Solomon Islands."

Ida looked at Alfred, and neither spoke for a moment. Then Alfred gripped the edge of the table with his huge hands, leaned back, and his laughter rumbled.

Ida said, "Tommy Baker wasn't in the Pacific. He never left Texas during the war."

"Almost made it to San Diego," Alfred said, and laughed again. "War stories!"

He stood up and turned toward the bathroom, stumbled, half-fell, and vomited in the bathroom doorway.

At home in bed that night, my head—I was awake, not

dreaming—tumbled with images of foxholes, the bodies of Japanese soldiers, Tommy Baker's skewed grin; again and again I heard Alfred Hadl's laughter and saw him coughing over a puddle of wine-red vomit. But most of all I saw a circle of squatting men and not quite outside the circle a small, intense boy, squatting too, and listening; then the men were gone and he was still there, still listening. I slept and woke up to feel the bed spinning, and I too became sick, but my nausea was as much from anger—fury at Tommy Baker, at myself—as from the wine.

In the morning, as my mother and I cleaned up the mess, she said, "You must have had an interesting visit at the Hadl's."

"I learned a lot," I muttered.

Back in Bixton in January, I quit ROTC. I graduated in 1960, the same year that Ida Hadl, tired perhaps of the endless procession of students, dull or precocious, gave up teaching. I was hired to take her place, and Carla Bastrop and I were married. Fifteen years later—we were divorced by then—I became the principal.

I wasn't drafted, but my brother Ted was sent to Vietnam, and he was killed near Da Nang.

Before he left, I told him, "Take care of Number One. That's you." Was it the kind of thing, I remember wondering, that Tommy Baker would have said? Had I gotten that phrase from him? If Tommy hadn't been such a liar, I thought later, I might have died there instead of Ted; once I had imagined I was ready for that.

I was never a very good teacher, although not bad enough to be fired from Comanche Valley. I cared little for the students' interest in history, or lack of it. Sometimes I questioned our textbooks. "Books are written by people, not God," I would say; "People make mistakes about facts. This book is just one person's idea of what the facts are."

Seven years after I became principal, a young man came into my office one July day to apply for a position teaching biology. His name was Willis Baker, he said. His family still owned some land in Comanche Valley, the Clark place it was called, and his father had grown up in the community—had, in fact, known me when I was a boy.

"So you're Tommy Baker's son."

"Yes, sir." He had Tommy's face: plumper cheeks, the skewed grin less pronounced, his voice softened. "Dad said to see if you were still here, that you might remember him."

"I remember a couple of little girls," I said; "no son."

"I was born in Seattle. I probably wasn't even a gleam in Dad's eye when you knew him."

I smiled. "How is your dad?"

His eyes dropped. "He died in May. He had malaria, you know, from when he was in the Philippines during the war. The doctor said it finally caught up with him."

I felt a malaria-like chill myself, as if the mimosa outside my window was bending from a January, not a July, wind. I said, "He died of malaria?"

"Yes."

I thought of teaching history for fifteen years in a country school, of seven years of making schedules for teachers. I thought, with a nostalgia that made me shiver a second time, of men dying in the mud and in glory in forgotten, terrible places: Tommy Baker's hard, grinning men.

The young man asked, "Did you know Dad well?"

"He never spoke to me, that I can remember." I added absently, "But I used to think he had told me more than anyone else."

He looked across the desk at me with a puzzled expression then, and I in turn regarded him suspiciously, wondering whether he, or I, or both of us, or neither, was telling riddles.

3 | » Talking at a Slant

THE winter I was seventeen the main thing my family talked about at the supper table was poverty, in the form of the Alf Keeler family. Actually my mother and I did most of the talking. My father and my brother Ted, who was fifteen, just listened. Ted was never there without David Newgiver anyway, and they were always snickering about something else between themselves.

This talk about the Keelers started because I had suddenly resumed a friendship with Ira Keeler, whom I hadn't had much to do with since our sophomore year when I caught up with him in height, boxed him evenly, beat him out on the basketball team, and decided he was too dumb to waste time on. So when, one Friday in December, I went over to the Keelers' house to meet Ira instead of taking out Gaylene Helm, the preacher's daughter, my mother was primed with questions all the next week.

"You probably had a nice supper," she said Monday evening.

"Had fried ham."

"Get your elbow off the table. Did Mrs. Keeler fix it real nice? Or one of the girls?"

"Birdie—Mrs. Keeler did it."

"Ted, put your knife down before you eat that. Who served it?"

"Irene—or Onda, I don't know. They just set it on the table."

"On a nice plate, I guess," my mother said.

"Um."

"Did the girls set the table real nice?"

"I guess."

It was pretty complicated and oblique. This was meant to get me to how many plates the Keelers had, and knives, forks, and spoons; to whether the plates matched and there was room at the table for Birdie Keeler and her daughters to eat with us—the Keeler males and me, and, although my mother did not know he was there, Junior Goacher—or afterwards; and mainly to where Irene Keeler was.

That was how we got to poverty by talking about the Keelers. My mother was interested in poverty only because, in her eyes, the Keelers *were* poverty, and she thought I wanted to get mixed up with Irene Keeler. She was right.

That was my senior year in high school, 1961. One morning the previous summer our milk cow Blackie started riding, which was what we called it when a cow was in heat. Across the road our herd bull—my father had bought him from Harold Newgiver, David's father, and his registration name was Domino Apocalypse III—had caught Blackie's scent, and he leaned against the fence, bawling. After we finished the chores my father said, "Put a halter on Blackie and take her over to the animal before he tears the fence down." I saddled the horse, led the cow across the road, tied the halter to a mesquite so her romance wouldn't carry her off into the range pasture, hooked my leg over the saddle horn, and watched her and Domino go at it. My father, I knew, intended this to be my education in sexual matters, all of it; we would not discuss what I saw, or whether snubbing a cow to a mesquite in a pasture might differ from a human relationship.

I mention this because it was the way we told or did not tell each other things, for my parents were at least as reticent to find out as to reveal. My father wouldn't even use the word *bull*: cows were cows, but Domino was an *animal*, and the way my father used the word it sounded like the underside of the unspeakable.

None of us had much acquaintance with real poverty, but my mother had been closer to it than my father. Once, while she was snapping green beans, she told me about when the bank foreclosed on her parents' farm near Goldendale, Kansas. She was eight years old. She started crying while the milk cows were being auctioned off, and an old woman said to her, "Well, your papa's ruint, ain't he?"

In Comanche Valley we were neither poor nor rich. Harold Newgiver drove a Buick and could have afforded a Cadillac, but I think he had, as we all had, some antiquated notion of the evenness of things, despite the evidence to the contrary, or at least he wanted to keep up that appearance. He owned all the bottom land in the valley, the land that, in just a few years, would put you on the board of the Minnekah Savings and Loan and of any church in town. After the homesteaders had broken the sod and themselves in those desperate early years, his father had come with money during a dry spell and simply bought them out. No one ever talked of these things, however, and I think we were all grateful to Harold for buying only a Buick Roadmaster, just as we were grateful to General Motors for making the Chevrolets our neighbors (whose land wasn't quite as good as Harold's) bought, the same Chevrolets which, when they were traded in, people like my parents bought, and which, when they were completely worn out, we sold to people like the Keelers.

My mother was also grateful to the Newgivers because Harold's wife, Marie, encouraged David's friendship with my brother Ted, even though Ted was a year younger. Ted had a 4-H Club way of planting his feet apart and looking you straight in the eye; his voice made you think of sincerity, and he made straight As. The Newgivers probably thought some of this would rub off on David, and my mother thought the rich would rub off on Ted. She wouldn't have put it like this.

My parents had differing notions about the Keelers. Alf Keeler's father had planted cotton and ruined the Keeler farm just as my grandfather had ours, so when my father saw him squatting in the shade at the bank corner he always stopped to shake his hand and talk. If he knew that Alf had been known to sleep off a binge on bootleg whiskey in a Minnekah alley, he never said so.

But my mother had never spoken to Birdie Keeler, who sometimes could be seen in the White Rock Bar with a glass of beer in one hand and a cigarette in the other, her head thrown back in hoarse laughter that revealed her broken and missing teeth. This was beyond damnation in our valley, where no woman was acknowledged to be a drinker, or an adulteress. The worst she could do was smoke; that was enough, that was what we'd say she did, for it encompassed all other abominations, even dancing Saturday nights at the Rancho. Understand, I'm not saying my mother would have snubbed Birdie Keeler if she met her in Lowder's Grocery; I'm saying the meeting was impossible to imagine.

Cedars hid the Keelers' paintless house and crippled cars on an otherwise bald hill where the dust blew north in summer and south in winter. Three of the Keeler boys, Elmer, Orville, Ira, and one daughter, Onda, were older than I; Irene was fifteen, and then, after Birdie Keeler must have thought she, like their sand-swept farm, would never produce again, she bore twins, Yvonne and Elvin.

I said "Keeler boys," but this is also how we talked around things, for Elmer, the tough one, was at least twenty-eight, and Orville, who was a little crazy, maybe twenty-five; Ira, a senior like me, was twenty-one, and Onda, also a senior, nineteen. Irene was a sophomore, the one Keeler who had never failed a grade. All the Keeler

children except Elmer, who was chunky, had thin straight
legs and out-curved spines like question marks. When Ira
and I boxed, I thought of that curve in his body as a de-
fense: somehow I could not land a blow, could not reach
his body.

David Newgiver pointed once at a picture in a biology
book of a Neanderthal man with slanted forehead and
ridged brow and said, "Look. There's Ira." Ira didn't understand the joke, but he knew he was being laughed at,
and I had to separate him and David, who was big for sixteen, with thick, rounded shoulders. I too had thought of
Ira when I saw the picture, but long before that I came up
with a theory about how the Keelers looked. The first time
I went home with Ira, we had homemade bread soaked in
coffee for supper. Nothing else. And the same for breakfast. By lunchtime back at school, I *felt* the way the Keelers
looked.

Ira and I became friends in the seventh grade. We must
have made a comical pair. I was scarcely waist-high to him
and mostly big mouth, and he was everything I wanted to
be: sixteen years old, taller than our teacher, and the center
and best player on our basketball team. That was the year
the teachers decided to pass him on, and Onda too, from
grade to grade no matter what, rather than have them on
their hands forever.

My mother, whom I could persuade of anything when I
was younger and almost nothing as I grew older, approved
of our friendship then. Her attitude about Ira changed because of Irene. Puberty had by-passed Onda: her mouth
hung open good-naturedly; her face was blank as the thin
question mark of her body, and she was so innocuous that
the students in our country school, normally malicious,
protected her like a Raggedy Ann doll. But when Irene was
fourteen, suddenly—probably the suddenness was not in
her change but in our belated realization of it—her hand-
me-down dresses fit her very well, and some of the women

in the valley groused about people giving her good clothing
before its time, not realizing she flattered it instead of the
other way around. Her gaunt face smoothed; her breasts
filled the held-breath hollow of her Keeler chest; lower,
where the curve of the question mark straightened, her
newly rounded hips thrust forward with a frankness that
obsessed me, and this my mother somehow knew, this was
what worried her, though she never, ever, would have said
so.

"Do the girls do the dishes for Mrs. Keeler?" she asked
Tuesday night.

"Yes," I said.

"I suppose the boys don't hang around the kitchen much."

"Not much."

In Comanche Valley taking a girl out was a public decla-
ration. The neighbors saw you driving to her house and
back down the road, saw you at the only movie in Minnekah, and the party-line telephone spread the news long
before you took her home. There was decorum about it
too: our neighbors were happiest when I took out Carla
Bastrop, whose father rented some of Harold Newgiver's
poorer land and bought used Chevrolets as we did; my
mother wanted me to take out girls like Gretta Bixby, who
was ugly and stupid, because Lawrence Bixby owned better
land and bought a new Chevrolet every three years after
wheat harvest; Gaylene Helm's father, being a preacher,
had no land, but he drove a better car than we did, so she
ranked between Gretta and Carla. What I'm saying is that
every mother wanted her child to move up toward the
Newgivers and everybody else wanted you to stay even.
And that my simply taking Irene out some Saturday
evening was impossible. So my plan was to pick up on my
old friendship with Ira and get next to her without going
public.

On Wednesday I went home with Ira from school,
knowing my mother could hardly object to what I'd been

allowed to do for years. Thursday night the slanting questions started again.

"Well, is there lots to do at the Keelers?"

"We went rabbit hunting," I said.

"I guess you boys enjoyed that," my mother said, meaning "Did Irene go with you?"

"Uh-huh." I tried not to grin. David Newgiver was sitting across the table with Ted, and they were walling their eyes and poking each other in the ribs. I had told them about rabbit hunting with Ira and his brothers, and Junior Goacher. My mother imagined Ira and me walking across the pastures late in the afternoon, guns cradled on our arms. Actually we had driven along the country roads that night with spotlights shining in the borrow ditches. Elmer and Orville had ridden on the fenders. Ira and I had shotguns poking out the windows, and Junior drove, holding a jar of moonshine between his legs. Twice he hit the brakes hard and sent Elmer and Orville flying off into the bunchgrass along the road. The second time Orville jumped up shouting, his glasses askew, and fired his gun right over the car while we dived for the floorboards. This was what I had told Ted and David, although instead of Elmer I put myself out on the fender with Orville.

"Who's Junior Goacher?" David had asked.

"Keelers' second cousin. Just out of reform school." I wasn't sure about the reform school. I *was* sure my parents had not heard of Junior, and I meant to keep it that way. He had become a second reason for my going to the Keelers', for he was outside what I understood to be the possibilities in our valley: he had no parents, home, history. He chain-smoked. His skin was dark as a Comanche's, but freckled, and he had a gold tooth squarely in front; he combed his long black hair from a part even with his ear all the way across his head, and after he roughhoused with one of the Keeler boys he jerked his head and tossed his hair back in place like a saddle blanket. When he smiled his mouth curled as if he knew what you were thinking. He was about my age.

"Take some more cornbread, David." My mother knew he ate it like candy. She said to me, "You can't hardly see the house for those cedars."

"Um."

She wanted to know how many rooms there were and who slept where, but I knew better than to tell her. The kitchen had a kerosene cookstove and a table. A second room had a bed in which Alf and Birdie slept, a pallet that was unrolled for the twins, a rocking chair, and a small table crowded with prizes Orville had won at a carnival—a silver-colored horse with a bead-chain bridle, a wooden horseshoe with a garland on it, a green mermaid with red glass nipples, Chinese finger traps, and plaster dolls. The third room had three double beds in which slept, respectively, Elmer and Orville; Onda and Irene; and Junior and Ira, all fully clothed except for their shoes. I had crowded in with Junior and Ira.

If my mother had asked me in earlier years about the Keelers' sleeping arrangements, directly or otherwise, I might have told her, because I saw nothing wrong with them. I scarcely noticed Onda and avoided Irene, who had been a chattering nuisance. Or I might not have, for I learned early the habit of obliqueness in our family. I never told my mother about the supper of bread soaked in coffee, for example, which was often repeated, or that we ate with spoons because that was all they had, or about Birdie Keeler's toothaches, when she moaned for hours in her rocking chair, rocking, rocking, a rag stretched across her mouth, while the rest of us played dominoes in the kitchen. Even as a seventh grader, I was sure my mother did not want to know this.

"I guess the older boys are off working somewhere," she said sharply. She didn't like not being answered.

"They're home right now," I said; "hard to get a job in

cold weather like this." Elmer and Orville had done a year
each in the penitentiary for stealing cars. Ira had told me
this, and I knew it anyway, because it was in the paper.
My parents had a way of not reading things like that, and
it was not something my mother would hear when she listened on the party line, where there was decorum too, and
some things that weren't said, even though the Keelers
didn't have a telephone and wouldn't have heard it. Elmer
also got into fights at the Rancho dances on Saturday
nights, fights he always lost, and he often spent the rest of
the weekend in jail. And Ira had told me that Orville
shacked up with a woman older than his mother in Minnekah, but she threw him out about once a week.

"Who's the lucky girl this Saturday night?" my mother
asked.

"Think I'll go over to Ira's."

She raised her eyebrows at this, but didn't say anything.
The whole Keeler family was going to the Rancho, so I had
invited myself along, figuring I could just leave my car at
their house and probably maneuver around to sit with
Irene both directions.

And that's what happened. I danced—badly—with Irene
and Nancy Thomas and other girls from along the river
and up in the blackjacks or cedar canyons, girls who
moved in their cheap dresses with a springy freedom that
Carla Bastrop and Gaylene Helms would never know. Two
men got in a fight, and I saw Hook Stambaugh, the big,
square-jawed bouncer who was a cowboy the rest of the
week, throw them out into the parking lot, where they
started swinging again, changed their minds, and walked
off arm in arm. Ira and Orville showed me how people hid
their bottles under their cars, and Orville helped himself,
but Ira and I declined.

I told a different story to Ted and David Monday night
as we drove the cows in. In it Hook Stambaugh threw *me*
out, and I sampled bottles from under a dozen cars.

"You're going to wind up in jail," Ted said.

"Probably so," I agreed. "But Irene's worth it."

"Irene?" David stopped, and his mouth dropped open like Onda Keeler's. "You do—*do* her?" He had trouble with straight talk too.

I said no more. On the way home after the dance, I had managed to push into the back seat with her, and when the others drowsed off after a few miles I got past more buttons than Carla Bastrop and Gaylene Helm had ever allowed me, but not as far as I wanted.

"Did you have a good time?" my mother asked at supper.

I nodded. "Fooled around in town with Ira."

"I suppose you two boys just drive around town."

"Up and down Main Street."

On Tuesday night I went home with Ira to go coon hunting, but not the way my mother would think of it, two boys shivering around a fire somewhere while the hounds trailed and bawled, waiting for them to tree. Junior Goacher had talked the Keeler boys into following the hounds on horseback in the darkness, crashing through brush and trees and barbed-wire fences, over hills and creek banks and into ponds and quicksand.

"All you got to do is keep the horse's head up," Ira told me as we plunged into the darkness, the horse snorting and stumbling. "Horse can't fall or roll with you if his head is up."

I wanted to believe this, clinging to the cantle behind him, the saddle skirts chafing the insides of my knees until the blood ran, but I didn't. What kept me from begging out of the stupidity that night, besides my wanting Irene and thinking that was part of it, was an idea I was beginning to have of myself as a caste-breaker; a man for all seasons, if I had known the expression. I was doing things with the Keelers no one who could afford a new Chevrolet, much less a Buick, would do. David Newgiver, I thought, would never ride a horse into the dark to risk breaking his neck or slicing himself open like a watermelon on barbed wire. I began to think of myself as the only free person in the valley, and when Orville fell off his horse around midnight and broke his arm, it seemed to corroborate this feeling. With me laughing as loud as the rest, we drove into Minnekah to the doctor, Junior giving him nips of moonshine along the way.

After that, at least one weeknight a week, I went home with Ira to get into whatever foolishness Junior dreamed up. On Saturday nights I went to the Rancho with the family. My answer to my mother's questions usually amounted to "fooled around town with Ira," and that seemed to satisfy her. If I told her less than the truth, I told Ted and David more. One night at the Rancho, Ira and I refused to join a line of men that had formed before a drunken woman in the parking lot. Clutching some dollar bills in her hand, she leaned against a car fender and pulled her dress up. Elmer and Orville were there with their money, and after Orville had his turn he skipped back to the end of the line again, cackling and holding his pants up. My brother and David Newgiver believed I had been in the line at the Rancho, believed a tree limb snatched me off a horse while we were coon hunting, although I had no broken arm as proof, believed that Irene generously rewarded my wild doings, and that I gladly risked being killed by her brothers to have her.

"You're crazy." Ted shook his head as we drove the milk cows in.

"Yeah," I grinned, looking off as if I could see beyond our little valley, maybe see my own glory or death out there. David listened even more closely than Ted, and if I had no new story to tell, asked me for an old one.

"Did they have a good wheat harvest?" my mother asked at supper. "One of the girls dresses real nice."

"Greenbugs got their wheat," I answered.

"Nothing for greenbugs to eat on that hill," my father
said.

"Which one of the girls dresses so nice?" my mother
asked.

"Can't tell them apart," I said.

I gradually realized that Junior was my rival for Irene,
although, given the logic I knew, this was impossible. He
whirled Irene, Onda, Nancy Thomas, and many other girls
around the dance floor in fast and intricate patterns that
would have left me in a hopeless tangle. He could talk to
the girls too, and their mothers, and open car doors for
them and have his arm just right so they always took it,
could do these things I thought a man would be better off
not knowing. And a lot of others: he could roll a cigarette
perfectly with one hand; siphon the gas, every drop, out of
one car and into another, usually his own; he could wire
and start a car before you could bring the keys from the
house; he could make whiskey if he wanted to, he said, or
sell what someone else had made. He bragged of walking
right past the sheriff in Minnekah to deliver two pints in
each cowboy boot. He had a eye for fancy hubcaps, and
new ones often appeared on his car. Ira said he had quit
school in the third grade and couldn't write his own name.

Sometimes I thought my desire for Irene was as simple as
Domino's for Blackie in the pasture; at other times I felt
noble about it and wanted to carry her off in some public
way that seemed far more dangerous than riding into the
darkness with the Keeler brothers.

To placate my mother I took out the girls she approved
of, but they marketed themselves as grimly as Harold Newgiver sold seed wheat. The price of a kiss from Gaylene
Helm was attendance in her Sunday School class; a held
breast, communion. One night I opened the steamed-up
windows of the car so we could breathe, pointed at her
breasts still safely under her sweater, and said, "All right.
What do I have to do just to see them, bare?"

She frowned for a moment, then said, "Be a missionary to Africa."

"Okay."

"You have to sign." She fumbled in her purse, then shook her head. "I don't have a form with me."

Carla Bastrop, who was a little flour-faced, wasn't quite as bad, but she made it clear the price of going much below her neck was a class ring. Sometimes that winter I lay shivering next to Ira, on the other side from Junior in the Keelers' bedroom, listening to the snores, the north wind howling over the bald hill and around the uncaulked windows, I as stinking and unwashed as they, sleeping in our jeans, socks, shirts, and even our jackets. Less than an arm's-length away lay Irene, I thought, but was not sure, for the sisters always went into the bedroom and got into bed first. I tried to work up my nerve to cross that narrow space, to move under the tattered quilt with her: we would make love while Onda did not awake to protest the shaking bed, the brothers slept through its creaking. I wondered which of them would do what to me, Elmer with his heavy fists and small red eyes, crazy Orville, Ira. One night at the Rancho, Alf Keeler had tried to slap Orville away from the steering wheel; Elmer and Orville, and Ira too, had swung on their father, and he had grunted, doubled up, and vomited over the front of the car. Probably they would stove in my ribs and break an arm, maybe both. The moon shone through the window on what I thought was Irene's hair, within a foot of my hand. I reached over and pulled the quilt down until the light glinted on an open mouth. Onda watched me, her eyes blue and empty.

So I was afraid to cross that space, but I found other ways that were tantalizing, if not satisfying. On the dance floor my hand felt the pliancy in the small of Irene's back and, in the press of the dancers, slid down until she pulled it up again, frowning and smiling. Sometimes I got around Junior and into the back seat of the Keelers' car with her

for the long ride home, and when she set her teeth or
gripped my hand fiercely in both of hers I simply pushed
harder, while her mother snored through rotten teeth in the
front seat, and she gave, a little more, a little more, gave in
to the strength of where we lived and who we were, I
whose parents bought three-year-old Chevrolets and whose
mother set a fork on the left of every plate and knife and
spoon on the right every meal of every day, so that she had
no choice but to give in as Gaylene Helm or even Carla
Bastrop would not.

"Does Irene make better grades than the other Keelers?"
my mother asked.

"Don't know what the others make," I said.

The last Saturday night in February I found out Irene
had a price, too. After she'd pulled my hand back to her
waist several times as we danced, she said, "Why don't you
just ask me out like you do Gaylene and Carla, and maybe
you'd get what you want? Wouldn't that be easier?"

"Maybe I'll just do that," I said.

"Sure. Maybe you will." She laughed and turned to
dance with Junior.

All week I tried to work my nerve up. She had unsettled
me, calling my bluff like that. I was put off by her ambi-
tion, yet I wanted her, and her offer was better than those
of the "good family" girls, as my mother would have
called them. Still, I postponed asking her from day to day,
until on Saturday evening I pulled up into the cedars at the
Keelers' as usual.

An extra car was there, a new Buick Roadmaster, looking huge among the Keelers' rusty Chevrolets. I sat for a
moment, puzzled, and then Irene stepped out on the porch,
blushing, and right behind her was David Newgiver with
his hand on her waist.

We must have spoken. I couldn't remember as the
Buick's dust drifted across the yard from the road. When I
turned back to the house, Junior was leaning against a

porch post, grinning. He said, "Son of a bitch tuck her right out from under us, ain't he?" He had his makings on the porch railing and was rolling himself a cigarette with one hand.

"He can't do that," I muttered.

Junior cocked his head as if he hadn't heard me. Then he laughed. "Can't do it? Course he can. He can do anything he wants, same as me. It's people like you that can't. Don't you know that?"

David had told Harold and Marie Newgiver that he was going to our house, but the news that he was taking Irene out passed and re-passed on the party line before they got to Minnekah. When he and Irene came out of the movie his parents were parked beside the Buick in Harold's pickup, and they followed him back out to the Keelers' house. That news, too, was all over Comanche Valley Sunday morning, and I was delighted: David hadn't stopped in some pasture where, I was sure, Irene would not have been able to resist the Buick's velvet seats. And Junior had been wrong, too.

On Monday my mother was waiting in the yard as I got off the school bus, her arms folded, her face splotched white and red. Whatever was up, I knew there would be no oblique talk this time.

"Do you know a girl named Nancy Thomas?" she asked.

"A little. She lives over by Rafer Springs."

"I know where she lives," she snapped. "She called Irene Keeler today and said she danced with you at the Rancho Saturday night."

"Well—"

She put her hands on her hips and leaned toward me. "Do you know how many people listen in every time someone calls on that line?"

"Probably twenty or thirty."

She leaned closer. "When they hung up Marie Newgiver

called me and started yelling that you and Ted put David up to taking out Irene Keeler."

"*We?* We didn't put him up to anything."

"You know what I'm talking about. Now Ted's not supposed to have anything to do with David, and I just don't know how we're going to hold our heads up in this valley. I'll tell you this: you're not going to the Keelers' again, or to that Rancho place."

"I'll do what I please when I please," I shouted as she went into the house. She didn't answer.

In a way I did do what I pleased the rest of that, my senior year, but what I pleased changed: I didn't go back to the Keelers', or the Rancho, and I had no more to do with Irene.

I started to school at the teacher's college in Bixton that fall and muddled along with Bs and Cs. President Kennedy was killed the next year, and that was something else we slid around at the supper table when I came home from school. We didn't talk about Vietnam either. By the time Ted graduated from high school in 1964, however, I was uncomfortably close to 1-A, and that had something to do with my marrying Carla Bastrop that summer, and even with the birth of our child the following spring.

Ted made the honor roll at the state university every semester until he was drafted in the spring of 1966. Junior Goacher volunteered and went into the army the same time as Ted. He had married Irene Keeler in what no one bothered to call a shotgun wedding, since he was perfectly willing. When they left on their honeymoon the Keeler brothers followed them in one of their old Chevrolets for six hundred miles through Texas and into Louisiana until Orville went to sleep and hit a fence post.

Ted and Junior went through boot camp at Fort Hood together, but Ted went on to OCS at Fort Benning. Both of them were sent to Vietnam. Not long after Junior went Irene bought a better car and moved from their crackerbox renthouse into a brick veneer in a new suburb of Minne-kah. Rumors passed that Junior had something to do with the PXs over there, and other things, and he was making money hand over fist. He came home driving a Cadillac, and he and Irene moved into an even larger house. Ted was stationed near Da Nang. The day he was shipped out I gave my parents a world globe and a big map of Vietnam so they could keep track of where he was, but I never saw either the globe or the map again. Ted was awarded a silver star for gallantry, and after four months he was sent home in an aluminum box.

I teach history now at Comanche Valley High School. Memories do not fade quickly in our community, and because of Harold Newgiver, who was on the school board then, I was almost passed over for the job. Later I *was* passed over for principal, and that was certainly thanks to the Newgivers. Harold was getting old, though, and turned the farm over to David, who made some mistakes about buying big tractors and fancy herd bulls. Now Junior Goacher owns as much of the valley's bottom land as the Newgivers, and he does not make mistakes. He's on the school board, and when the principalship comes up again I'll get it, even though my divorce has given me another black eye in the valley. That's another topic my parents and I talk around. I sent them roses on the first anniversary of Ted's death, but my mother called and said, "Don't ever send us flowers again." It was the straightest thing she'd said to me since that day in the yard when I was a senior in high school.

4 »
On the
Wing

THE boy's father whispered it for the third time, "Wet butt, hungry gut," and for the third time Jeff laughed silently in the darkness, just a huff of air through his teeth to show he had heard. He understood that this was his father's way of being men together, using words like "butt" and "gut," his father whom he had heard say "damn" only once when a wily bucket calf, as impossible to drive as a cat, had escaped its pen. Duck hunters: wet butt, hungry gut. Someone had said it to Jeff's father, a small lean man whose fingers blurred when he tied knots that slipped or held, as he wished, and now he said it to Jeff.

Daylight would not come. They sat on a rotted corner post they had replaced the previous summer, his father facing south in their blind, Jeff north, their four-buckle overshoes sunk ankle-deep in mud that belched if they shifted their feet. They had broken through ice thin as paper when they crept into the blind, which was not really a blind, just a clump of tamaracks taller than Jeff that leaned inward around a little knoll. His father had pointed it out last summer in the August heat when they were setting fence in the shallow water to keep the cattle from crossing onto the Albright side.

"Make a dandy duck blind," his father had said, and Jeff had seen that it would, the thickly growing tamaracks at the end of the long low ridge of red clay jutting into the lake, water to the south, west, and north. So in December when the ducks had been coming in for two weeks, and even a vee of Canada geese and another of snow geese had passed over—the snow geese white and exotic in the little valley of meadowlarks and crows—when the rain had fallen steadily and begun to freeze, his father said at supper on Friday, "We'll try that blind in the morning."

"I heard Helen Albright say they were going to Minnekah tomorrow," Jeff's mother said.

His father snorted. "They won't go anywhere tomorrow on that road."

"She said they were going in the pickup."

"Pickup or no pickup, they won't go anywhere on that road."

They arose early to milk, the boy milking Belle, the part Jersey, with his new strength, squeezing the teats in a fast, steady rhythm that raised foam thicker than meringue on the milk, leaning his red cap with the flaps down into the cow's flank for warmth until the ice melted on her back and trickled down his neck. Leaving the horses in the barn and the milk for Jeff's mother to separate, they took their guns from the rafters in the milkroom, the boy's father the single-shot with the three-foot barrel, the boy his double-barrel, ancient but new to him, and they followed the path for a mile through the pasture that Jeff knew as well as his father, the ice on the mesquite thorns tinkling like vicious little bells. When they reached the redlands where nothing grew except bunches of yucca and cactus, they stopped to load the guns, the boy jumping at the loud *ping* of the shell ejector on his father's Long Tom. The red clay stuck to their overshoes and balled up until they dragged their feet sideways to break it off, then it balled up again.

"We won't see the sun today," Jeff's father said. They walked more and more slowly as they neared the water, then, crouching, followed the narrow ridge a step at a time out to the tamaracks.

They had seen nothing, could see nothing in the darkness, could hear only the hooting of mudhens and the
occasional quacking of ducks, the sliding hiss of wings as
ducks chattering in soft thin voices banked, came over
them with a *whoosh!* that hunched Jeff's shoulders, and
splashed noisily in the water somewhere in the darkness.
Once the hissing wings grew so shrill they became a shriek
that cornered just above him. He cringed and shivered;
then the sound flattened away and was gone.

"Teal," his father said.

Jeff nodded in the darkness, wondering if his father had
flinched too, knowing with irritation that he had not.

Jeff had already killed ducks with the old shotgun,
crawling up over the dams of smaller ponds near sundown
after school. At first he had not held it properly, and the
heavy-kicking twelve-gauge had bruised his shoulder, but
he had not told his parents. He had bought the gun himself
in Minnekah with his own money. In town with his
mother, when he saw the gun with its curlicue hammers in
Ben Bowden's shop window, he knew Ben would sell it to
him even though most people wouldn't sell a thing like
that to an eleven-year-old boy. But Ben was from out in
their part of the county too, the only man he or his parents
knew who was divorced, locked out of his own house by
his own wife, so Ben would sell it to him.

"Will it shoot?" Jeff asked.

"Sure it'll shoot." Ben opened the breech and inserted
two shells. They went to the back room of the shop where
a floorboard had been pried up just for the purpose, apparently, and Ben fired both barrels into the hole in the
floor. Jeff's head swam with the noise, and he gave Ben
eight one-dollar bills and carried the gun six blocks down
the alleys to where his mother was waiting.

On the way home he traced and retraced the upright
hammers like a pair of thumbs and rubbed at the dim
scrollwork on the sides, the muzzle of the gun on the floor

of the car and the barrel between his knees, the gun nearly as long as he was.

"That Ben Bowden," his mother said. "Your dad will make you take it back."

But when they got home, as Jeff had expected, his father opened the breech, peered down each barrel, closed the gun, cocked the hammers, and pulled each trigger. "Left hammer is loose," he said; "a copper washer will fix that."

Jeff's mother said something, a sound that wasn't a word, and turned to the stove.

"The tipstock's been carved out of pine," his father said. "Someone broke the old one off. They did a good job of carving it."

Daylight would not come. His father, not even an outline beside Jeff in the tamaracks, said "Wet butt, hungry gut" a fourth time, and the boy laughed soundlessly again. Then daybreak was there, the darkness bent into grayness, and Jeff thought he must have slept as his feet slept, numb in the icy mud. He inspected the small feeding black birds on the water before him: pointed bills, necks pumping like bicycle riders as they swam. All mudhens: coots, not worth the powder to kill. Then, beyond them—out of range, he realized even as his thumb tightened on the right hammer of the gun—beyond them he saw it, too stunningly white for belief, too large for belief: a snow goose, the question mark of its long neck dipping, instantly upright again.

"Dad."

His father peered for a long moment, then whispered, "I might reach him with the Long Tom."

Jeff stiffened. "He's on my side."

"Maybe he'll feed in closer," his father said, and they waited.

The sound of an engine came to them from the southwest. The Albright's pickup appeared on the muddy road coming over the hill and moved steadily around the rim of

the valley, climbed the hill on the other side, and disappeared.

. . . .

When Jeff was five, his father had strung three miles of
wire for a telephone. When it rang some number other
than theirs—two longs—his mother stood by the wooden
box on the wall anyway, her hand over the speaker, the
heavy receiver at her ear. After she hung up she would say,
"Bee couldn't get Alta's mother"; "Bee broke in because
Stahlmans had a long distance"; "Bee gave a general ring
for the Cornelsen's auction." Sometimes she turned the
crank on the box and called Bee—one long—to ask her
anything, what time it was, whether the Rayfields' pasture
fire had jumped the fence, if the river was up. So Jeff had a
Bee too, listened in long silences to Bee's news as he built
and destroyed in his sandpile, repeated what he had heard,
asked questions, argued with her—or him, for he never
wondered if Bee was she or he. That had lasted until he
had heard his father come into the house many times and
scold while his mother leaned against the wall by the
brown wooden box, her hand over the speaker, until he
heard his father mutter, "Just a waste of time. Prying into
other people's business." Had lasted until he had watched
his mother every day at the same pan of dirty dishes, every
day at the ironing board; until he had watched his father
spur and ride to a frothing, trembling standstill a wild
young horse, until in the heat of June harvest, in the driveway of the granary where the dust was finer than flour, he
listened to the steel song of wheat flung from a steel scoop
as his father emptied a trailer, and Jeff turned away from
his mother. When he was ten, he braced his foot and
pulled on a thin, limber rope to draw a bull calf's legs up
against its belly and expose the small wrinkled sack, and
his father with the short out-curved blade of his knife
made two deft lengthwise cuts through layers of skin white

then crimson, pressed out the testes like elongated eggs, snipped off one then the other, poured on the disinfectant with its high acrid smell, smeared the empty sack with tar to keep away the flies that laid eggs that hatched into screwworms that ate living flesh right to the bones, and released the calf to stand, uncertain, doomed, and for a moment beyond fear because of the thing they had done to him. Also when he was ten, while sleet stung his face, holding a thick, heavy rope that snubbed a cow with pain-glazed eyes to a post, Jeff had watched his father's arm, bare, wet, and blue with cold, disappear again and again into the cow and do something, right something despite all the cow's straining against him, and then the calf came out and lived. And so Jeff turned away from his mother.

· · · ·

The numbness in Jeff's feet had moved up into his legs and become ache. The white goose fed closer, within range, the boy knew, of the long barrel of his father's gun. They waited. Still the bird fed toward them, and in the gray light that did not distinguish the water from the air above it, Jeff could see now the black markings on its wingtips.

"I could reach it with the choke barrel," he whispered. He felt his father hesitate, then carefully remove his glove and fumble in the pocket of his jumper.

"Put this in." His father gave him a shell. "It's a goose load."

The boy exchanged the shells without taking his eyes from the goose. It had stopped feeding.

"Move slow," his father whispered.

Jeff cocked the hammer on the choke barrel and began to push the muzzle of the gun through the brittle foliage of the tamaracks. The snow goose, turned sideways toward them, was motionless.

"Set him right on top of your sight," his father said.

"I know," Jeff answered. The goose spread its wings, drummed the air, cleared the water as the boy fired, and fell. The mudhens fled squawking in all directions, some flying over the blind so low they flung water in the boy's face. The white goose was still, low and shapeless in the water.

"Got him on the wing," his father said.

Jeff trembled as he stood up to reload, the smell of gunpowder from the breech of the gun sharp in his nostrils, the gun's explosion, so loud after the long silence, still echoing, still deafening. He felt the pain in his legs above his numbed feet as if it were someone else's. He said, "I'll go get him."

The sound of shots came to them from over the hills to the northwest, weak and tinny, like lady fingers thrown in a rain barrel. His father said, "That's on Henry Slater's pond. Let's wait; maybe they'll chase some ducks over here."

The boy looked at the goose. Bits of white down had settled in the water around it. It had drifted closer to them.

"Don't worry about him," his father said. "He's not going anywhere."

They waited. A breeze out of the north ruffled the water, pushing the goose toward them until it caught on a mesquite snag. It turned slowly, a full circle, came loose, and drifted toward them again. Jeff looked for blood spotting the white feathers, saw none. If it had been summer, he thought, the big snapping turtles would have scented the goose's blood, would have come up under it and torn at it with smooth jaws sharp as the snippers his father used on the bull calves. But now they were buried in the mud of the lake bottom. Jeff caressed the hammers of his gun, aware of himself as a wielder of death. The mudhens, either forgetful of the danger in the clump of tamaracks or secure in their own uselessness, swam back into the area they had fled.

Again shots came from Henry Slater's pond. The sun broke through. Its rays glinted blindingly on the goose as it turned, and for an instant the white bird seemed to be the source of the light.

In a few minutes eight or nine ducks appeared, very high, and circled overhead. They swung out over the red-lands, then came in low directly at the tamaracks.

"They'll turn when they see us," Jeff's father said. "They won't light." He stood up and fired. The lead mallard closed its wings, dropped, and rolled on the bare ground near the end of the ridge. Jeff fired too, missed, cocked the other barrel, and missed again.

"Got one anyway," his father said. They heard a commotion in the water and looked around just as the snow goose lifted off toward the northwest, the black markings on its wingtips crisp and clear in the sunlight. Jeff threw off his glove, dug desperately in his pocket for a shell, broke open the gun, put the shell in, closed the breech, and fired futilely. The goose rose steadily beyond the far edge of the water.

"Well, I'll be—must've just stunned him," his father said. Jeff tugged his feet angrily from the sucking mud, then bent to retrieve his glove, keeping his face turned away.

The sky closed over, darker than before. As they trudged back across the redlands, they heard shots in the northwest again.

"That's still Henry's pond," Jeff's father said, stopping to listen. He was carrying the mallard.

Jeff said nothing. He remembered the goose in the water, shapeless in death, remembered its great spread wings beating the air, its taut neck and sleek body alive, fleeing toward life, and he thought, testing himself, "I'm glad it got away," but even as he thought it he imagined himself carrying the goose, the ache in his arm from its dead weight, and knew it was a lie.

At the barn they let the horses out, one into the horselot and the other into the pasture, and at the house they left their guns on the porch while they took separated milk to the barn to feed the bucket calves. Back at the house, they sat on the edge of the porch to clean and remove their overshoes.

Jeff's mother stepped outside, her arms folded against the damp cold. She said, "I heard Verna Slater talking to Alta. Henry just killed a snow goose on their pond."

Jeff's father began, "Well—"

"That's just a waste of time, listening on the phone," the boy shouted at her. "Prying into other people's business—"

His father slapped him cleanly. Jeff had felt it coming and took it without cringing. Stiffly, he faced his father, who raised his hand again, then lowered it awkwardly—foolishly, Jeff thought—to his side.

"What was that all about?" his mother asked. His father bent to clean his overshoes without answering, and Jeff turned away, turned away.

5 | »
Orielle
Bastemeyer,
Where Are You?

I HAVE, in a word, wandered.

And experienced: the sands of Sonora and Mauritania, the killer winds of the North Slope, the endless Steppes; oil rigs buckling under the waves of the North Sea, the cobblestoned web of Brussels, red wine in Athens, the beaches of Lomé and Cotonou, the sober boredom of Saudi Arabia; I have fled with the Irish from Tehran, drunk with the Germans in Melbourne, and gambled with the Indians in Nairobi.

And here three-fingered Ogun hurls the boulders of Idanre and leaps the curling Niger; Sango the axe-handed shatters the quailing skies; juju men peer through muddy hearts, rain drums mutter in the night forests, and shrieking women flee the raffia-bodied Ekpe; Fulani drovers urge their humpbacked cattle over invisible trails from the Sahara to the littoral swamps, the ebony paddles of the riverine Ibibio flash while Mammy Wata strokes her serpents and calms the tide and chides the greedy crocodile; I eat foo-foo, moi-moi, and soursop and walk among the wily Hausa traders, the fawn-faced beggar women of Chad, and the warriors of Tiv.

And along the perilous Kwa the children spit.

Hwttt! Compressed lips, taut silver stream: splat! Surprised gecko, tiny explosion on its milk-glass head. The children never miss. The rains come and then the drought and they never miss. The battered house girl, the boys

vending *oki agara*, the naked lads of Akim-Akim: hwttt!
They never miss.

Hwttt! Sinister, distasteful aqua fricative.

I wondered: *déjà vu?*

No.

You warders charged with caulking the chinks and
grouting the fissures against tangential nuisances, trouble-
some memories: Sluggards!

. . . .

Orielle Bastemeyer. Thirty years ago in Oklahoma it
was, my best friend when I was ten, Orielle Bastemeyer.

I first saw him at the Crawford Ranch roundup in August, the big event of the summer. The little farmers like
my father came to help, and maybe buy a steer to fatten
for butchering or a few yearling heifers. It lasted two days,
and on the evening of the second day Old Man Crawford
always barbecued a big steer.

Orielle was the only other boy there my age. He was
sitting on top of the corral fence in jeans and a work shirt
and beat-up old cowboy boots, watching the men work the
calves. His head was as square as a tractor battery, he had
blond, curly hair, and he didn't look at me when I climbed
up beside him.

I said, "Who're you?"

"Orielle."

"Orielle? What kind of a name is that?" I'd never heard
of anyone named Orielle in my life.

"Just Orielle," he said and spat hwttt! and hit a yellow
grasshopper right on the butt down in the corral dust.

"Where you from?"

"Texas."

"Texas!"

I wasn't sure where Texas was, but I knew it was huge
because everybody said it was, and wild and dangerous,
and the men wore Stetsons, sweaty gray with low menacing crowns and great brims that swept back from a vee like

a hawk's beak just over the nose. I sneaked a look at his curly hair. It was so tight and thick, I thought, you'd have to use a curry comb on it. My hair was brown and straight and stuck out in back.

"Well, Texas is big," I said, "but Oklahoma is bigger, ain't it? Over all, I mean."'

"I don't know," Orielle said.

A tall, sunburnt man on a heavy roan horse had been roping the calves for the other men to vaccinate and brand, and now he rested while another batch was being driven in. He hooked a leg over the saddle horn and rolled a cigarette from a tobacco sack, putting the sack back in his shirt pocket with pearl snap buttons and leaving the round Bull Durham tab hanging out.

"We got real cowboys in Oklahoma," I said. "Like him."'

"That's my dad," Orielle said.

My dad never hooked his leg over the saddle horn. He didn't have a saddle. Or a horse. Or a shirt with pearl snap buttons. He didn't smoke.

"Your dad work for Old Man Crawford?"

"Yep."

Old Man Crawford was palsied and wore high-topped yellow boots with the pants legs stuffed inside. He was sitting in a wheel chair under an elm tree by the corral, drooling tobacco juice over a filthy moustache down onto his collar and saying "goddamskinnysonsabitches" over and over again, as he did every year. We lived with my grandpa on his farm, but he had stopped chewing before I was born and was perfectly healthy and never said anything worse than "by golly." We raised chickens and guineas.

After a while a girl about sixteen came from the house with a glass of water and some pills for Old Man Crawford. Her face was plump and peaceful looking, and she had breasts like brood hens.

"Man," I nudged Orielle, "she sure has big ones."

He spat and hit a speckled grasshopper. "My sister Joyce."

I didn't have a sister. Later I asked Orielle where his mother was, and he said he didn't have one. I said I did. She was home canning peaches.

We spent the afternoon together, and by evening Orielle and I were best friends. He said so, when I asked him. That night I stayed with the Bastemeyers in what used to be the bunkhouse, Orielle and I sleeping on pallets on the floor.

Before we went to sleep, I asked him, "You ever heard of Rosemary Henderson?"

"Nope."

"She's my girl. She's been off visiting relatives in Little Rock or Georgia or someplace this summer. Her dad's president of the school board. They're rich."

"Had a girl in Texas. Charlotte Morphew. Her daddy owned the Brazos River."

"Me and Rosemary are the exact same height and the exact same age, except she's a month older," I said. "She wrote me about a thousand letters this summer." Which wasn't quite the truth. I'd gotten a card back in June, from Tulsa. It had a picture of the Grand River Dam on it. But the writing space was blank. "I guess she's crazy about me." But Orielle was asleep.

We were up at sunrise the next morning, Joyce serving us fried eggs and ham and biscuits and grits, which I had never heard of and didn't like. Orielle and his dad put butter and salt and a layer of pepper on the grits, tabasco on their eggs, and Orielle drank black coffee just like his dad. Joyce was wearing a long cotton housedress. Every time she set something on the table she swung like pumpkins on a vine and I nearly bit my fingers off. My mother was about as filled out as a lightning rod.

"Orielle, you'll have to help today," Mr. Bastemeyer said

as he pulled the Bull Durham sack from his shirt pocket. "You ride that paint horse." He turned to me and said, "You can ride too if you want. We got another horse."

"I guess I better not," I said. I wanted to do it, but I had an understanding with horses: they didn't like me, and I was scared to death of them. I could still feel the hoofprint my cousin Danny's pony had left on my rear the previous summer. "I got a bad back, and the doctor told me not to ride horses."

"All right."

So I sat on the corral fence alone and watched Orielle drive cows and calves up the lanes from the holding pens down by the creek while his dad roped the calves for the other men to work. Orielle could cup his hands together and blow between his thumbs and make that noise, "OHHH-*EEE*-OHHH," like an owl, or a wounded locomotive. I tried to do it about three hundred times, sitting on the fence. I couldn't make a sound.

His horse was one of those Indian ponies, small and white with brown splotches all over it, quick as a rabbit, and his saddle was the real western kind with a low cantle and a big flat-knobbed roping horn. The stirrups were drawn up to fit his short legs. When he got tired of spitting at grasshoppers and making that "OHHH-*EEE*-OHHH" sound, he untied the leather whangs holding the lariat by his knee and whirled the loop over his head, stiff as a cable, while he yelled "hi-yahh! hi-yahh!" at the cows.

It was a hot day, and after a while Orielle's dad sent me to the house for the water jug. I went up the hill past the elm tree and Old Man Crawford, who was saying "goddamskinnysonsabitches" as usual, and barged right into the kitchen and squarely into Joyce, who was standing there in her blue jeans, fastening her brassiere. My head was right under her chin. She smelled like sweat and Oxydol and biscuit dough. I felt like a calf in a loading chute.

She said, "What are you doing here, Walter?" I gaped.

She overflowed the stout white bra, like too much whipped cream in a bowl. "Go outside."' I went.

I yelled, "Your dad sent me to get some water!"

"Well, come and get it," she said, "It's all right now." I went back in cautiously, but she had her blouse on and buttoned. You would think, by the placid tone of her voice, that she didn't even know she had just initiated me into practically all the female mysteries of life.

I took the jug to Mr. Bastemeyer and then ran down to the holding pens to tell Orielle I'd seen Joyce with her shirt off.

"Clear off!" I said.

"I seen her naked lots of times," he said, and spat hwttt! and knocked a locust off a fencepost.

That evening, when Mr. Bastemeyer was cutting the barbecued steer and the men were putting planks on saw horses so the neighbor women could set out baked beans and potato salad and roasting ears and fresh tomatoes, and Orielle and I were inspecting the watermelons floating with blocks of ice in the horse tank, the Henderson's big blue Oldsmobile drove up. Mr. and Mrs. Henderson got out, and then Dorothy Drumheller, who was Rosemary's best friend and had hair cut short like an old whisk broom, and then a girl that looked like Rosemary, except she was a head taller and had red hair instead of brown and bumps on her chest.

I watched the red-haired girl while Orielle wandered back down to the corral. She was wearing white high-heeled shoes and a white dress with ruffles at the shoulders and flounces on the skirt, as lacy as a tablecloth, and lipstick. Pretty soon she came over where I was, Dorothy three steps behind, and said, "Hello, Walter. Aren't you even going to speak to me?"

My stomach bobbed like the watermelons in the tank. It was Rosemary.

I finally managed to say, "You dyed your hair."

"No I didn't." She took a comb out of a little red alligator-skin purse and began combing her hair down over one eye, watching me with the other. It was large and brown and limpid, and the watermelons bobbed like crazy. My eyes were about even with her collarbone. I stood as straight as I could and edged up on my tiptoes a bit, but it didn't help much. "My hair is naturally red," Rosemary said. "I just let all the natural red come out in it this summer."

I had known Rosemary all my life, and her hair had always been light brown, just like mine. But I didn't argue. Rosemary wasn't the kind of girl you argued with. I couldn't think of anything to say about how she'd grown, either, or about the lipstick and high heels, or the bumps on her chest. But I was thinking about them.

"Rosemary, I—"

"My name isn't Rosemary any more, either. It's Rose-*Marie*. My daddy's going to make them change it on the school records. All the ladies down South are named Rose-Marie."

She said "down South" like "day-yone say-yoth." And "either" like "eye-thuh." She got over "down South" in a few weeks, but pronounced "either" like that from then on, and I suppose still does to this day.

Orielle was making his "OHHH-*EEE*-OHHH" locomotive sound down by the corrals. The cows were all huddled against the far fence, watching him.

"What is that *horr*ible say-yound?" Rosemary—Rose-Marie— asked. She had taken a compact from her purse and was dabbing on more lipstick. It was red as blood.

"That's Orielle. He just moved here." I was secretly glad she hadn't come while he was still on his horse, whizzing that lariat around his head and yelling "hi-yahh!" I wasn't sure why. I cupped my hands and blew on my thumbs, but it just sounded *pffft*, like a wet balloon going down. Dorothy sniggered. She was a pain in the ass.

"I'm thinking about going to Texas," I said. "To work on a ranch—" But Rose-Marie didn't hear me. She and Dorothy were on their way down to the corral, Rose-Marie taking wobbly steps in her high-heeled shoes and holding her hair back so she could see where she was going. I tried to spit through my teeth at one of the ice chunks in the tank, but dribbled on my chin instead.

If I'd known the misery that was ahead of me, I'd have jumped in with the watermelons and drowned. Or frozen to death.

· · · ·

We went back to school in September, and on the first day while we were waiting for the teacher, Mrs. Moser, to come in, I decided to show Orielle the difference between Oklahoma and Texas. Rose-Marie was sitting in front of us combing her hair down over one eye, so I said loudly so she could hear, "Orielle, we got a map here. I'll just show you how little Texas is next to Oklahoma."

We went over to the map and of course saw Texas immediately, but I couldn't find Oklahoma.

"I guess it's too big for this map," I said.

"There it is," Orielle said, "right on top of Texas."

I squinted. It looked like a wart on a camel's back. Rose-Marie laughed out loud behind us. She had a blood-curdling laugh. Dorothy giggled.

"Are you from Texas, Orielle?" Rose-Marie asked, batting the long lashes of her free eye at him. I knew she knew he was. I didn't know why she asked him. She had on enough lipstick to paint a barn.

"Yep," he said, and spat hwttt! at a paper wad on the floor, right there in the classroom. He hit it squarely and knocked it down the row and all the way under the teacher's desk.

"We're thinking about moving to New Jersey," I said. "We might buy a big ranch there."

But Rose-Marie didn't hear me. She was watching Orielle scrape the cowshit off his boots. Dorothy giggled again.

We didn't come from any place, my family. We just came from right there.

All through the fourth grade Rose-Marie and I had written torrid, double-coded notes to each other, spelling our names backwards and using pig latin for key words so dumb Dorothy, who tried to read every note before she passed it on, never had a clue. I still have one filed away somewhere:

> Earestday Arlingday Retlaw,
>> Do ouyay avehay any uicyjay uitfray?
>> Ithway all my ovelay,
>>> Yramesor.

But there were no notes from Rose-Marie in the fifth grade. She never answered mine. I accused Dorothy of not passing them on.

"I'm not," she admitted.

"How come?"

"Rose-Marie told me not to."

"Well, give them back to me," I said. "You can't read them anyway. They're in code."

"I can too," she said. "I eadray ouryay otesnay eryvay ightnay, Retlaw."

I discovered that I had no chin whatsoever, compared to Orielle. I walked around the house for hours with my chin stuck out, until my mother said my jaw must be broken and threatened to have the doctor put it in a cast. That sounded like a good idea to me, since a cast certainly would give me a bigger chin, but then she said I wouldn't be able to talk for three months, so I gave it up. My hair wouldn't curl, or even bend. I stole her hair curlers and used them every night, and poured on gallons of Wildroot

Creme Oil. Nothing helped. It still looked like dead Johnson grass.

Rose-Marie screamed every time Orielle cupped his hands and went "OHHH-*EEE*-OHHH!" When I wasn't working on my spitting, I practiced the whistle. I would spit twenty times, then blow on my thumbs ten times. My chin became chapped and raw when winter came, and so did my thumbs. I was dry as a salamander all the time. I never produced a sound. Orielle, I observed, had a small gap between his upper front teeth, and I thought that must be his secret. At night I stood before the mirror, alternately trying to pull my teeth apart and wave my hair with Wildroot. Wildroot tastes terrible.

In January, Rose-Marie discovered country music. She talked of nothing but Hank Williams and Hank Snow and Merle Lyndsay and the Oklahoma Nightriders, and she sat around combing her hair over first one eye and then the other and humming things like "I'll Sail My Ship Alone" and "Take These Chains from My Heart."

"I've sent off for a guitar," I said. "I'm going to take lessons." We were sitting on a bench in the warm sun on the south side of the school house, Orielle on one side of Rose-Marie and I on the other. But somehow Dorothy had squeezed in between Rose-Marie and me. I was sitting mostly on air.

Rose-Marie was interested. She leaned to look around Dorothy with her free eye, and said, "What are you going to play?"

"Nothing but country music," I said. "I'm crazy about it." I felt squiggly inside whenever she looked at me, no matter which eye she used. I hadn't thought of buying a guitar till that moment, but I had developed a fantasy during my chin exercises of suddenly appearing in the classroom, tall and deeply tanned, my chin jutting out like a truck bumper, a Bull Durham tab dangling from my shirt pocket, wearing black denim jeans, black shirt, black Stetson, and black boots, playing a black guitar and singing something like "Heartaches by the Number" in a bottom-octave bass. Everyone would listen, awed. Tears would stream down the hairless side of Rose-Marie's face. She probably would drop to her knees. She would have a chest like Orielle's sister Joyce's.

"Orielle, why don't you learn to play something?" Rose-Marie said. "You and Walter could be a band."

"Don't need to learn," he said. He spat and hit a Camel cigarette butt six feet away. "Done know how. French harp."

"Oh sure," I said. My legs were aching because Dorothy has squeezed me completely off the bench. "You could just up and play us something right now."

Rose-Marie was batting her eye at him. "Could you?"

He splattered the Camel butt again and said, "Guess so," and to my utter disbelief pulled an old French harp from his jeans pocket and played the worst "Wabash Cannonball" ever heard in or out of Nashville. Rose-Marie was practically holding his hand when we went back to class, and I, looking down at my bib overalls, perceived my heart as a ragged chunk of fresh liver ready for frying. I saw myself flopping under a train coming out of Nashville, a black guitar strapped across my back.

I began training a month early for the class picnic in April. It was always held at Jimmie Cowley's farm, in the hackberry grove, and Jimmie's dad always put up a quarter for the footrace. This year, I reasoned, it would probably be a half-dollar since we were fifth graders. Every evening at home I practiced running with my chin stuck out. I developed a secret technique, holding my fingers and thumbs straight out and tightly together, vertical for streamlining. I didn't mention the race to Orielle. He would, I figured, wear his cowboy boots with the big, heavy heels. That would cost him about ten miles an hour. I would wear my sneakers. I even went home with Jimmie, whom I hated, and practiced secretly on the real course while he was helping with the evening chores. The course began at the edge of the hackberry grove, went up a little hill to an old hay barn and straight back down to the hackberries, where everyone would be standing, cheering. I had won the race two years straight; I knew the taste of glory. My legs were long and skinny, runner's legs, I thought; Orielle's were short and muscular, hopeless. I envisioned myself pulling steadily away from Orielle and the others as we went up the hill, my streamlined hands knifing through the air, sure-grip sneakers skimming the red dirt; whizzing around the barn, flying back down the slope, glancing back at the others as I slowed, trotted, even walked with dignity across the finish line, spitting hwttt! casually at a black tarantula about to leap on Rose-Marie, drowning it. I practiced spitting. My chin chapped again. The presentation ceremony, I thought, would be dramatic: Orielle and the other awed competitors in a little group to one side; murmurs of praise in the background as I stood with my thumbs in my hip pockets, tall as—no, taller than—Rose-Marie; a tear trickling from her eye. After a long, eloquent, heart-felt speech by Jimmie's dad, who was a stutterer and usually didn't say anything, he would give me the half-dollar and I, taking it with a humble, but significant, "I am indeed grateful to you, Mr. Cowley," would turn to Rose-Marie and say in a rough, kind voice, like a cement mixer, "You want this half-dollar, Rose-Marie? I got plenty."

The morning of the picnic was hot and windless. Mrs. Moser held classes hopelessly, for everyone was thinking about the potato chips, bologna sandwiches, and cold pop the mothers were bringing—everyone except me; I was concentrating on the race. Orielle as usual had on his boots. My plan was working. I held my hands at my sides in their streamlined position as I sat at my desk, imagining they were jet-propelled sails. Dorothy was busy passing notes between Orielle and Rose-Marie, and smirking at me. I smiled grimly; that would come to a screeching halt.

At last we were piled into the bus and driven to the

Cowley farm, Mrs. Moser making worried remarks to the driver about the thunderheads building up in the southwest. Nobody paid any attention. We all knew she saw cyclones in every cloud. When the bus stopped the kids flew in every direction, some to climb the scrawny hackberries, some to wade the forbidden creek, others to slide down the gullies and ruin their jeans. I was doing the same thing till I realized Rose-Marie and Orielle were walking—walking!—in the grove, Dorothy tagging along. So I went to check the racetrack for loose rocks that I might avoid and Orielle stumble over in his boots and break his leg on.

Finally Mr. Cowley blew his whistle to line us up for the race. Mrs. Moser was still watching the thunderhead, which was now huge and black and moving toward us with small wispy white clouds flitting beneath it, and some of the mothers were listening to her.

"On your m-m-mark!" Mr. Cowley said. I was poised on all fours, almost feeling sorry for Orielle, who, poor ignoramus, was standing straight up beside me. Hwttt! he spat. I remembered I hadn't learned to spit, but that was a small matter.

"Go!" All I saw was the heels of Orielle's boots churning dust in my face; my streamlined hands seemed like parachutes holding me back. By the time I reached the corner of the barn where his muscular butt had disappeared, people were clapping, and when I emerged on the other side Jimmie's dad was already giving Orielle, not fifty cents, but—God! Injustice!—a silver dollar. I didn't even come in second. The liver, I saw, was unfit for humans; it would be thrown, raw and bleeding, to a snarling pack of mongrels in the back yard.

Before the clapping had stopped there was a tremendous crack of thunder. The clouds were careening in every direction, and no one had to tell us to get on the bus and head back to school and the storm shelter. Every kid in western Oklahoma knew what tornado clouds looked like.

We were all packed into the long, low-ceilinged, damp

concrete cellar with the other classes just as the winds and rain hit, the girls screaming and some of the little kids crying. The thought occurred to me that Orielle probably didn't know about twisters and had stayed out there to be blown to Jamaica or at least fried right down to his pointed boot toes by lightning. But there they were on a bench in the darkest corner of the cellar, Rose-Marie hanging on to his arm like he was gold-plated.

I squeezed in beside them, despite Dorothy's protesting I was scrunching her. I said, "Orielle, I guess you don't have these storms in Texas. There'll probably be a flood. It almost washed away the bridge on Cattle Creek once, on our place."

"Brazos River flooded us out in Texas," he said. "Took the barn. Took my horse. Took the pickup. GMC pickup."

Rose-Marie gasped and tugged on him like he was in quicksand. I ground my teeth and acted like I hadn't heard. "But of course that's nothing compared to a tornado. Twister, now that's something. Blew our windmill down last year."

Orielle looked for a place to spit. I tucked my sneakers under the bench. He said, "Same night as the flood, twister blew our house away. My mom was in the kitchen. Never seen her again."

Rose-Marie shrieked and groaned and buried her face, hair and all, on his shoulder. I hated his guts.

The storm passed—no tornado—and we were herded back to the classroom, all but Orielle and Rose-Marie. Jimmie Cowley and I were sent to look for them, but my heart, reduced to minced liver, wasn't in it. My heart wasn't anywhere. The mongrels of despair had eaten it, even the bitter bile was gone. I knew where they were, still in the cellar, and I didn't want to find them, but my feet carried me there.

They were standing in the darkest corner. Rose-Marie

had his neck locked in her arms, his nose smashed against her bony chest and the bumps, and she was kissing the tight curly locks on top of his head and crooning, "Orielle, my poor, poor Orielle." I backed out and sent Jimmie to get them. I wasn't up to it.

The Bastemeyers moved away when school was out that spring, and I never saw them again; nor, I suppose, did Rose-Marie. But it was too late. What I had assumed to be a benevolent universe had manifested itself as malignant, or even worse, indifferent: I had looked into the storm cellars of life and found betrayal, peered down the racetrack of love and seen disappearing bootheels. When Rose-Marie returned from summer vacation in Santa Fe with her hair dyed black and a pair of castanets and her name changed to Rose Maria and calling Dorothy Drumheller "señorita," and I saw interest once again flicker in her limpid brown eye for me, I could not respond. The watermelons were gone, the tank empty. And when she fell in love with Randy Muncie, who was in the eighth grade and had a sombrero from Juárez and a Cushman motor scooter, not a molecule of envy stirred me. I had sat on the bench of hope, and it was air. Orielle had ruined my life.

· · · ·

Orielle Bastemeyer, who could spit like the children along the ancient banks of the Great Kwa, where are you now? Who in your tenth-year glory could splatter a Camel butt at six feet and steal my girl with a rusty French harp, who had curly hair and a cowboy dad, whose barn was washed down the Brazos and mother whisked to kingdom come in her own kitchen, who showed me your heels in the picnic race and in your expectoratory uniqueness could bridge space, yea even time, flaunting in the New World that runic craft unknown except in the heart of darkness, cradle of the species, where are you? I have seen the Pyramids, the Pantheon, the walls of China and Benin, the women of Yala and Annang, traveled from Niamey to

Timbuktu by Range Rover, boat, and camel, and where are you and what are you doing and what have you done? Orielle Bastemeyer, despoiler of my life, can you top this? I'm in Africa, where you could lose a dozen Texases, where the sands of the desert bubble glassily in the midday heat, the harmattan withers the soul, mambas kill from baobab trees, fish walk in the mangrove labyrinths, and the palms bleed wine, where every mother's son can spit hwttt! and where the hell are you? Can you still set a katydid awash? Can you still cup your hands and blow OHHH-*EEE*-OHHH to the wonder of brown- or red- or raven-tressed girls who comb their hair over one eye? Orielle Bastemeyer, may Esu god of disruption dog your churning heels, may your battery-square head gleam baldly, may the very teeth you spat hwttt! through be dentist's porcelain!

6 | »
Nineswander's
Fence

"GREETINGS from the chickenhouse," I wrote to my parents. I made it sound like a joke, but my real intention was to impress them. No heaped decades of manure under a sagging roost here: the concrete floor was spotless. The screen door hung true. Yet Mrs. Doty assured me that my room, my part of the long, low building—to the east it was a machinery shed, west a storage room, and beyond that a workshop—had been a chickenhouse. The bed, the chair, and dresser were new, as was the shelving for Mrs. Doty's books. There wasn't a chicken on the place.

"When Doty decided to farm, I said all right if he did it within reason," Mrs. Doty said the first evening at supper. "Chickens and milk cows are not within reason."

I had to look to be sure Doty was laughing: a sudden rush of air and expanse of gold-lined teeth above a jutting chin, small shrewd eyes shining behind rimless glasses. He didn't dress like a farmer in overalls or coveralls. He wore khakis, knit shirts, and golfing caps—Mrs. Doty called them that—instead of straw hats.

Mrs. Doty also explained the outdoor shower, the fifty-gallon barrel Doty had set up on the corral fence behind the long building: "I don't need any grease and field dirt in my house." Shivering in the breeze of the first refrigerated air conditioner I had ever seen, I savored this. The chicken-less, cowless farm, Doty's knit shirts and golfing caps—all agreed with the fence that ran both directions from the house to the section lines and half a mile north.

I said, "As soon as I saw your fence I knew I wanted to work here."

Doty laughed soundlessly again, and Mrs. Doty sniffed in what I took to be agreement. "That was old Nineswander's last hurrah."

"Nineswander?"

They were silent. What I had said was true. I had seen Doty's notice posted at the bus station in Kirchfield and caught a ride with a farmer, who pointed out the fence when we were ten miles away. I watched it as if it were a mirage. Four strands of barbed wire would hold any cow worth keeping, my father had taught me long ago; five were luxury. He had not prepared me for two miles of six-board, eight-foot-high white fence.

I pointed out the window at the backboard and goal on the edge of the garage driveway. "Who's the basketball player?"

Mrs. Doty set dishes of fruit cocktail by our plates. "That was here when Doty bought the place. It was for Nineswander's grandchildren."

I learned that everyone called him Doty or "His Honor." He had been the mayor of Kirchfield, where he had managed and later owned the grain elevator. His mailbox had "Horace L. Doty" stenciled on it.

Mrs. Doty spoke with her thin, bluish lips pursed to one side in what I at first took to be a mutter of disapproval and irritation. Often it was. A certain tone of hers would snap off a topic. When she used it Doty never replied, and I soon learned not to either. She used makeup only when she drove the new Kaiser (maroon, matching the trim on the house) to Kirchfield in the afternoons to play bridge. Her food differed from the meat and potatoes, the endless fried chicken a hired hand expected to eat: potatoes did not taste of the meat's grease, peas and green beans held their color. The plates and bowls matched and were unyellowed, unchipped. The knives and forks were graceful yet heavy, without garlands and flowers. Folded napkins. Formality, alertness: I could not set my empty tea glass down so quietly that Mrs. Doty did not hear the rattle of the ice and refill it immediately. They had a dining room with a large table, lace-covered, but we three ate in the kitchen on a smaller one of stainless steel and thick glass. Except at breakfast, there was never a sign—not a dirty pot or spoon—that she had cooked.

In the mornings I heard Doty's heavy step on the gravel, then the wakeup call: "About that time, James." When I came to the kitchen, Mrs. Doty, her eyes still puffed with sleep, curlers under a plastic cap, would be poaching Doty's eggs, having set my plate on the table. I could smell shaving soap, could hear through the floor above me Doty's hawking, the thump of his boots.

Harvest is desperation, fear of high winds, hailstorms, fire; the heads of wheat suddenly ripen and bend on thin stalks, and there is a held breath until the grain is safe in the bins, or is trampled down, worthless, the year's work lost. Doty used this rush, this desperation, I realized too late, to cheat me. Not until after harvest was over and the plowing well started did he discuss wages.

"Hundred twenty-five a month."

"I could have made more than that in two weeks working by the day," I said.

"You want to quit now, I'll pay you a little more."

The sun cast the pickup's long shadow ahead of us. We were driving to his Corwin field, fifteen miles from the home place. We had brought the tractors the day before, and Mrs. Doty had picked us up and taken us home. Doty pointed toward Corwin. "About ready to cap those tanks." Corwin consisted of a co-op elevator, a few stores and

houses, and some elm trees, just a spot of green in the corner of a wheatfield, the concrete elevator a gray stump
above it. Six new tanks were being built.

The elevator tanks blurred in my anger at my stupidity
for not settling with him before harvest, at my notion—I
hadn't put this in words to myself, I was so sure of it—that
a gentleman farmer with an expensive fence around his
place would pay fair wages. I thought about quitting, but
there were no more jobs by now; his "little more" would
be a five-dollar bill, and I would have less than two hundred dollars to show for the summer. I did some bitter
arithmetic: Doty's wheat had made thirty-five bushels an
acre. Wheat was selling for two dollars a bushel, and he
had over a thousand acres. I snickered at the incongruity.
Doty glanced at me angrily, but said nothing.

I said, "One-fifty a month would probably break the
bank, wouldn't it?"

He turned the pickup in at the Corwin field. "One
twenty-five."

We began to pump diesel into the tractors.

As a boy Doty had scooped wheat in the boxcars beside
the elevator at Kirchfield. When he was fifteen a football
player from Georgia, an All-American, went to work beside him one hot July day, collapsed in half an hour, and
died before they could get him to the hospital. Doty was
manager of the elevator before he was thirty and bought it
when he was thirty-five. He ran it for twenty years. When
he told me these things, I reflected that our negotiations
over my pay had been a mismatch: farmers were willing to
quibble over a nickel, and Doty had dealt with them suc-
cessfully for forty years before I tackled him.

He seemed to ease up after he saw that I wasn't quitting.
We still were in the field shortly after sunrise and worked
till sundown, but he gave me Sundays off, and often we
quit earlier so he and Mrs. Doty could go to Kirchfield, or

he sent me to work by myself. Sometimes he invited me in to watch the fights on television—Kid Gavilan, Hurricane Carter, Archie Moore.

Mrs. Doty tried several experiments with her new deep-freeze that failed, except to irritate Doty. Since I drank a lot of milk, she brought home several cartons and froze them, but neither Doty nor I could eat the splotchy stuff on our cereal. She froze tomatoes and attempted to serve the resulting mush. She also tried some new dishes on us as practice for her bridge club: tomato aspic, a pâté, stuffed crab.

"What's this?" Doty asked.

"Tomato aspic."

"I like it," I said.

Doty pushed his aside. "Doesn't look like a tomato to me."

Mrs. Doty removed the plate. "At least James has an open mind about it."

Even during harvest, I had been reading Mrs. Doty's old Book-of-the-Month Club selections on the shelves in my room: *Brideshead Revisited*, *Green Grass of Wyoming*, *East River*, *Raintree County*. Now I read more. I told her I was reading *Cass Timberlane*. "Sinclair Lewis is really sarcastic," I said at breakfast. I had read long after the lights in the house had gone out. "He's funny."

"Sarcastic, yes; there's nothing funny in that book."

Doty hawked loudly and started down the stairs. I said, "I mean the way he describes people, like the dentist's wife and her relatives that smell like soap."

"Nothing wrong with soap."

"What's wrong with soap?" Doty asked.

"We were talking about one of my books." Mrs. Doty set his plate on the table, and we ate in silence.

Despite that abrupt ending, Mrs. Doty and I began to discuss my reading, sometimes even when Doty was at the table. I read *Giant* and *The Silver Chalice*, started but did not finish *Tallulah*, and read and re-read *Catcher in the Rye*. That one I did not mention.

Mrs. Doty didn't know it, but we also talked at times other than at the kitchen table. I spoke for both of us on the tractor, and in these conversations she was so swept up in my intensity that she had no choice but to capitulate intellectually and, naturally, bodily. I smoothed her face and unpursed her mouth, and in my usual version—Doty was at a meeting in Wichita—she whirled from the kitchen stove, tore her housedress open, and revealed herself as very much like a girl on a calendar in the gas station at Corwin. As the afternoon wore on, however, the realist took over and I told an imaginary friend she had "lost a fight with Ugly"; "she eats corn on the cob through a picket fence"; "it was a choice between her and the dog, and the dog won."

I didn't say anything to her about *Catcher in the Rye* because it didn't seem like a book she would read, or even own. More important than that was this Holden Caulfield, the boy in the book. He was my age, but to me he was an alien. For one thing, he was being kicked out of his fourth or fifth private school. I had never heard of private schools, much less of being kicked out. He was casual about losing things, like the fencing team's foils on the sub-way in New York City, or even his money. I didn't know what foils were—swords, maybe—but I was as careful with Doty's screwdrivers, which probably cost less than foils, as I was with his tractor, which cost more than my father made in three years. I had never seen a fencing match, a subway, or a taxicab. As I got off the tractor and bellied under the plow to pull out Russian thistles that had clogged the colter disks, I wondered why he would say getting in and out of taxicabs was a pain in the ass. Thinking of the flour sack in which I had brought my extra clothes, I wondered why he disliked cheap suitcases and what an

expensive one would look like. I wondered, with all the
sophisticated things he knew—what musicians in New
York night clubs were good or bad, where to go in the Village, wherever that was—why he seemed so obsessed with
people who squeezed pimples or picked their noses or far-
ted. I wondered how he would react to a cow with her
nose eaten off by screwworms, or to holding a calf while it
was being castrated. He seemed like a whiny little pissant
to me, yet some things in the book rang true, like his inability to get a brassiere open, or the part with the
prostitute and her boyfriend, which I read every night.
While the tractor droned around the field I took his place
and gave the scene very different endings in which the
whore emerged as not only sensitive but a grateful virgin as
well. Still, I acknowledged the truth of the scared kid in the
hotel room.

One day when it rained we went to Kirchfield to get
some disks sharpened. While Doty waited at the black-
smith's, I bought a basketball at the hardware, and after
supper that night I shot goals on the driveway. Doty came
out and watched, hands in the pockets of his khakis.

"You ever play?" I had just gotten the size and strength
to shoot a jump shot that year, and I leaped again and
again, following each shot to the backboard.

"Played a little football. Had to work too much." He
went back into the house.

Doty had poured a small square of concrete for his outdoor shower, sloping it so the water ran into the corral. He
had hung an old tarpaulin around the slab. Sometimes the
water in the barrel would be so hot by evening we had to
let some out and run in cold well water, but often Mrs.
Doty showered earlier—I knew because of the mud in the
corral—and the water would be pleasantly cool. If we were
late coming in from the fields, she would call from the
back door, "Hurry up and shower," and Doty and I would
take turns getting wet, then soaping up and rinsing off. His

shoulders were muscular, deep chest matted in gray hair, beefy thighs. I thought of the hang of his stomach as mirroring his prominent chin, of one as a verification of the other.

After a windless day when the dust enveloped the tractors no matter which direction they went, he handed me the soap and said, "Soap my back for me. I can't reach a spot there."

"Old age." I lathered the place, which was sickly white compared to his sunburnt arms.

"I never was able to reach it," he snapped.

I was deep into *Kon-Tiki* then. Heyerdahl's journey was as remote as the Milky Way, yet I had lived it that day in a wheatfield. I could not stop talking about it at supper.

Mrs. Doty seemed amused. "There should be another book out there by Heyerdahl. Something about an island."

I nodded. "*Easter Island*. I'm going to read it next."

Doty said, "You'd better turn that light out earlier tonight. Might go to sleep on the tractor."

I grinned at Mrs. Doty. "I can plow in my sleep."

Practicing jump shots before I went to my room, I imagined Mrs. Doty watching from the kitchen door or a bedroom window upstairs, comparing me, my long-muscled legs ("long-muscled," which I had read somewhere, was infinitely better than "skinny"), my agility with Doty's. I knew how the sound of a bouncing basketball carried, and I kept thinking of words like "throbbing" and "pulsating." The last light faded. I took a final shot, then looked expectantly at the house. But it was Doty's heavy shoulders and thick trunk that turned away from the screen door.

After I had finished *Kon-Tiki* I lay in the dark thinking not of Heyerdahl's odyssey but of Mrs. Doty. I invented gaps between the buttons of her dresses, a thigh exposed under the glass top of the table (but hidden from Doty), a carelessly tied robe and the scooped neckline of her gown

under it, and with these indiscretions her wordless surrender. I arose, stepped outside, and, my eyes on the dimly
outlined window where I imagined her to be lying, completed our betrayal of Doty with a few quick strokes.

The next morning Doty drove on to Corwin instead of
turning off toward his field. He parked within inches of
the elevator wall and pointed toward the top of the new
tanks. "They're about finished up there. Let's have a
look."

All my life I had seen the steel ladders running up the
sides of the grain tanks eighty, ninety, a hundred feet or
more, but it had never occurred to me that anyone climbed
them. Doty had already hoisted himself into the pickup
bed, and from there he could get on the first rung of the
ladder. He started climbing.

Before we were a quarter of the way up we were higher
than any other building, any tree in Corwin, anything else
on that Kansas plain. My hands began to sweat, and I
stopped to rub them against my jeans. I thought I had been
climbing fast, but Doty was drawing away from me. I
knew better than to look down; instead I looked up, and
that was just as bad. The tank seemed to lean, to swell
outward and fill the sky; I felt I was climbing out over
nothing, that my body might swing free from the ladder.
The tank swayed, I began to realize, maybe just a fraction
of an inch, but it seemed like a vast distance. I felt heavier,
and an iron stiffness crept through me. Each rung took
more effort, and I thought how slippery it was, how, as I
reached for the next, my life depended on one clenched
hand. I climbed more and more slowly. Doty had slowed
up too, but still the distance between us was widening. I
hated him, hated the son of a bitch and every step he took,
knowing he had been doing this since he was fifteen years
old, that he had trapped me again, just as he had trapped
me over my pay.

Finally he disappeared over the top. The ladder ended

right at the edge, so there was one last breathless scramble
with nothing to hang onto.

He must have been catching his breath and waiting to
see the top of my head, because he was just starting toward the new tanks when I looked over. There was a
single plank laid across to where the men where working.
It was a foot wide, spanning about six feet that looked like
much more to me. Doty took it in one stride. I was still
getting scared then; in another half a minute I couldn't
have done it. I crossed behind him, my stomach flipping at
the give in the board.

While Doty talked to the men pouring the last concrete,
fear hit me. I could see Kirchfield ten miles west, Anthony
thirty miles east, and all the gray elevator shafts that broke
the patterns of the plowed fields. The new tank swayed
with us, and as I moved out of the way of men with wheel-
barrows of cement and sand I looked back at the edge
where the ladder was, where I would soon have to poke
my legs out backwards and grope for the ladder. I shivered
uncontrollably for a moment; I hoped Doty would fall
screaming and splatter over his pickup, and then I would
refuse to climb down and make them lower me in the basket they hauled up cement and sand in. Maybe my anger
dulled my fear. I stopped shaking, and when Doty called I
followed him across the plank, waited until his cap disappeared over the edge, dried my hands on my pants legs,
and climbed down.

That night Doty said, "They're capping the Corwin
tanks. I talked to Johnny Bucher up there today."

"You climbed it?" Mrs. Doty frowned. "I thought that's
why you got out of that business."

"Little climb never hurt anybody," Doty said. "That
right, James?"

"He climbed up there too?"

"Yep."

She ate in silence. I said, "I've started another book.

Catcher in the Rye." Actually I was starting *Easter Island*, but I wanted—what? I wanted to leave Doty hanging on his damned elevator ladder and speak to her in another language, our language.

"I thought you were going to read *Easter Island*," she said.

"I opened this one by accident. It's good."

Again she frowned. "Maybe I ought to censor those books out there."

"What about the books?" Doty rattled his iced tea glass, and she reached for the pitcher.

"Nothing," she said in the tone that stopped things.

But I didn't want to stop. "I know how that guy feels in the book. He's lucky to live in New York and have all those experiences."

"I certainly wouldn't call it luck." She stood and began to take the dishes from the table. "And I don't think we need to talk about it."

I stood up too, feeling Doty's eyes on me. "Anyway, I understand that guy."

As we started out the door, Mrs. Doty said, "We're going to Kirchfield tonight. There's a movie on, if you'd like to go."

"Sure."

The movie was just Nat King Cole opening his enormous mouth and cooing syrup I didn't like. About ten people were in the theatre, and we all left.

I walked the streets. The kids driving around looked me over and went on. Once I had to explain to the town constable who I was, but when I said "Doty" he left me alone. Finally, while I was reading a plaque on a street corner that said Carry Nation had smashed a saloon there, a girl in a ratty old Willys station wagon stopped.

"Who are you?" she asked.

I told her my name and said I worked for Doty.

"Oh. Doty. Want to ride around?"

We talked about our schools and friends, none of whom

the other knew. She was pretty, I saw when the streetlights caught her. Her name was JoBeth Horton, and her parents owned the dry cleaning shop.

"Old Doty is really tight," she said.

"I know."

"He used to be mayor."

"Big deal."

At ten-thirty she stopped by Doty's car. I put my arm around her, but she leaned over quickly and opened my door, so I got out. The Dotys came out from the party just then, and she honked and waved as she drove away.

"Who was that?" Mrs. Doty asked as Doty started the car.

"JoBeth Horton." I was still thinking about how deftly JoBeth had gotten me out of her car.

"You found one with a reputation soon enough," Mrs. Doty said.

"Reputation?" She didn't answer.

I wondered about that the next day. If JoBeth was easy, how did she get me out of her car so neatly? If she wasn't, why had Mrs. Doty said it? We finished the Corwin field that evening and brought the tractors home the following morning. We had just one more small, sandy field to plow.

August had begun then, the dead-air days when you could see tall funnels of dust miles away that sat in one place and spun themselves out. It had been hot for so long that there was no coolness even in the newly turned ground. Doty had exchanged his cap for the first pith helmet I had ever seen.

After lunch, instead of refueling his tractor, Doty climbed on mine and took the steering wheel. "I'm taking the afternoon off," he said; "I'll make the first round with you."

The sandy field, which ran along a shallow creek, had not been in cultivation long; a row of bulldozed cottonwoods and willows was rotting next to the creek. It was another still day, and sweat had already darkened our shirts. As we neared the creek I could see ahead of us what I first thought were gnats, big clouds of them, but then I realized they were much larger. We hit the first swarm, gray-winged, dark-bodied flying ants, and they began to light on us and bite. We slapped at them, but they got tangled in the hair on our arms and necks, doubled up, and bit until they were crushed. Finally we reached the corner, and Doty turned the tractor away from the creek. I looked back: where the plow had passed, the swarms were milling furiously. The next round would be worse.

Doty got off the tractor by the gate and started toward the house. I looked toward the creek, then at his diminishing figure, headed toward air conditioning, a can of cold beer, and a nap. It wasn't harvest; plowing the field a day or so later when the ants had finished swarming wouldn't make any difference. There were worn moldboards and disks to be replaced, oil in the tractors that needed to be changed, a grain bin that needed cleaning: plenty to keep me busy. Doty didn't have to leave me out there. I drank from the water jug slowly, letting the tractor idle, knowing that Doty was listening for the engine to rev up. But he was too smart—not feeling too guilty; I knew him better than that—to look back when I was watching. I waited until he disappeared behind the farm buildings, then gunned the tractor toward the creek bottom and the ants, saying "Son of a bitch, son of a bitch" over and over again. I finished the field at sundown.

That night I came in to watch the Carter-Flanagan fight, although they hadn't invited me or even answered when I mentioned it at supper.

During the third round a car drove up and two couples about the Dotys' age came in. Doty was suddenly talking loudly in a way I hadn't heard before. Mrs. Doty's mutter became clear and excited. The women kissed Doty and called him "Your Honor." He took some bottles out of a

cabinet, and in a few minutes Mrs. Doty was bringing
drinks. I left the television on but turned it down. I suspected that if Doty caught my eye he would jerk his head
toward the chickenhouse, but I wasn't going to look at
him.

They settled on the couch and chairs at the other end of
the living room. I had seen one of the men in the bank at
Kirchfield. He was kidding Doty about playing blackjack
in Las Vegas. The sour smell of whiskey came to me. I
heard one of the women ask in an undertone if I was the
hired hand, and Mrs. Doty's "Yes." They spoke with a
loud, hard edge to their voices, as if they had a captive audience. Like me. The man from the bank said something
about "a good credit risk like Nineswander," and Doty
laughed.

Mrs. Doty asked, "James, would you like a drink?"

"Yes, Ma'am." My knowledge of drinks was from
names in books—Manhattan, Tom Collins—which meant
nothing to me. I was elated.

I turned the television off, and when one of the women
looked at me I said, "I'm reading *Easter Island*. Have you
read it?"

She shook her head. I said, "I'm where they're exploring
some caves that are so narrow they can barely get through
them. It makes me feel claustrophobic to read it."

"James." Mrs. Doty handed me a tall glass filled with
ice, the liquid clear as water. I drank. It was water.

I choked and bent over, sloshing water on myself.

When I stopped, Mrs. Doty asked, "Are you all right?"

I nodded, my face hot. I said loudly, "It was too strong,
I guess." Her mouth snapped shut, and she turned back to
the others. Then Doty caught my eye, and I went to the
chickenhouse.

Doty took a five-gallon can of paint from the storage
room the next morning and started me painting the corral.
He set my lunchpail inside the workshop. When Mrs. Doty

came out of the house, he said, "We'll be back by this evening," and they left.

Doty had started me on the west side by the shower, out of the morning sun, but by noon I had painted northward to the loading chute, the sun was right over me, and I was baking. I went in my room, read *Easter Island* for a while, and slept. When I finally got back to work, I kept cool by soaking my shirt in the shower. In fifteen minutes it would dry out, bone dry. I took more breaks in the afternoon to read, keeping an ear cocked for Doty's car.

I kept thinking about the boy in *Catcher in the Rye*, all the things he did, and the one thing he didn't do, which was work. That was the difference, that was why his life was exciting: work was boring, especially farm work, in spite of all the crap about farmers chewing milky grains of ripening wheat and feeling up the moist soil. What they really did was kill everything they didn't want to grow and think about going to Arizona for the winter. They hired stupid boys like me, and the work was even more monotonous than factory work because it was done alone. I thought back over the summer: the few paltry things I could remember—reading books, talking with Mrs. Doty, riding around with JoBeth—had happened when I wasn't working. Caulfield was rich, so he was interesting. If he acted like a nut, his parents would hire a psychiatrist; if I did, Doty would fire me. I was a peasant.

"You didn't get far yesterday," Doty said at breakfast. There was a letter from JoBeth by my plate.

"Took a while to get the hang of it. I got faster in the afternoon." I spread extra jam on my toast without looking up.

"Not much to learn about painting a fence."

Mrs. Doty nodded at the letter. "She didn't waste any time."

I went back to work on the corral, stirring the paint in the five-gallon can, then pouring it into a gallon can to carry to the fence. By mid-morning I had started back southward and was across from the shower when I ran out of paint. I was about to climb the fence when someone turned on the water in the shower.

If this sounds silly, that's because it is—now. Doty was mad because I had loafed yesterday, so I needed to keep working. I was out of paint, and it was across the fence—two fences. I didn't know who was in the shower, but if I went over the fence—I had to climb it right there because the machine shed was to the south and the paint was wet farther north—if I went over there I'd be looking right down into the shower and at whoever was in it. I thought of all this in about five seconds. Then instead of climbing the fence I walked around the long building, and just as I came in sight of the shower Mrs. Doty stepped out holding her towel at arms-length before she wrapped it around herself.

I went straight on to the paint, refilled the can, and climbed over the fence. I didn't hear Mrs. Doty go to the house, but in a minute or so Doty came striding across the gravel driveway, swung up on the fence by the shower, lunged over, climbed the second one, and stood on it above me.

"How's it going, James." It wasn't a question.

I kept my eyes on the paintbrush. "All right."

"Your lunchpail is in the workshop. You run out of paint, there's more in the storage room."

"Right." If I looked up, I knew, I would see him with his fists on his hips, balanced up there to show how easy it was to climb a couple of fences instead of walking a hundred yards around a building to see a man's wife coming out of the shower.

"We're going to Kirchfield. You finish here, start on the fence at the road. See if you can't get more done today." He grunted, jumped down inside the corral, and climbed out the other side.

Sometimes you mull over your motives, and others': had I really walked around so as not to seem like a peeping Tom? Couldn't I have swung over the fence quickly, my back to the tarp? Couldn't I have heard as I rounded the corner that the shower had stopped, and backtracked? Why hadn't Mrs. Doty said something, so I would have known for sure it was her? Or would that have mattered? She had told Doty; she didn't have to . . . I wondered why she had.

I said I went straight on to the paint, which was true, and I *was* looking straight ahead, but you see a lot when you're not supposed to, the pink shower cap, the hang of her stomach, like Doty's, and two scars, a long one across her stomach and another short and vertical on her right side. The funny thing was that before I got to the big paint can I was already confusing her with a picture I'd seen once. It was in a book about the German concentration camps in World War II that got in our school library by mistake. The picture was of women being run naked down a street in front of German soldiers, and one of the women you could see very clearly, the bush at her crotch and the shame on her face, you could see that even though she was old her lips were set tight like Mrs. Doty's and she was running fast to escape the shame, her hair flying and her breasts flapping awry. I couldn't separate the two, her and Mrs. Doty.

After that, in the morning Doty would take me, the paint, paintbrushes, water jug, and lunchpail to where I had stopped painting the fence the day before. He picked me up at sundown.

I understood that they were trying to run me off. One evening at supper Doty laughed soundlessly and asked, "You still like that fence as much as you used to?"

"There's burnt wood all along behind it," I said. "What's that from?"

"Shelterbelt."

Mrs. Doty muttered, "No wonder old Nineswander went bankrupt, with that and the fence."

"Fence is a damned nuisance," Doty said. "Should have burnt it too."

But for the most part we ate our meals silently. Silence, I thought, was important to both of us, Doty and me. He could fire me any time, but that wasn't enough. He wanted me to say, "I quit." I knew it was a kid's game, something like climbing an elevator or seeing who could tough it out with a wheat scoop in a boxcar.

Even the weather seemed to be on their side. Six days straight the thermometer by the workshop door was still over a hundred when Doty brought me in at dark. It was stupid; I wasn't sure why I was sticking it out. Doty was smart, and maybe he was sure I *would* stay if I thought they were trying to get rid of me. I thought about this possibility, then forgot it; *what* Doty wanted was *his* business. I decided I was staying to make it up to myself for being awed by whatever I had mistaken the fence for, and more than that for confusing Doty with it.

This will sound crazy, but I got to know old Nineswander while I knelt in the cinders washed from the plowed ground where the shelterbelt trees had been. The creosoted posts were first-quality, the boards extra thick and heavy with scarcely a knothole in them. They fit so tightly in the notches cut in the posts they could have grown there, but nevertheless they were held with heavy galvanized nails. Nineswander had built his fence to last a hundred years in a place where maybe a dozen people would see it, mostly farmers who would grouch at the wasted money every time they passed.

I hated the heat, the dirt, and the loneliness out there, where waving at the driver of the bulk milk truck was the high point of the day. I hated the fence too, but finally I began to think of it as a huge grin, like Nat King Cole's: the Nineswander I knew, bankrupt, dead, or whatever, was having a long last laugh. Years later when I read that someone had buried a bunch of Cadillacs in Texas with their tailfins up in the air, I immediately thought of Nineswander's fence. I decided to try to finish it before the end of the month when I went back to school.

During the second week that I was painting, one of those storms that pound the earth with huge raindrops passed through in the night. The humidity the next day was unbearable, and that was the closest I came to getting sick. The minutes dragged. The sun seemed to stop straight overhead. I pulled up Russian thistles and piled them against the fence to make a shade to eat lunch under.

When Doty brought me in that night the shelves in my room were empty and the books gone, even *My Cousin Rachel*, which I was reading and had laid face down on the dresser, and *Catcher in the Rye* too, with the hotel room scene marked. The Dotys said nothing about the books at supper, and I wouldn't have said anything if they had piled them on the table and set fire to them.

There was a letter addressed in JoBeth's big round handwriting, but I didn't open it. I practiced jump shots and layups until pitch dark, dribbling up and down the driveway. I tried to imitate one of my teammates at school who could bounce the ball so hard and fast it sounded like pistol shots.

The next evening the poles that held the goal were lying beside the driveway. The backboard and goal were gone.

"Had to take that basketball goal down," Doty said at supper. "Need the poles for a gate at the Corwin field."

I yawned. "It was an eyesore anyway." Mrs. Doty looked at me sharply. I rattled my iced tea glass, and she reached for the pitcher.

I finished the east half of the fence two days later and

started on the west side. There were eight days left before school started, and I was sure I could do it all; I was getting faster every day.

Doty went into the field after calling me the next morning. He came in late for breakfast.

"That storm packed the ground," he said as Mrs. Doty took his plate from the oven. "Needs springtoothing." He looked at me. "How much longer do you have?"

"School starts a week from tomorrow."

He chewed his toast, then nodded. "Put the painting stuff away."

As I stacked the paint cans in the storage room, I felt as if someone had just let me out of a cage. I went into the chickenhouse.

In a few minutes Doty called "James!" from the machine shed. I came out carrying my flour sack. Doty was bolting another section onto one of the springtooths. He began, "Hook up that—"

"I want my check," I said.

He looked at the sack, then finished tightening a bolt. "Bad time to quit. Ground needs working."

"I want my check."

He began loosening the clamp on one of the curved teeth that was broken. "Pay you eight dollars a day the rest of the time you're here."

I shook my head.

"You quit now I can't pay you for a full month."

"I can work fractions," I said. "You owe me ninety-two dollars."

He went into the house and came out in a few minutes with a check. Mrs. Doty stepped out on the back porch, her hands on her hips. The check was for a hundred dollars. I said, "There's eight extra here."

"That's all right."

I put the check in my billfold, and we shook hands.

As I turned toward the driveway, I said, "You asked me

if I still liked old Nineswander's fence. Well, I do. I would have stayed to finish it."

Mrs. Doty shaded her eyes. "I'll be going to Kirchfield, if you want a ride to the bus station."

"There's a milk truck coming by pretty soon," I said. "I can catch a ride with him."

She went inside. Doty was working on the springtooth again, his back to me. I walked down the driveway with long country strides, whistling, and turned east onto the road. If there was time before the bus left, I thought, I might look up JoBeth. The fence grinned at me so white in the morning sun it hurt my eyes, and I grinned back, and that's when, for no reason at all, I started crying.

7 | »
Tearing
the House
Down

WILLIAM couldn't remember when he hadn't known how badly Grandpa Toll had located the house. The bare hill and the red dirt road ten yards away, the cedar planted before he was born and scarcely waist-high when he was old enough to hoe the weeds around it, sometimes encouraged by his father's tamarack switch, and now, thirty years later, not much taller than his head; the curve in the road where summer dust rose with each passing pickup or cattle truck, drifted northward and settled over the house; winters with not a mesquite or fencepost for a quarter of a mile to break the north wind. Remembering his icy flesh as he used to burrow under the quilts, trying to flee the urgently human sounds of the wind under the eaves, William suddenly shivered and began to slide. He grabbed the chimney.

"Careful," Theodore said. "It's steep."

Brad grinned. "Whatcha doing, Dad?"

"Slipped. Boots are worn out." William set his heel in a hole where the wind had already torn the shingle away and worked the wrecking bar under the metal gable again. The boy seemed delighted with the weekend project. A chance to tear a real house down, to rip his jeans and risk his neck: heaven. Every shriek of a nail pried from its eighty-year resting place seemed to be music to him. His ragged, over-sized sweatshirts—one apparently filched, William noted, during the boy's last visit to his apartment—flapped in the wind. Always the wind.

And the rattlesnakes. Maybe the piles of junk—Theodore would never call them that, not even now—the twisted scrap iron, disks, moldboards, horseshoes, oil barrels cut in half, hitches, drawbars, magnetos, sickle blades, gear housings for mowing machines and rakes and drills, Model T frames, presswheels, sprockets, sprocket chains, clevices, axles, and God knows what else that even Theodore would have to study for half a minute before he named by name and function and origin—maybe the pile of junk on the hill drew the rattlesnakes, like magnets. Or the shade of the house, any shade, the cool ground under the broken masonry of the cistern—something drew them, early spring to late fall, to lurk as thick muscles of death along the foundation, to block the screen door—that had happened when he was five, and he had been the one trying to open it—and shatter his mother's lonely days and test her aim with the .22 rifle.

"Grandpa. What'll we do about the chimney?" Brad asked.

"Use the sledge hammer on it. It just goes down to the attic floor. We'll break it up when we get the roof off," Theodore said.

"Wow."

This was the fast part. The gray brittle shingles snapped easily over the nail heads, and they let them slide off the roof. Later, his father would insist that they save every board, William knew, and that meant not throwing them.

Theodore stood astraddle the gable, feeling the roughly mortared bricks of the chimney. "Your Grandpa Toll must have been in a hurry when he built this," he said apologetically. "I've seen him do a better job."

"Lasted eighty years," William said.

"We boys used to sleep on pallets up in the attic. Sometimes the snow'd blow in. We'd get right up against the

chimney, but by morning it'd be cold. We'd really tumble
down those stairs and run for the cookstove in the mornings."

"Dad!" Brad was on the very edge of the roof, ripping
off the last shingles. "Did you sleep up here too?"

"No. Downstairs." Small and wiry, William thought: the
ten-year-old and the septuagenarian, gamboling over the
roof like mountain goats. His own back already ached.

"Your grandma wouldn't let William sleep up here,"
Theodore said.

So it was a place of delight, not discomfort. Here, on
rainy days, William had found in a sturdy wooden box his
father's childhood toys, of such quality as he had never
seen then or since—cast-iron cars and a horse-drawn fire
engine with a dalmatian on the seat, all brightly painted;
an intricately carved puppet; an ark full of animals. Another box held spent mortar shells, an ammunition belt, an
army cap that had been his Uncle John's, and a bayonet,
blade oiled and shiny, in a heavy scabbard. He found his
mother's tall, clumsy typewriter, played with it and eventually ruined it. Here he had come to read in the dim light of
the four-paned window, sometimes with permission, more
often without, and here, for a breathless minute, he had
once explored a cousin's newly sprouted breasts.

When William stopped to smoke a cigarette after the
shingles were off, Theodore said, "Be careful where you
put that out. The grass is dry."

"Right."

"Your Grandpa Toll used to smoke a cigar once in a
while. None of us boys ever smoked, though."

They began to pull up the shingle lath sheathing from
the rafters. As William had anticipated, his father meant to
save them.

"They're full of nails," William protested.

"I'll have plenty of time to pull them this winter."

"I could help you," Brad said. It was nearly mid-morning, and Brad had shed two sweatshirts, flinging them off the roof, leaving a third, faded orange one with half a sleeve missing. His grandfather had climbed down to discard his denim jumper and switch from felt to straw hat. His blue workshirt under his bib overalls, however, was buttoned at collar and cuff and would remain so, William knew, no matter how hot it got.

He said, "You'll never use these, or anything else here. What's the point in tearing it down?"

"It was raining in where the shingles came off. I didn't want it to rot down."

Back in the pastures, William as a boy had searched out dozens of better places to build a house: valleys where the low bluffs curved to the north so a house might be tucked out of the winter wind like a chick under a hen; in the midst of the chittamwood grove at the spring; or in the mountain itself—it was only a low butte, but they had always called it a mountain—burrow into the soft gyp rock and the harder red clay and live warm in the winter, cool in the summer in the deep, safe silence. Grandpa Toll had, after all, lived in a cave, less than a cave—rough-cut cedar trunks thrown over a narrow ditch, brush and rock and then dirt heaped on them—for five years while he homesteaded the place, while he broke the sod covered with buffalo grass fine as hair and turned it under and readied it to be tilled by his son Theodore and Theodore's son William and. . . .

"Leave the outside ones till last," Theodore said. They had taken up the shingle laths without cracking a single one, eased them to the ground, and stacked them neatly, Brad racing up and down the ladder; then they had knocked the rafters loose from the wall plate and ridgepole, and now William, half a head taller than Theodore, stood on the attic floor holding the ridgepole while the other two worked with hammers and wrecking bar at the outside rafters. Brad was wearing an unmatched pair of

Theodore's old gauntleted work gloves. He had snagged a
pants leg and torn it from knee to ankle, an elbow was
scraped and bleeding, and his red baseball cap was covered
with cobwebs.

"Stack the rafters over by those fence posts," Theodore
said. "By the cellar."

The Fraidy Hole, as the neighborhood called it, but
William remembered that fear had been real enough on
nights in late spring when lightning had exploded and
clouds hurtled chaotically ahead of that unmistakable
freight-train roaring in the southwest; and under the two
broad boards that were its door awaited other terrors in
the cellar—rats, scorpions, a rattler, or a whole nest of
them. Theodore used to loop a rope around the boards,
and one night, when the roaring grew deafening, William
and his parents had clung to the rope and felt themselves
for one timeless instant lifted from the ground, then
dropped as the thing passed. The woodshed was gone the
next morning, a swath of mesquites east of the house
mowed like grass.

William bent with an armload of rafters near the gray
cedar posts, rotted off at ground level over three or four
decades and thus useless, but nevertheless collected and
neatly stacked with two posts crossed under them to keep
them dry. Drop them, William thought irritably, not wanting to admit that he intended to put crosspieces under the
rafters. Kneeling to pull off two of the posts, he felt a
movement, contraction against his boot, saw under the
posts the yellow-brown coil, and leaped backwards.

"Son of a bitch!" he gasped as the angry warning buzz-
ing began.

"What—he get you?" Theodore shouted.

"No!"

"Where is he?"

"Under the posts."

"What, Dad?" Brad shouted as he came running.

"Stay back. It's a rattlesnake," Theodore said to Brad; to William, "Watch him. I'll get my snake killer."

It would be, William knew, a limber chittamwood stick, newly cut that spring: long, light but hard as iron, kept in the pickup ready for use like the sledgehammer, several pairs of gloves, an extra coat and hat, plus a cap, two spades, two flashlights, coils of bailing wire, an extra jug of water, a gallon of kerosene, an axe, a rifle and maybe a shotgun, blocks of wood of various sizes. . . .

"Probably taking a snooze under there," Theodore said.

The killing of the snake was predictable, if exciting to Brad: the higher, incredible intensity of its rattling as it was punched out from under the posts, its too-late attempt to flee, the whistling arc of the stick four, five times, the draped body over the stick, the ritual cutting off of the rattles, Brad's delight in taking them.

You just killed them. That was the law of the farm. There was another way of thinking, doing things—the snake hadn't harmed him, wasn't going to harm him—that William fully believed in elsewhere, but not here. It had started with Toll, the patriarch, who had determined that this land, and the land of his neighbors as they starved out, or, a little more reasonable than he, had simply left, was to be Stephens land, no one else's, no other creature's. No, William thought, it started with the Stefanovich who handed on not a word of his mother tongue, not a word about his origins, thus killing off the past, and with the Stefanovich who killed the last vestige by changing his name to Stephens, and then Tolliver who named a son after Teddy Roosevelt, Theodore who named William after Bryan, and William who chose a harsh monosyllable of the Sixties . . . if it can't be nailed or plowed, if it's a nuisance, kill it.

Toll had also killed something else: the thin skin of dark soil, the topsoil, fragile as a dragonfly's wing. He had over-grazed the land; worse, turned it under and planted it to wheat; worse, to broomcorn; worse, to cotton, killing, tearing down even as he built, and after a short burst of prosperity the land began to die, only wheat would grow and less and less of that, and Theodore tried to turn it back to buffalo grass, nearly too late.

By noon they had bared the joists of the ceiling, and Brad had put his foot through the plaster underneath several times. They ate bologna sandwiches on the floor in the old living room, sharing apples and a piece of cheese.

"This is great," Brad said.

"Like that old baloney?" Theodore asked.

"You bet." At home he wouldn't have touched it, William thought.

"Grandpa. You ever wear those overalls out?"

"Got an old pair. You want them?"

"You bet."

"I'll give them to you tonight."

Brad stretched out on the floor, "Dad. How come you don't come live out here? You could fish and round up cattle, drive around the pastures in the pickup. . . ."

William rattled the ice in the water jug. Luxury is luxury so long as it awes you, he thought, remembering how as a child he had stared at the ice in a glass of water in a restaurant, how the roar of the first flush toilet he ever saw startled him.

"You don't know," he said, glancing at Theodore's oversized knuckles; "you're just out here a day, in an air-conditioned pickup. You don't know what it's like, day in and day out."

Theodore stirred, shuffled his feet. William remembered, years ago:

"*You're what?*"

"Going on to graduate school. Going to teach history."

"But who'll take over the—"

"I don't know. Not me."

Brad said, "What what's like?"

"Living here. Working here. Sunup to sundown on a tractor—"

"Man!"

"Not 'Man!' Just boring."

"A Dutchman built the house," Theodore said. "Name of Speer. Your Grandpa Toll said he—"

"Not a Dutchman," William said. "German. All those 'Dutchmen' you talk about were Germans. *Deutsch* they were; not Dutch."

Theodore said after a pause, pointing to the short, narrow staircase that now led to nowhere, "He did a fine job on those stairs. It's a tricky thing, building stairs. You have to figure the rise and the run and the angle, then cut stringers to hold the steps. These had to turn a corner, so that made it worse for old Mr. Speer. Grandpa Toll said he figured it all out in the dust right there at the corner of the house one morning. Said if a whirlwind had come up, he'd have lost a day's work."

William lit a cigarette. "I've never understood why Grandpa Toll built on this bare hill. There are all kinds of better places in the pastures, down out of the wind and dust."

"He was kind of proud of it," Theodore said. "It was the first frame house out here. Most folks had soddies. There wasn't much dust then. The road was just a track, and people didn't drive by sixty miles an hour."

"The soddies made more sense anyway. Warmer in winter, cooler—"

Brad jumped up, whistling the new tuneless shriek he had acquired. "Let's go back to work."

"Grandpa hauled this shiplap from Fort Worth," Theodore said, standing in the front doorway and running his fingers over the gray, ribbed siding. "Took him four days. We can put it up in the barn loft."

"There's nothing you can use it for. Why do you want to keep it? Throw it away. Burn it," William said.

"Let's go to work," Brad called from the top of the stairs.
"Coming," Theodore said.

What right, William wondered, to impose on future generations? Presumptuous. . . . He felt the darkened indenta-
tions in the living room floor where a succession of stoves—
oval-shaped wood heaters, a tall black coal burner, various
kerosene models—had failed to keep the room warm. He
recalled his earliest memory: sitting on the floor by the
south window and tearing pages from a book, some book,
and suddenly realizing the foolish waste of it, or perhaps
that he would be punished . . . and one winter day he had
lain on the couch before the same window recovering from
mumps and dreamed of a faceless woman whose body
swelled and shrank, swelled and shrank, until the sun was
full in his face and he awakened, sweating. In his old bedroom, the cowboy-and-cactus wallpaper still hung intact.
He stretched his arms, nearly touching both walls, traced
the line where the red chest of drawers had kept the wallpaper from fading, the chest where he had hidden a paperback with what had seemed a torrid sex scene in it, and
later a package of prophylactics, both of which his mother
must have found. He remembered Grandma Stephens,
hands grotesquely misshapen from ninety years of work,
repeating someone's sage advice: "For God's sake, keep
them on the farm." No right.

He went into the other bedroom, his parents'. So much
mystery here: the drowsy, never-quite-understandable mur-
mur of their voices; his mother's powders and perfumes—
though a meager supply it must have been; his father's ties
and tie clips, spats, a huge pair of bearskin gloves which he
never wore, the Kodak in its yellow box which came out
only at Thanksgiving and Christmas, a lockbox which
William had never seen open, worn-out dollar watches,
dainty pearl-handled knives, a little .38 pistol that had
been Grandma Stephens'. Glancing up at a hole where
Brad had stepped through the ceiling plaster, he frowned

and smiled. A monument here, a bronze plaque: *Here, following excellent spring rains and a cotton crop worth a fortune in the first instance and a wheat crop which made the mortgage payment in the second, were duly engendered Theodore Stephens and thirty-two years later his son William Stephens.*

William helped Theodore remove the doors and load them in the pickup to be taken to town and stacked in the garage—"People steal doors," Theodore said—while Brad leaped from joist to joist battering down the ceiling lath and plaster until he was stung on the arm by yellowjackets and came flailing down the ladder.

"Thought I'd gotten rid of all those rascals," Theodore said, bringing bicarbonate of soda from the pickup to put on the swelling arm. "Must be a new nest." He waited until the wasps had quieted down, then went up with a tin can of kerosene and splashed the nest. "Got them all, I think."

In the walls, William thought as he pried off the once-green (but not in his memory) trim around the narrow windows, uncovering a square of white paint at the end of each shiplap strip; if the house is eighty years old, there'll be eighty generations of dead yellowjackets in the walls, those that crawled in for the winter and come spring couldn't find their way either back out or else into the house and our clothes to sting us. And he was right: they filled the spaces between the studs high as the windowsill, dust at the bottom, larger fragments, then dry but recognizable shells, and finally the curled, browning bodies from the past spring.

Lath inside, plastered over; outside, the shiplap nailed directly to the studs; not an ounce of insulation. The flame in the kerosene lamps used to dip in the winter gales, and sometimes even the Aladdin lamp fluttered. It was a sieve, not a house.

William began pulling away the shiplap, starting with a small triangle at the gable above the attic window.

"Look there, Brad," Theodore said, "you start at the top with that little piece because it was the last to go on."

"Can I have it? And the one from the other end too?"

"What do you want with that?" William asked.

"Can I have it?"

"Make a good souvenir," Theodore said. "Crazy thing people do now with that stuff. They use it *inside* the house—old barn siding, clapboard, anything."

The shiplap came off quickly, and they had nearly bared the north side when a new Oldsmobile, windows up and an air conditioner roaring, stopped behind the pickup in the driveway and a tall, elderly couple got out.

"We're tearing it down, Arthur!" Theodore shouted with a little coughing laugh, like an apology. The woman shrilly echoed his laugh.

A few more inches of topsoil, pedigrees for the herd bulls—even now, William thought, you'd think old Jensen was the county squire.

"All the fine old landmarks are disappearing, Theodore."

"A wonderful house," Cora Jensen said. "It was always my favorite."

"Just like a sharecropper's," William, crouched in the stairwell while his mother's "club" was meeting, had heard Cora whisper. Later, when he asked what it meant, his mother had cried.

Jensen looked at William. "The younger generation has left us."

"They say you can't keep them on the farm." Theodore coughed again.

"All our institutions are coming apart."

Such as marriage. Amendment to the plaque in the disappearing bedroom: *Toll, husband to Hannah for fifty-three years; Theodore to Martha, forty-five years and*

counting; William to Diane, eleven years only; Brad. . . .
Institutions, William thought, are revered when convenient,
as in old Jensen's case, Methodist piety from ten to twelve
Sunday mornings, and a relentlessly demanding landlord
the rest of the week.

Suddenly William had a thought that made him blush:
back when he and Diane were dating, even before they had
lived together, he had brought her out here from Tulsa one
Sunday afternoon, not telling his parents or stopping by
their house in town, had brought her straight to the old
house intending to make love there, found it locked, and—
it had seemed a perfectly reasonable thing to do—was
about to break the door in when she stopped him. It being
a fine fall day, they had instead found a sunny slope and
put a blanket down in the brown buffalo grass.

He thought: we're like salmon.

By five o'clock they had the shiplap neatly stacked and
had begun heaping the plaster and lath beside the driveway
to be hauled off. To William's surprise, Theodore didn't
want to save it. William was aching in every joint, but
Brad and Theodore were going strong. Brad, given free rein
at the plaster by Theodore, was banging away with the
wrecking bar, and Theodore and William were taking
turns loading the wheelbarrow and dumping it when
William stepped on a nail.

"Damn it!" He sat down, half falling, pulling the wheelbarrow over. The nail, its rusty head flush in a broken
lath, was deep in his foot, right through the crepe soul of
his boot. He grabbed the lath, closed his eyes, and jerked,
fighting down the quick empty sickness in his stomach.

Brad came running, Theodore behind him. "What'd you
do, Dad?"

"Nail." he stood up, putting his weight on his heel, and
limped to the pickup. "I need to get this boot off."

As he sat down on the running board and started unlacing the boot, he saw Theodore pick up the lath and study the red, wet nail.

"That's one of those old thick eight-pennies," Theodore said. "Your Grandpa Toll bought a keg of them when Carl Lowder quit the lumber—"

"I don't give a damn what it is or where it's from." William threw the boot down and pulled off the stained sock. "If you didn't want the house to rot down you could have saved me a wasted day and a hole in the foot by having it bulldozed over the hill. Why in the hell do we have to keep everything, like packrats?"

"You might get tetanus, Dad," Brad said. "They said in school about rusty nails."

"We can soak your foot in kerosene," Theodore said. "It'll get up in there and disinfect it. I've got an old pan under the pickup seat that'll work about right."

While he has pulling out tire chains, wrenches, overshoes, and a small tarp to get to the pan, Theodore mumbled, "I thought about the bulldozer."

They filled the pan with kerosene, and William put his foot in it, stretching the wound to open it while Theodore and Brad watched.

"Go on back to work," William said. "I'll let it soak for a while."

"That kerosene'll clean it out," Theodore said. He and the boy started toward the house, Theodore stopping to right the wheelbarrow and push it ahead of them, but Brad suddenly turned, came back to the pickup, and stood before William.

"A Dutchman built it," he said, fists on hips.

"What?"

He brushed something from his cheek with the back of his hand and shouted, "A Dutchman built it!"

The smell of kerosene, William thought: as familiar, as close as the musk of cellar air, as a milk cow's flank warm against a boy's forehead on a dark, cold morning.

"Son," he said, "I didn't want to tear the house down at all. I'm sorry we're doing it."

Brad frowned and looked back at Theodore, bent over the wheelbarrow behind the stripped, rib-like studs. He said uncertainly, "So am I."

They were knocking loose the doubled two-by-fours that formed the wallplate by the time William rejoined them.

Theodore glanced at him. "No sense in fooling with that shiplap. I'll wait till we get a good rain so the grass won't catch fire, then pour a little kerosene on it and burn it."

William said, "Let's put it up in the barn. Maybe I'll use it. I suppose I'll build a house one of these days."

He held the loosened end of the wallplate while Brad hammered at the other. Muddling up the creek, he thought; fish muddling up the creek.

8 | »
Interim
in the
Desert

I feel, Marcus—I am sure—that all people in
the world ought to be, each of them, more
than one, and they would all, yes, all of them,
be more easy at heart.
>   —Isak Dinesen,
>   "The Dreamers"

ON a Monday evening in June, on a quiet
street (all of the streets were quiet) in the
West Texas town of Cabora, Andrew Corwin was kneeling in the moist soil of his
garden plot, pulling the bindweed around his tomatoes.
Now and then he glanced across the sparsely grassed yard
at his house nestled in the pecan trees, where he could see
his wife's silhouette behind the latticed windows of the
breakfast nook, her head bent over the lab reports she was
grading. Atop the fireplace chimney, a mockingbird was
scolding; doves, fat and not much wilder than chickens,
were pecking at pecans on the bare ground beneath the
trees; swallows were repairing the mud nest under the
front porch.

The house was a compromise. The Corwins had come to
Cabora eleven years ago, fresh from what Andrew had
thought was, surely must have been, a revolution—he had
seen the killings at Kent State, had been whacked on the

head by a policeman's billy in Chicago and dragged off to
jail from a demonstration in Washington. They had, hadn't
they, stopped a war, deposed a president? Granted, his hair
had been combed when he and Barbara came to Cabora,
his beard trimmed, and they had been properly married,
but these were superficial conformities; certainly not signs
of disillusionment. At Andrew's insistence, despite Barbara's
puzzled misgivings and the frowns of John Canuteson, Andrew's boss in the political science department, they had,
in the Hispanic area south of the railroad tracks, rented a
sand-colored adobe house with cement-patched cracks in
its thick walls, closetless bedrooms, and a slanting floor.
They parked their Volkswagen on the unpaved street
among pickups and low riders, and that first winter Andrew had referred to Sanderson Heights addition with its
three- and four-bedroom, brick-veneered, double-garaged
ranches as "the faculty ghetto." By the next fall, however,
when he had seen that, so long as he rocked no boats,
achieving tenure at Cabora State would require little more
effort than breathing, he complained about the plumbing
in the adobe, its tiny rooms and windows, its creaking
floors. He stopped calling Sanderson Heights "the ghetto,"
although he did not share Barbara's interest in buying a
house there. They settled on a house north of the tracks,
three-bedroom, brick-veneered, double-garaged, fairly new
but in an older area. On one side was a house just like it—
owned by Vinny Singleton, the registrar—but the Pratt
house on the other side, small, unveneered, and run-down,
had allowed Andrew to salve his conscience. That, and the
little garden by the back fence, built up with hauled-in topsoil, had won him over.

"It's not the dirt under your fingernails that you like,"
Barbara had scoffed later. "That garden appeals to your
vanity."

"Nonsense," Andrew replied, but he knew she was right.
A garden in the desert was a luxury.

They had grown potatoes, onions, radishes, jalapeños, okra, cherry tomatoes and slicers, carrots, leaf lettuce, cabbage, and turnips, and they had tried but failed with watermelons and cantaloupes. Barbara had wanted to cut down the Chinese elm that sent its roots up into the garden, but Andrew said, "It's not right to kill anything that can grow in a desert." After a couple of years Andrew was ready to cut it down, but by then Barbara wouldn't allow it. By then she had also ceased feigning any interest in the garden, and Andrew became less ambitious. He gave up on the early and late crops, the cabbage, onions, and radishes; he thought of the work of digging out the potatoes, and didn't plant them; the okra was a nuisance. Finally he grew nothing but tomatoes.

And during their second year they agreed that West Texas' endless highways were not hospitable to cramped, rackety Volkswagens; they bought a small, used Pontiac, and the VW became their second car; a year or so later they bought a larger Oldsmobile, new, and the VW disappeared.

The bindweed was stubborn, persistent stuff. Andrew had to dig out all of each white, corkscrewed root, for otherwise it would come up again in a few days. It was good, mindless work that let him think of, for example, the taste of beer in his throat. Victory beer: he grinned, seeing again the pain, more real than pretended, in John Canuteson's face as he had paid off his golf bet earlier that afternoon. Andrew had, on the eighth and ninth holes (the country club had a nine-hole course), hit perfect approach shots and rolled in successive ten-foot putts to come from nowhere and win ten dollars from Canuteson and five apiece from Maury Harper, the head of the theatre department, and Vinny Singleton.

Andrew thought also with mild regret that his vacation was over, that at nine o'clock the next morning he would face a class of graduate students beginning a three-week workshop. An old professor browsing in the library stacks at Kent State once told him, "You will find, Mr. Corwin, that the only real drawback to university teaching is the students." It was true; the good part was the leisurely vacation reading in the mornings, learning on paths of your own choosing without goals or deadlines; golf in the afternoons. The other side—facing classes with trumped-up energy and zeal, announcing narrow boundaries of interest and achievement for a few weeks or months, naming the game and the rules—was drudgery.

Glancing at Barbara's silhouette in the window again, Andrew thought, or rather refused to think, of something else. He frowned and dug deep in the dark soil, felt it coming over him again, vague but very certain, what had never quite formed itself in words, that conviction that—over how long? The past year, two years?—had loomed as the single menacing fact of his life: in the midst of comfort, of, given any reasonable interpretation of the word, compatibility, his marriage was inexplicably, ever so gradually falling apart.

He shrank under the force of this nameless fear for an instant, as from a jet of cold water; then it abated. And that was when, beyond the fence separating the Corwins' property from the next lot, someone began playing a recorder.

Andrew stopped to listen, surprised. The Pratt house had been vacant for over a year. The piped notes, hoarse and childish, were disparate at first, then began to fall into patterns. It was definitely, Andrew thought, in the Pratt's yard. He stood up slowly. The yard was brown and bare except for a few dandelions with incongruously bright yellow blooms. In the middle of it a woman was sitting on a straight-backed chair. Andrew looked beyond her at the house. There was no car, but boxes were piled in the carport. The windows and front door of the house were open, and he heard—he realized he'd been hearing it for some time—the scrape of furniture being moved.

The woman was tall; that was clear, even though her back was toward him. She was dressed in white, loose pants and a long-sleeved white blouse; a scarf, also white, was wrapped around her head like a turban. Light glinted from a large ring on her finger and bracelets on her wrists. She played the recorder slowly, as if concentrating on an unfamiliar song, bending forward and rising from the hips in time with the music, her neck arching. Yet, Andrew thought, hesitantly though she was playing it, the tune with its runs of high notes and the irony in its slower, lower echoes was urban, hardly what one would expect from a bare yard in a lonely desert town.

When she stopped Andrew applauded and said, "Bravo."

For a moment he thought she was not going to reply. Then, without turning, she said in a pleased voice, "Thank you. You're very kind."

"I didn't recognize the tune," Andrew said.

Holding the recorder up as if she might begin playing again, she asked, "Do you like it? It's my own composition."

"Very nice. Nice to have a new neighbor who's a composer."

"You don't sound like a cowboy." She lowered the recorder to her lap. "I was told there were only cowboys in Cabora."

Andrew laughed and told her that he taught political science at the university.

"Political science. It seems like a contradiction in terms."

Her name, he learned, was Virginia Stone. She sat very straight with a seeming ease that, Andrew had observed, few women, or men, knew. Her voice was strong and full, although it broke higher occasionally, reminding him of the way his grandmother had talked. At first he had thought she might be in her late twenties; then thirties, then forties. She still had not turned toward him. He moved a few steps to the right along the wooden fence until he could see the curve of her breast.

"And what do you do?"

It seemed to him that, hearing the new direction of his voice, she turned her head slightly away. "Principally, I've been a physician. I lived in Colombia for many years."

"What has brought you here?"

"Here? Oh, I came to die."

Andrew started to laugh again, but the flatness in her voice stopped him.

"I've made a foolish purchase," she said. "I bought this house in which I cannot live—that is, assuming I were to live."

"Can't live?" Andrew remembered that Walter Pratt had complained about the poor workmanship in the house. "Well, it needs some repairs probably, but—"

"It's been built with petrochemical materials, which I'm allergic to," she said; "I'm allergic to fuels, insecticides, synthetic clothing and carpets, plastics—all these, and more." The fullness in her voice that Andrew had noted earlier seemed to fade as she spoke. She hesitated, stumbled, as if she were searching, not for the right word, but the strength to utter it.

Andrew said, "But what—I don't understand what you're going to do, if you can't live in the house."

"I have a hammock. I'll put it up in the carport and sleep there."

"That's fine for now, but the winters can be very cold here. Then what?"

She lifted and dropped her shoulders. "We have the summer ahead of us. Perhaps I'll die before winter. The hardware store has sold me something called screw eyes. Do you know of someone who can install them so I can hang my hammock?"

"I could probably do it."

"If you would be so kind."

"We have a new neighbor in the Pratt house," Andrew told Barbara as he got his toolbox from the utility room. "She was sitting on a chair in the yard playing a recorder."

The lab reports were in two stacks on the kitchen table beside Barbara's coffee cup. She was wearing her oldest wraparound skirt, and her bare feet were crossed under the table. As always when she graded papers, she had teased her short brown hair until it sprang out in all directions. She glanced over her glasses at the toolbox. "Was she piping up a handyman?"

Andrew grinned. "Maybe so. I'm going to hang a hammock for her."

Barbara nodded and picked up another paper as Andrew backed out the door with the toolbox. Of the many things he admired about her, one was her confidence. She did not play "mine" games like Vinny Singleton's wife, who would have followed Vinny straight across the yard and through the back gate, arms folded under her breasts, to greet the new neighbor with a sugary smile while she found out what danger had loomed up in the Pratt house and to show that danger that Vinny had a wife, and a vigilant one. Barbara went about her business. It was a trait, Andrew knew, that did not endear her to some of the other faculty wives, who, Barbara grumbled, "talk about nothing but their husbands. Don't they do anything themselves?"

Or if it wasn't Barbara's confidence . . . Andrew felt a bit of the chill from the garden again; but he didn't allow himself to think, Maybe she just doesn't care.

Dr. Stone was, he decided, in her sixties. She was as tall as Andrew, perhaps taller; close to six feet. The long oval of her face was nearly unlined, but marred by deep red patches. Her hair, what he could see of it at the edges of the turban, was blonde. She had no eyebrows. In their stead were unevenly arched lines which might have been hurriedly penciled, Andrew thought without basis, while he was getting his toolbox. The bracelets were bangles, all glass except for one with intricate geometric patterns which appeared to be of heavy gold. She drew a small flowered handkerchief from the sleeve of her blouse to dab at her eyes, which were watering, and he had the feeling that she could not see him distinctly. She followed Andrew into the carport, moving carefully, and sat on a chair matching the one in the yard.

"I apologize for this imposition," she said. "I'm sure you have better things to do."

"This will just take a minute," Andrew answered.

After one miss he sank a screw eye into a stud in the wall of the house. The carport had been built with heavy beams as uprights, so it was a simple matter to sink a second screw eye into a beam across the concrete floor and, after he had reknotted one end rope to lengthen it, hang the hammock.

While he worked, another woman, middle-aged, shorter, and stouter, watched from behind the screen door to the kitchen. She spoke in a mocking tone in rapid Spanish, and Dr. Stone answered more slowly and, it seemed to Andrew, who despite his years in Cabora had not learned Spanish, very elegantly. The younger woman interrupted herself with sharp, good-natured laughter. At first Andrew thought she was commenting on his work, but as the exchange continued he decided Dr. Stone was her target. Dr. Stone answered in an amused voice, her laugh a clear sound deep in her throat that made Andrew smile even though he hadn't understood a word.

"Do you speak Spanish, Dr. Corwin?" she asked.

"I should. I've lived here eleven years. But I don't."

"Then I will explain," she said. "My maid says I've lured a perfect stranger under my roof the very day we came to town."

"A serious accusation," Andrew said.

When he had finished, Dr. Stone said, "How can I thank you? Would you like a glass of wine?"

Andrew hesitated. "That sounds good, but my wife and I are going out for dinner, and I should be taking a shower. She's just had a research paper accepted at a conference—a national conference, in fact—and I'm taking her out to celebrate."

"Wonderful! Ask her to join us for a quick glass. I would like to meet her. Concepción! *Nos horías el favor de traer dos vasos?*"

"*No tenemos vino,*" the second woman shouted from inside the house.

"*Está segura?*" Andrew's new neighbor frowned.

"*Sí, estoy segura.*"

"We have no wine," she said. "I am sorry. We have just arrived from Austin. In a few days we'll be better organized."

She rested her hands in her lap then, and her shoulders seemed to draw together in weariness. Andrew said good night, agreeing to her offer of wine at a later date.

· · · ·

"What's she like?" Barbara asked as Andrew came into the bedroom. She was standing at the chest of drawers wrapped in a towel. Andrew knew that, out of habit, she was debating whether or not to wear a bra. It was a decision that in their pre-tenure years at the conservative little university had not, at least in Andrew's opinion, been so simple, and that, oddly, had not been a problem when they first came to Cabora. Barbara had not been a bra-burner in the Vietnam days. She had grown up in Lubbock—her parents later moved to Houston—and done her undergraduate work at Texas Tech. When they first met, she had listened to Andrew's stories of besieged administrative offices and club-swinging deputy sheriffs as if she had never looked up from her test tubes and centrifuges during the years of unrest, as if it had all been dreamed on another planet. Only after they had been in Cabora for two years or so had she, suddenly and unaccountably, Andrew thought, decided that brassieres were nonsense.

"She's in her sixties," Andrew said. "Her name is Virginia Stone. *Doctor* Stone, as in medical doctor, but I assume retired. There are two of them; the other woman is her maid. They speak Spanish to each other. Dr. Stone said she lived a long time in Colombia, so maybe the maid is from there."

Barbara straightened up, her bra in place, and fastened the catch. She had, as Andrew had observed admiringly over the years, kept in better shape than he. She had been a jogger before it became fashionable, and, at forty-one, she still ran a few miles each week at the university track. She said, "Isn't it a little odd to put up a hammock the day you move into a house?"

"It's a strange situation," Andrew answered. "She says that she has allergies and can't sleep—actually she said she can't *live*—in the house. By the way, when I first talked to her out in the yard, she said she'd come here to die."

"Oh, that's sad."

Andrew laughed suddenly. "After I put up the hammock, she wanted us to come over for a glass of wine. But the maid told her they didn't have any."

"What's so funny?"

"Nothing, actually." In truth, nothing was funny. When they returned from dinner, Andrew was still puzzling at the rush of pleasure he had felt, still felt, at the notion of an elderly woman apologizing for not bringing wine along when she came to Cabora to die.

Dr. Stone was not in sight as the Corwins drove past her small house on their way to the university the next day, but they saw the other woman, Concepción, watering the yard, her thumb held over the hose-end to make a spray. The hammock appeared to have been slept in, for bedclothes were piled on it. The watering, Andrew

thought, was a waste of time on the rocky desert soil. He
thought the same thing when he saw Concepción scattering
grass seed Friday afternoon from a large box. Dr. Stone
was lying in her hammock, apparently asleep. Later that
afternoon he saw Concepción returning from Safeway carrying a large bag of groceries. Saturday, from his yard, he
heard men hammering and shouting in the house, and
Concepción's brisk Spanish.

2

On Monday evening Dr. Stone called. "I thought I might
not die for several weeks, so I had a telephone installed,"
she said. "You're the recipient of my first call."
"I'm honored," Andrew said.
"I now have wine. Would you and your wife join me for
a glass?"
Concepción was watering the nearly bare ground again
when the Corwins passed through the rickety gate in their
backyard. Gesturing toward her, Andrew said to their
neighbor, "Not much point in that here in the desert."
Dr. Stone—Virginia, as she invited them to call her—
replied, "My husband used to say, 'The difference between
a tropical rain forest and a desert is water.'"
She was pleased to learn that Barbara taught in the
chemistry department at the university, for her husband
had also been a scientist, a botanist. He had gone to Colombia first on a grant from the University of Texas. Later,
as other organizations became interested in his research, he
stopped teaching except for an occasional lecture. He sent
his young wife back to Texas to medical school, and they
had been separated for many years. She returned to
Bogotá, where, while her husband divided his time between
his laboratory and expeditions on the Guaviare River, she
practiced medicine and was involved in a large expatriate
community.

"Then my husband died," she said with what sounded more like exasperation to Andrew than sorrow. She had moved to Cabora on the advice of a colleague in Austin. The town was recommended for allergy sufferers, she said, because of its dry air, its extreme isolation from traffic and industrial pollution, and its high altitude.

Their glasses of syrupy wine rested on a three-legged table. While Virginia questioned Barbara about her paper and the conference in St. Louis where she was to read it, as well as about what the present college generation was being taught in chemistry classes, Andrew observed their host. She was again dressed in loose white clothing, coarsely woven cotton, he thought, and her eyes were still watering. Her hair, somewhere between gold and silver in color, was piled in intricate, harmonious tiers. Although it was obvious that she could not see well, she wore no glasses. Her eyebrows were now traced in perfect arches. Her lashes, which Andrew hadn't noticed before, were dark and extremely long. Lipstick, a pale pink shade, had been traced frugally across her upper and lower lips, and her cheeks were lightly rouged.

Barbara pointed at the heavy bangle on Virginia's wrist. "I've never seen anything so beautiful."

"Isn't it?" Virginia held her arm across the table so Barbara could see it more closely. "It was given to me in Calcutta by a very dear friend."

And while Barbara and Virginia talked, Andrew became aware with pleasure, even relief, that Barbara liked their new neighbor, that the two very different women, Barbara, seven or eight inches shorter, who disliked jewelry, Barbara with her heavy, dark-framed glasses and short, neat hair, unpretentious as she herself was, and Virginia, their—*ornate* seemed a fitting word to Andrew—ornate host, liked each other.

The yard was muddy from Concepción's watering, so they sat in the carport on wooden chairs, two of which

Andrew had fetched from the tiny dining room, stepping over boxes which had not been unpacked. Through the door to the living room, he had seen leaned against the wall a portrait of a woman both regal and voluptuous. It reached from floor to ceiling. The woman wore a shimmering silver gown. Her tiny silver hat was shaped like a garrison cap and decorated with pearls; it looked more like a crown than a hat. Holding a small silver poodle by a jeweled leash, the woman looked from long, veiled lashes over the viewer's head with calm assurance. Andrew was reminded of a print of Elizabeth I in Canuteson's office, and of portraits of Isabella he had seen in the Prado. It was a bad painting, in his opinion, but its subject was clearly beautiful, and clearly Virginia.

"I've made a small purchase." Virginia pointed behind them at a long, narrow mirror atop a corrugated cardboard box on the floor. "Concepción and I were able to unpack it, but we haven't the slightest idea how to hang it."

"I'll bring my toolbox," Andrew said.

When he returned, Virginia said, "Please don't think that taking advantage of my neighbors is my usual modus operandi. I simply haven't found people who do these things yet."

"Not at all," Andrew said. Using a level and tape measure and following Virginia's directions, he installed brackets on the house wall near where he had attached the screw eye for the hammock. The mirror was about six feet in depth and had an arched top. With Barbara's help he set it in the brackets and tightened them.

"Concepción has discovered how Cabora furnishes its homes," Virginia said when they had finished and she had thanked them. "It's through the Sears and Roebuck catalogue store."

"That's true," Barbara said. "These days they just call themselves Sears."

"They are reluctant to deliver, however. I had to explain

to them several times that I had no automobile. It appears to be immoral to live in West Texas without one."

"But they finally brought it," Andrew said.

"For a few dollars extra. In my childhood, my mother regarded Sears and Roebuck as the epitome of bad taste, but sometimes she had no choice but to buy from them."

Smiling, Virginia stood up slowly and held out her arms before the mirror. "Isn't it lovely! Isn't it lovely how mirrors deceive us and give us space where there is none."

"It's very nice," Barbara agreed.

"They're the secret to being a good host. I learned this long ago: a guest with a mirror to look into is never bored." Virginia turned to them with her fingers over her mouth as if to shush herself. "I didn't mean to sound epigrammatic. It's an infirmity of old age."

Barbara watched Virginia sit down again, then said, "So you moved back to the States after your husband's death?"

"That was over twenty years ago. I've been many places since then."

Her face seemed less splotchy to Andrew than when they first met, but still inflamed, as if covered by a rash. She spoke with the hesitancy he had noticed before. Since her husband's death, she had been in the mountains of Afghanistan on a research project of her own concerning allergies, which, ironically, had been her specialization; had been in charge of an army hospital in Vietnam during the war there, serving with the rank of colonel; had traveled in Europe on the usual tourist circuit, and in other places westerners seldom visited—Mali, Chad, Botswana, Tibet, Bangladesh.

"You have a lovely wife," she said to Andrew. "Both lovely and intelligent. You're a lucky man."

"I agree," Andrew said.

"And your husband is very handsome," she told Barbara. "I was swept off my feet when he spoke to me from his garden."

"He does that."

"You were sitting down," Andrew reminded Virginia.

Virginia laughed. "However, he's much too literal." She pointed toward the house. "We've made progress here. I hired some men to tear out the carpeting, which I'm allergic to. The hardwood floor is unvarnished, so it won't harm me. Now I suspect the wall paneling; I'm allergic to something in it. But I've run out of money, so we must wait."

She blamed her allergy, her present condition, on a man in Austin who she said had wanted to marry her.

"His idea of a lively evening was to sit before a television set for several hours." She stopped Concepción after the woman poured a finger of wine in her glass; she weakened it with water from a small clay pitcher, sipped, weakened it again. Her hands, thickly mottled with age spots, shook as she poured. "I didn't agree, but I was newly arrived back in the United States, and I thought I might be missing some deeper meaning. So night after night I sat beside him in a room with a deep-piled carpet made of synthetic materials, and I became sicker and sicker until I was nearly too weak to understand what was happening. Now, thanks to that idiot—and my own idiocy— I'm dying. The allergy has affected my eyes, too. I can't read without a magnifying glass, and then only for a few minutes; I'm useless. It's maddening, not being able to read. I've always read."

A telephone rang, and after a moment Concepción called to her.

"Gracias, I'm coming," Virginia said.

"Harry!" Andrew and Barbara heard her cry from the dining room. "How are you, my darling, and how did you find me?"

Concepción spoke loudly to the Corwins from the kitchen door, laughing merrily. Andrew nodded and shrugged his shoulders.

"*Cómo?*" Barbara asked. Concepción spoke again, and Barbara laughed too. "She says Virginia has a boyfriend in every country."

The telephone conversation, punctuated by laughter and what sounded like an occasional scream of protest, lasted a good ten minutes before Virginia reappeared, her face more deeply flushed and her eyes livelier than before.

"That was an old, dear friend in London," she said. She emptied her glass. "This is terrible wine. Concepción's talents do not extend to choosing good wine. Can you imagine? He tracked me down here, though I left no forwarding address."

"That took some perseverance," Andrew said.

"He's persevering, all right. He insists on sending me some money."

Andrew chuckled uncertainly. "That must be the best kind of old friend to have."

"Not at all," Virginia snapped. Her exuberance faded then, and weariness seemed to catch up with her.

"What do you think?" Andrew asked as the Corwins walked back to their house.

"She's beautiful," Barbara said.

"Beautiful?" Andrew was surprised. "Why do you say that?"

"Because she is."

The idea pleased him. He said, "Her hair certainly is; it's dyed, right?"

"Darling, it's a wig. And those were false eyelashes. I wish we could do something about her reading. Aren't there specially printed books for people like her?"

During the break between his classes the next morning, Andrew called the Texas Department of Rehabilitation to ask about help for Virginia. He was told the Division for the Blind and Handicapped at the Texas State Library in Austin would send her tapes and large-type books.

"Funny," the secretary said, "another Dr. Corwin just called about her. A lady."

That afternoon Andrew received a call from Virginia at his office. "I neglected to ask you last night about your specialization in political science," she said. "Could you use my expertise in South American politics in your classes? Or what I know about Russian-Indian relations? That's what the war in Afghanistan is about, you know."

Andrew had three graduate students worried about their comprehensive examinations facing him across his desk. He laughed a bit sharply and said, "I'm afraid I'm strictly domestic."

"Perhaps you could direct me to the proper person."

The graduate students shuffled their papers impatiently. Andrew thought about John Canuteson, who taught the Latin American courses from notes yellow with age. "We don't have anyone in the Indian-Russian area," he said, "and I suspect the specialist in the first area you mentioned would not welcome another point of view."

Virginia's voice rasped. "I need someone to give me something to *do*."

"She couldn't stay in our classrooms more than a few minutes," Andrew said at dinner after he had told Barbara about Virginia's call. "Much of the building is carpeted, and maintenance sprays insecticide at least once a month."

"But that's not why you won't introduce her to your colleagues."

"No? Then why won't I?"

"Because she's old."

"That's nonsense," Andrew said, knowing it wasn't. "How do I know what she really knows about Afghanistan, or Colombia?"

"She lived there."

After a pause he said, "The truth is that I can't imagine a class of graduate students, let alone undergraduates, sitting still while she reminisces about Bogotá. They don't want to know what it was like, they want lists; they want pat answers to pat questions."

As they rose to clear the table, Barbara said, "Isn't it ironic how no one wants to listen to an old person? We spend our lives learning about living, and then what? What use is it? People go out of their way not to hear about it."

"They want to learn for themselves."

"Do they? I don't think so. I think most people just want to coast. To be safe."

Andrew knew they were approaching uncertain ground. During their third year in Cabora, he had talked long and persuasively of tenure and the stability of a state-funded school, if undistinguished and unknown, when Barbara had been offered a low-paying post-doctoral fellowship at Princeton. Later, she had researched jobs for both of them in West Africa, the Middle East, and Papua, New Guinea. Andrew squirmed as he remembered one of their third-year arguments:

"I do not see what encasing my breasts in a stupid, uncomfortable garment has to do with my academic career, much less yours."

"Logically, nothing; but Canuteson was staring at your nipples all through dinner."

"They grow on the body, like ears; why didn't he stare at my ears?"

"And his wife was eyeing you and him both."

"That's her damned problem. Or his."

"No, it's ours."

But she had played the game, although she hadn't worn heels, pantyhose, and makeup often enough and hadn't gushed enough to get into the Pilot Club. And she had never suggested that her steadily growing list of publications should have gotten her tenure and a promotion ahead of Andrew.

He said, "At least we heard about living from Virginia last night."

"All day I kept remembering things she had told us. Thinking about her with that mountain tribe in Afghanistan. About the excitement of her life. No, that's wrong; the depth of her life."

Andrew said carefully, "Compared to ours."

"Is that the point? I'm not jealous; not even wistful, I don't think. Just glad. Glad for her confidence: can you imagine her wanting to give lectures, when she can barely stand on her feet?"

"There's a life-sized portrait of her in the living room," Andrew said. "She was a knockout in her prime."

"I can see that in all her gestures."

Andrew grinned and brushed back Barbara's dark hair to kiss her cheek. "What you need is a call from an old boyfriend in London."

She smiled. "Why not?"

Later Andrew said, "Obviously she's fluent in Spanish. Maybe you could take lessons from her."

"That's an idea."

The next evening Barbara said, "We're all set. She refused to take money. It's to be an hour of conversation twice a week."

3

About three weeks after they had called the Department of Rehabilitation, Barbara set a bottle of Chateau Neuf de Pape on the table for dinner.

"What's the occasion?" Andrew asked.

"Virginia got her first tape yesterday. *Anna Karenina.* This is her thank you."

As Andrew uncorked the bottle, Barbara said, "I've never seen her so happy. She was quoting long passages this morning. She was so happy I nearly cried."

Barbara taught a class only during the first summer session because she wanted to work without interruption in the university laboratory on another paper, an extension of the one she was to present in St. Louis that fall. Andrew, however, was in charge of graduate workshops in both sessions. He sometimes saw Virginia when she played her recorder during the hour before sunset while the mountain breezes were coming up to banish the day's heat. He listened while he weeded or watered his tomato vines. It annoyed him that the neighbors' children paused to watch her curiously, tittering, balancing their bicycles with one foot on the ground. After a few weeks, however, they ignored her. When she stopped and went into the house, white and straight in the dust, he too went inside with a queer twist in his heart that he first thought was sadness, then changed his mind.

"She doesn't play well, actually," he told Barbara. "She tries this note and that until she finds the right one, and sometimes she doesn't find it. But that lonely sound is woeful, isn't it? That and her loneliness, out there in the middle of the yard."

"Or her aloneness," Barbara said. "I don't think she's lonely in a bad sense."

"It makes me think of—I thought once of that morning when we saw Long's Peak from the tent."

"Oh, that's nice."

"It's a kind of communion," Andrew said. "That doesn't make sense; wait, here's what doesn't make sense: communion that I'm left out of. That high, lonely sound: she's in it, and I'm not."

"You sound like a poet," Barbara said. "But that's what I mean about her not being lonely. Her life is too full."

"Was, maybe; it isn't now."

"No, is. It still is. I understand why you say that, but when I go over there, she's never idle. Yesterday she was

playing Indian music when I came in. It was a Ravi Shankar tape, and she wouldn't talk until it had finished. How
many people in Cabora know who Ravi Shankar is?"

"Still—"

Barbara smiled. "She's very fond of you. Maybe you're
in love with her."

"Nonsense."

"Why? Because she's old?"

"Partly, I suppose."

"I would be in love with her, if I were a man, if it were
just because of what she's been, and done."

"What she says she's been and done," Andrew said.

"Even for that, I think I would be." Barbara rubbed her
lower lip with her forefinger. "I like her matter-of-factness
about death. She talks about it as we would about the
lawnmower—if we were standing right there looking at
the lawnmower. That kind of proximity."

Andrew said, "That's an act."

"Or could she really be so indifferent, do you think, because of her training and experience? She said her hospital
in Vietnam was like a primitive factory, and one of its
products was dead people."

Andrew recalled when his mother had been hospitalized
with a bleeding ulcer. He had been shocked when he read
the "in-out" record on the door to her room: so many mil-
liliters of liquid in, so many out. The body was simply a
container, a temporary container; when the flow stopped,
the body stopped. He said again, "It's an act. It's one thing
to be indifferent about somebody else's death; your own's
another story."

Barbara nodded. "She says now she's living an Indian
summer."

It seemed to Andrew that activity around his neighbor's
house increased steadily, concentrating at first on the carport area, where two Hispanic men built wooden frames to

fit the spaces between the support posts, then covered them with screen. They installed screen doors in the front and back frames of the carport.

Concepción's constant seeding and watering of the lawn, along with, Andrew noted, wholesale scattering of compost, topsoil, fertilizer, and even potting soil, was paying off: she had grass thicker and greener than the Corwins' had ever been. An old man began to come once a week with a lawnmower. A curved walk of red flagstones leading from the sidewalk to the front door appeared, shortly afterwards flowers on each side of the door, and then trellises. One evening Andrew saw the two women pass his house together, Virginia upright as a Prussian soldier, her hand on Concepción's shoulder; after that he often saw them slowly walking at increasing distances from the house. Concepción carried a large stick, not to lean on, apparently, but to fend off dogs. On Sunday mornings he sometimes saw Concepción leaving the house alone, for mass he assumed, wearing a dark dress and a hat that reminded him of those his grandmother had worn thirty years ago. Later in the summer he saw a Hispanic couple in a late-model car picking her up on Sunday mornings.

When his vines began to produce, Andrew offered Concepción a bag of ripe tomatoes over the fence, which she accepted with smiles and rapid Spanish. Two days later she brought a dish cooked with tomatoes, highly spiced and delicious, to the Corwins.

"It's a chutney she learned to make from a British cook in Bogotá," Virginia said over the telephone. "She sends it with her thanks for the tomatoes."

When the university's theatre department began its outdoor productions in July, Barbara asked Virginia to go with her to the opening night for two short plays.

"The interior of the car is all synthetic materials," Andrew warned Barbara.

"We've talked about that. We'll drive with all the windows open. That's how she came here from Austin."

So Andrew watched them drive off the next evening, Virginia leaning her head out the window. When Barbara returned at eleven, he asked, "How was it?"

"Virginia loved one, something by Moliere, and hated the other," Barbara said. "The second has a small-town Texas setting, and the language shocked her."

"I wouldn't expect her to be shocked by anything."

"It wasn't the profanity, though there was plenty of that. It was—how do I say it—the *commonness* of it? The ignorance, maybe. I don't think she saw any point to it."

As he left the campus post office the following Thursday, Andrew was stopped by a red-faced and puffing Maury Harper. The local paper was clenched in his hand, and he waved it at Andrew. "Who the hell is this Virginia Stone, anyway? Vinny Singleton said she lived next door to you."

"She does," Andrew said. "Why?"

"She just set us back fifteen years. In the letters to the editor. Says we're a bunch of degenerates for doing *Bourbon and Lone Star*."

"She wrote that?" Andrew tried to keep a straight face, couldn't, and began to chuckle.

"The damned letter is too clever to say it in so many words." Harper turned away, swatting his thigh with the paper. "I don't see what's funny. The last thing you need in this town is to be charged with immorality. Damned old bitch."

While Andrew was working in his garden later, Virginia appeared at the back fence, her white turban in place. She said, "I wrote a letter to the newspaper, and it seems to have stirred up a hornet's nest. My telephone has been ringing all day."

Andrew smiled. "I heard about it on campus today."

Virginia's laugh was deep and rich in her throat. "A

preacher—his name is Marlatt, and he's a fundamentalist, I think—came by to thank me for chastising the devil." Her voice became bland, her face innocent. "He wanted me to get down on my knees and pray with him, but I said Concepción hadn't swept the floor yet."

Andrew said, "Maury Harper from the drama department is a friend of mine. He thinks you've sabotaged his program."

"Nonsense. The controversy will triple his ticket sales, despite the poor quality of his plays."

And in fact Harper's production enjoyed full houses that weekend. The following Thursday the paper's editorial page was full of answers to Virginia's letter, evenly divided between support and opposition.

Andrew interrupted Virginia's recorder playing that evening to ask, "How's our drama critic taking her notoriety?"

"Oh, I love notoriety." She rose from her chair in the yard and came slowly to the fence, still holding the recorder in playing position. "But I was horrified that that preacher—Marlatt—called me a 'defender of Christian morality.' I spent the afternoon at my typewriter writing another letter to deny that, and also to answer Mr. Harper's letter, which was well argued. I said in my reply that I don't object to his idea of celebrating the common man; I just don't believe there *is* a common man."

Thinking of the faceless names to which he gave Cs and Ds each semester in his huge freshman classes, and thinking also that he must be nearly as anonymous to them, Andrew said, "Surely you're not denying us drones our place in the scheme of things."

She smiled. "You work—you teach—so by definition you're not a drone. Anyway, we're not bees. I believe we all do what we can, given a chance, and we do it with taste and individuality."

"For example?"

She looked at Andrew with, he thought, amusement. He resisted an urge to brush away a fly that had crawled from her turban down onto her forehead. "Let me fetch my chair," she said. "Then I can lecture."

She brought her chair to the fence and sat down. "Once I was caught in a traffic jam in Calcutta. While we were stalled I saw a group of fifty or sixty laborers take their tea break. They had been carrying cement blocks to a building site, balancing five or six at a time on their heads. They were wearing lungis, which look like diapers to Westerners, and they were barefooted. Each was given tea in a tiny clay cup, not much larger than a thimble. Their pleasure, and the dignity with which they took it, was very evident. And each man, I thought, looked like a person one would like to talk to. A person of significance."

She paused, sitting in her not-stiff-but-erect way, her hands on the recorder in her lap, her eyes focused on something, Andrew thought, in some other time. What would she have looked like then, he wondered: would she have been in a battered taxi; a ricksha drawn by a small, wiry man; in a Rolls-Royce? It wouldn't have mattered.

Virginia laughed. "A better example: during the same traffic jam I saw a man bathe himself, every square inch of his body, at a public hydrant by the street. I remember thinking that no king could have taken a bath in his palace with more dignity, and certainly not with more modesty."

Andrew was silent, and then he nodded. "I see your point."

"That's why I could never have condoned the protests here during the Vietnam War; even if I had agreed with all the college students, the hippies shouting and chanting slogans were perfect examples of the mindlessness they claimed to be protesting against. That wasn't democracy; those were mobs. They debased themselves."

Caught off guard, Andrew grinned sheepishly and said, "Well, since I was one of the protesters, I'll have to disagree. I was certainly thinking like an individual, and hurting like one after a policeman wrapped his night stick around my skull in Chicago in 1968."

"Oh dear, I've committed another faux pas." Virginia clasped her hands at her breast. "Are you teasing me? I wasn't in the States during those years, but you don't *look* like one of those wild hippies I read about."

"I was in the demonstration at Kent State when the National Guardsmen opened fire, and I spent two nights in jail in Washington after a protest."

"And you marched and braved the policemen's clubs and engaged in passive resistance, all those things?"

"And occupied administrators' offices in two universities, and organized a draft card burning," Andrew said.

She looked at him, he thought, with new respect, with something like camaraderie in her expression. She said, "I'm having difficulty reconciling this information with my quiet neighbor who has a garden. Do you teach revolution in your classes?"

Andrew was sure a flush was spreading over his face, and he felt a distinct urge to squirm. "I teach traditional subjects."

"Then your ideas have changed." She said it neutrally, not quite a question. Andrew felt she was watching him closely. A little wistfully, he tried to think back to those days, those times of . . . certainty, he thought: when he, and so many others, had been so sure of their rightness, had taken every manifestation of opposition—preachers condemning from their pulpits, just-deputized plumbers and butchers' helpers swinging baseball bats, all the lies about military victories—as evidence of their just cause. What had it been like? The packed, intense meetings of graduate students, the boy-men bearded and unwashed like himself, the girl-women with their long straight hair, the endless cigarettes and bullshit and fuck and pigs talk talk talk, the gleeful fear when they finally did something, always half-baked, always half-hoping that they would get caught. It had been like . . . Andrew realized with surprise that he couldn't remember. He had shut the door on it, as had, he suspected, several others his age at Cabora State, though they would never admit it. Trust no one over thirty, they had said, and now *they* were over thirty, over forty, and couldn't trust themselves. Faces, marches, cloak-and-dagger games they had played to fool the law, or thought they were playing, the VW buses, the girls with Indian blouses, wooden beads, and ready thighs in dank basement apartments—he couldn't see them, could summon up only a cloudy remembrance of danger, the vague taste-smell of it, the incomprehensible suspicion that he had once liked it.

"I'll have to think about that question," Andrew said to Virginia. "I'm not sure whether my opinions have changed from those days."

"And I must adjust my conception of you." The admiration in her voice seemed to say "Fellow adventurer!" As she moved her chair back to the middle of her yard, he found himself wanting to ask: "But how do you sustain it? After all those years when you're so sure you're immortal that it's easy to be fearless, where do you find courage?"

• • • •

A few evenings later Virginia told Andrew with a bit of coyness in her tone, "I have a male friend now. I will invite you and Barbara to join us for wine soon."

"Someone we know?"

She shook her head. "His name is Lawrence Coke. He's a retired doctor like me, from Beaumont. He has allergies too. We met through our mutual colleague here, Dr. Paddock."

After a moment, she said, "Oh. And I'm expecting a visit from my old friend in Bogotá, Rudy Dietrich. I must stop Mr. Marlatt's visits now because Rudy would decimate him."

"Decimate?"

"Rudy's a great talker, and a bit ruthless. I was present once in Bogotá when he demolished the American ambassador in an argument about U.S. policy in Latin America."

. . . .

The controversy over the play lasted into August, when the Corwins went on vacation. The evening before they left they drove out to Comanche Overlook south of Cabora with Virginia. While Virginia leaned against the railing and peered down into the deep canyon lined with junipers, cactus, and yucca, then northward toward Cabora and beyond the town to Lancer Peak and the purple, jagged ridges of the Davis Mountains, Andrew and Barbara set up three folding chairs and a card table. Andrew drew a bottle of wine from a cooler and opened it, and Barbara spread a checkered tablecloth and set three glasses on it.

"This is lovely," Virginia said as she sat down. "I wasn't aware there was anything so beautiful around Cabora."

"If you catch it just right," Andrew said. He pointed out the path of light and shadow which the sun, already hidden to them by the ridge across the canyon, was tracing over the red brick buildings of the university on the mountainside at the east edge of Cabora.

"*Salud!*" Virginia said. "To my lovely neighbors and good friends. To my good luck in having them."

Barbara smiled and raised her glass. "And to ours."

Virginia said she had grown up in a small cowtown in south Texas, the daughter of a saloonkeeper—her mother. "Although she would have whipped us—her two daughters—if we had ever said 'saloon.'"

Her mother was French, Virginia said, but she never told her daughters anything about the circumstances of her coming to the United States or to Texas, or about their father. She ran the saloon with an iron hand, never allowed her daughters in the bar area, and sent them to a convent school in San Antonio.

"I remember her as very beautiful, and I suppose she

was something of a legend in the town. When I was about ten, one of my friends told me that everyone knew she carried a pistol under her dress. I never got up the nerve to ask her if that was true, and I don't think anyone else ever did either."

They heard a commotion on the bluff above them across the highway and looked up to see a small mule deer, two, then three, all antlerless, watching them over a clump of creosote brush. A pickup roared by, and the deer backed away.

"Tell me about your vacation," Virginia said. "You're going to Spain."

"First our parents', then to Spain," Andrew said.

"Spain." Virginia closed her eyes. "Madrid. The Prado. Huge bottles of red wine on the tables. Someday I will tell you of my adventures in Madrid."

Barbara said, "You could tell us now."

"Not now."

While Virginia questioned Barbara about the conclusions in her research paper, which she had finished that week—it had to do with accelerating the dialysis of certain solutions, and Andrew had long since stopped pretending to understand—Andrew realized with puzzlement that Virginia's remark about adventures in Madrid had pricked him unpleasantly. Remembering Barbara's suggestion, facetious, he thought, that he was in love with Virginia, he rejected it again. His annoyance had to do with some sense of being unimportant in Virginia's life, of having little significance in a life that had been significant, of appearing at its tag end. And that, he thought as he watched the dark shadow move swiftly beyond the university campus and up the mountain at the east edge of Cabora, that made no sense either.

The topic had changed from chemistry to D. H. Lawrence. Virginia had just finished listening to a tape of *Sons and Lovers.* She was beginning *The Rainbow,* and she had requested *Lady Chatterly's Lover.* "I met Lawrence when I was quite young," she said. "It was on the train from Mexico City to Veracruz. I decided to go to the last car for some reason, and he followed me."

She sipped her wine and looked northward, looked, Andrew thought, at scenes he and Barbara could not see.

"D. H. Lawrence was not a nice man," Virginia said.

• • • •

The Corwins flew first to Houston to Barbara's parents' home, then to Philadelphia to visit Andrew's mother. In Houston, while Barbara caught up on the gossip with her mother and younger sister—both were elementary school teachers and, Andrew thought, a bit in awe of Barbara—Andrew played golf early and late with her father, a retired geologist. They watched baseball in the den during the heat of the day. Barbara joined them on the golf course on the morning of the second day, then visited an acquaintance on the University of Houston campus that afternoon "to see what they're doing in chemistry that I've never heard of." By late afternoon of the third day when they went to the airport, she was more than ready to leave. Remembering his cool reception the first time Barbara had brought him to Houston, Andrew reflected that now he was more at home with her parents than she, it was he they turned to more easily with their suggestions for beer and charcoaled hamburgers, an evening watching a TV rerun. Barbara perked up in Philadelphia with Andrew's mother, who had studied the museum offerings, had the times and locations of the latest movies, and was eager to be taken to her favorite restaurants.

From Philadelphia they flew to JFK and thence to Madrid, where they divided their time between the city and day-trips by train to villages in the mountains. It was their third vacation in Spain and the best yet to Andrew, who enjoyed watching Barbara gain confidence by the hour with her Spanish until she could flawlessly rattle off orders to waiters and addresses to taxi drivers. Her sessions with Virginia, he saw, had been useful.

4

When they returned late in the afternoon on the day before registration was to begin at the university, they saw that lawn furniture had been added next door, a white table with four white chairs and a bright pink umbrella. By the sidewalk—ludicrously, Andrew thought—two posts had been set at the end of the flagstone walk and a thin, curved piece of pink plywood nailed across the top. On it the words "Los Arcos" had been shakily painted in large blue letters.

Andrew had just unlocked the house when Virginia called. She said, "A terrible thing has happened. One of my oldest friends, Rudy Dietrich, has just flown into El Paso from Bogotá. He rented a car to drive here, but he's been thrown in jail in a place called Beltsner."

"What did he do?"

"He was arrested for speeding. He also told the constable he shouldn't chew gum while he was on duty. Apparently one shouldn't talk like this in West Texas."

Andrew groaned in agreement. Virginia said, "He's always been such a bungler. He was supposed to come two weeks ago, but there was a mixup about the tickets. He has no dollars, only pesos and credit cards, and they won't take those. But I don't keep cash here in the house, and the bank is closed."

"How much does he need?"

"He says he needs forty-eight dollars to pay his fine and costs."

Andrew said, "All right. I can cover that."

"I would be terribly grateful. That Rudy! All his life he's done these things."

Barbara offered to ride with him, but Andrew saw no reason to waste her evening too. It was fifty-five miles back across the desert to Beltsner, and an hour of paperwork before the officer—Virginia's friend had run afoul of a highway patrolman, not a constable—finally told the jailer through an intercom to bring the offender out of the square brick jail.

The patrolman, who was still chewing gum, said, "You got yourself a real smart-ass friend there."

"I'm picking him up as a favor for someone else," Andrew replied. "I don't know him."

"You ain't missed much."

Rudy Dietrich was a short, round- and red-faced man of about sixty with thick hair combed straight back from his forehead. His teeth were bad and very short, as if they had been ground off, and he had small eyes. He did not seem at all abashed by his incarceration, although he refused to drive the rented car any farther.

"They can come and get it," he said, locking the keys inside after he had removed a denim dufflebag and a suitcase that appeared to be made of cardboard. "If they complain I'll sue them. I was thrown in jail because of their bloody faulty speedometer."

Darkness had fallen while Andrew waited in the courthouse. When they had passed the last brown adobes beyond the cattle-loading pens at the edge of Beltsner, Andrew set the cruise control on the car and settled back for the long drive over an empty highway to Cabora. He said, "I believe you've known Virginia for a very long time."

"All my life," Rudy said. "Through good and bad. I have known her the longest. I was present when she hired Concepción as a young girl from the mountains."

"Virginia was a terror in Bogotá," he continued after a silence. "She was a beauty, and she knew it. She set many pairs of horns on old Professor Stone's forehead. So many it was a veritable bed of nails."

Andrew joined in reluctantly with his passenger's loud laughter. Rudy continued, "Has she told you she's rich?

That's a joke. All she has is an annuity he left her. It brings
her about $800 a month. She would have been rich, if she
weren't so stupid—she could have married eight or ten different millionaires, from as many countries. Even now
some of these old fools would marry her just for the sake
of the memory of what she was like half a century ago. She
let herself be cheated out of an apartment building in
Bogotá that would have kept her rolling in money. I didn't
speak to her for two years after she lost it; it would have
been mine someday. Has she told you she had an affair
with me?"

"No."

"That's a joke too. I suspect she started the rumor herself; she's old enough to be my grandmother. She did have
an affair with my father. My father and Professor Stone
were great friends; someday I'll tell you how great. Has she
told you how old she is? Of course not. She's eighty-five if
she's a day. Seven years ago she had an affair in Madrid
with an airline pilot who was forty years younger."

Andrew braked to avoid several gray mule deer crossing
the highway. Rudy braced himself against the dashboard
and peered through the windshield at them. He said, "Why
have you driven across this godforsaken desert to get me
out of jail? Has she told you she'll leave you something
when she dies?"

"I don't know anything about her finances," Andrew
said, "and I don't care to know. I just live next door."

Rudy cackled. "My friend, we are all interested in money."

"That may be, but I'm not interested in hers."

"Good. Because whatever else may be said of Virginia,
she's loyal to her old friends, and I'm her oldest. She'll take
care of Concepción first; Concepción will go home to her
miserable village and live like a queen. Whatever Virginia
has left after that, she'll leave to me."

"Congratulations."

"Meanwhile, till she dies, you will enjoy knowing her."

Virginia's telephone call awakened the Corwins the next morning. Andrew unwillingly accepted an invitation to dinner that evening.

"I don't like this Rudy character," he said as he got back in bed. "He has about as much class as a carnival shill."

"We've been in West Texas too long," Barbara answered. "We're used to people talking around things. Haven't you ever wondered what would happen to her things when she died?" Andrew had repeated what Rudy had said about inheriting Virginia's assets.

"No. At least I never projected us into the picture. What I don't like about him is the way he talks. He speaks English as if he learned it from books, but what he says is from the gutter."

"Anyway, it won't be a late evening. Virginia tires easily."

Virginia had also invited Lawrence Coke, the retired doctor, and Frank and Clara Lunsford, whom Andrew knew slightly. The Lunsfords were professors from Minnesota, also retired. They had discovered Cabora and its high, dry climate while touring the country in a camper, liked it, and stayed. Andrew had met Clara when she filled in for an ailing history professor at the university the previous term.

Dr. Coke's allergies seemed to have taken more of a toll on him than Virginia's had on her. He was a tall, almost fleshless man—his torso, back to chest, could not be more than three inches in depth—who seemed physically ill at ease. He arrived carrying a cushion, of pure wool, he explained, which he placed in his chair before he sat down.

The Corwins brought a bottle of white wine which Virginia told Andrew to chill. When he opened the refrigerator, he saw that it was full of medicine: racks of vials, dozens and dozens of them with rubber seals; neatly separated rows of bottles, tubes, and jars with labels on them, long latinate names, and dates typed in large letters.

He was startled by Rudy's laughter behind him. Rudy

said, "There you are, my friend, what's ahead of all of us: heart medicine, allergy medicine, liver medicine; something for every defective organ in the body—and they all become defective."

While the Corwins had been on vacation, a mimosa tree about ten feet high had been planted in the center of the yard, and a concrete birdbath placed near it. Honeysuckle had been planted on both sides of the front door; already it reached five feet up the trellises. Virginia's lawn furniture, minus the pink umbrella, had been moved into the carport for their dinner, and two matching chairs added to the original four. Three more of the long mirrors from Sears had been added along the wall, and Andrew caught himself looking at the others and his own image as they appeared at four different angles in the window-like reflections. It was, he thought, as if he were spying on four small festive parties.

There was now a white-and-gold desk with delicately carved legs in the carport too, and Andrew noted letters to Virginia on it with "Los Arcos" as part of the address. Under the thick glass protecting the top of the desk, several yellowing letters were displayed.

"You see," Rudy pointed at a letter with a gold insignia at the top; "here *el presidente* congratulates Virginia for her service to humanity in the slums of Bogotá. And in more luxurious and private environs as well."

"Rudy!" Virginia snapped.

"And here the United States Ambassador to Colombia thanks her for exercising her peculiar and renowned talents to influence a stubborn anti-imperialist—"

"That's quite enough!" Virginia said, but Andrew noticed that she was smiling.

Rudy raised his wineglass. "To influence! Whatever its provenance."

"Hear, hear," Dr. Coke said.

"Most especially if God's personal envoy wields it," Rudy said.

Virginia laughed. "Rudy met Reverend Marlatt this morning. I'm afraid it was a collision."

"He'll convert her, mark my words!" Rudy shouted. "He'll have her groveling on her knees one of these days. Repentance! Atonement!"

Rudy told his version of his arrest, vigorously mimicking the patrolman's gum-chewing and portraying himself as so aggressive that Andrew, knowing a little of the temperament of West Texas lawmen, believed about ten percent of the story. The visitor from Bogotá eventually monopolized every topic of conversation, particularly when Andrew and the Lunsfords protested the deeds of the Somozas in Nicaragua, Pinochet in Chile, and Duarte in El Salvador.

"You know nothing of these things!" he shouted.

"We know they stayed in power through the use of terror," Frank Lunsford said.

"And what of the Communists? Are they strangers to terror and bloodshed? I tell you, you who support these Communists from your comfortable armchairs in the United States, you know nothing of these matters."

"Rudy's point is well taken," Dr. Coke said. "I—"

"The weeping Liberal heart of the United States is the joke of Central and South America," Rudy said loudly. "You know nothing! You—"

"Rudy, you're sounding positively omniscient," Virginia murmured, and he said no more on the subject.

Virginia sat on one of the wooden dining chairs; she dozed for half a minute now and then, Andrew noticed, seldom joining in the talk except to ask questions, although Rudy's references to men or events from the past sometimes brought a chuckle or a little shriek of protest from her. Every few minutes Rudy shouted at Concepción in a torrent of Spanish that she answered in kind with peals of laughter. Despite Andrew's protests, Rudy presented him with a poncho woven of fine soft wool "for rescuing me from the calaboose." Virginia's wine selection had improved, Andrew noted: it was a good dry chablis.

At the back of the carport a large flat box had been leaned against an upright, and beside it was a partially un-crated television set. Pointing at the box, Virginia said, "Good news. My friend Harry in London"—Rudy said something in Spanish of which Andrew caught only *amigo*, and Virginia replied sharply, in Spanish as well—"my friend from London has found a mattress for me that is pure wool and cotton. It just arrived today. Tonight I'll sleep in a bed for the first time in four months."

"*En la cama, en la cama*—" Rudy began to sing.

"Rudy, hush!" Virginia said.

Before dinner, Andrew and Frank Lunsford helped Rudy move a bed and bedsprings to the carport, uncrate the mattress, and put it on the bed. Then they carried the tele-vision console, which Rudy said Virginia had bought for Concepción "as a sop to the rabble," to Concepción's bed-room. Lawrence Coke followed the other men about, apolo-gizing for his inability to help.

Concepción served chicken enchiladas arranged in a cas-serole, bland by West Texas standards, with a thick cheese sauce containing spices Andrew did not recognize. Law-rence Coke was given a separate dish of cooked vegetables which he explained that his allergic condition required and which Rudy said had been inspected and certified harmless "by God himself in person." By the time Concepción brought coffee, Virginia was clearly exhausted, so Andrew and Barbara and the Lunsfords soon left.

A few days after Rudy had gone, the Corwins found cur-rent issues of the *Smithsonian, National Geographic, Har-per's,* and *Atlantic* on their doorstep with a note: "My sub-scriptions have caught up with me. I can't read them, so you take them. Virginia."

5

By the end of September the honeysuckle had crossed and joined on the trellis over the door of Virginia's house. A sycamore nearly twenty feet tall was planted in the yard in the front corner nearest the Corwins. The hole, Virginia told them as they drove out to Comanche Overlook, was eight feet in depth and diameter, dug by half a dozen men. Concrete statues of a bare-breasted nymph and a young satyr appeared at opposite ends of the yard. The house was repainted a light pink. Barbara reported that Virginia had had the dining room and the hallway to her bedroom lined with the arched mirrors, "at least nine or ten of them."

The first cold snap came in late October, just after the Corwins—Andrew had decided to go along at the last minute—returned from Barbara's conference in St. Louis. Andrew heard the wind hit in the middle of the night, and thought immediately of Virginia. He was glad that Barbara was a heavy sleeper. The next morning he stepped out, felt the bite of the north wind swirling the pecan leaves and pine needles, and went back inside for his topcoat.

As he passed Virginia's house he saw her sitting on her bed. He stopped the car and walked to the carport. She was wrapped in several blankets and was reading a large-type book with a magnifying glass. Her papers, he saw, had been scattered about by the wind.

"Virginia," he called.

"A brisk morning," she said, closing the book. Her face was deeply mottled, as on the day they met, and her hands were blue with cold.

"Are you warm enough?"

"Yes, but I believe I've been cheated. Concepción was told this new blanket was pure wool, but I'm getting a strong reaction to something. Would you come in and have a look?"

When Andrew located the label, he said, "You're right. It's fifty percent acrylic."

"My god." Virginia tugged it off.

Andrew said, "We have a down comforter. I believe its covering is cotton. Let me bring it."

He went back to the house and, with Barbara's help,

found the comforter, checked the labels, and saw that it was cotton.

He watched as Concepción wrapped it around Virginia. He said, "Virginia, you just can't do this. You don't realize how cold it gets here."

Virginia's laughter had, he thought, an edge of scorn. She picked up her book and said, "Who knows what one can do? My deepest thanks for the comforter; I'm warmer now than I was all night. You'd better go to work."

At dinner that evening Barbara said, "She claims she's perfectly comfortable now. But the wind was blowing through that carport so hard during our lesson that our coffee was cold before Concepción set it down."

Andrew nodded. "Her hands were blue this morning."

"And her lips were already badly chapped." Barbara rose from the table and turned toward the kitchen counter. Andrew stood up too, suddenly aware that Barbara was trying not to cry.

"She absolutely refused to talk about her discomfort," Barbara said. "She wanted to hear all about the conference, and how my reading went, and what response I got. She talked about doing amputations in Vietnam. And she's very happy because she's found a perfume that doesn't have a petroleum base."

The temperature dropped lower during the night, and by morning the wind had churned up a haze of yellow dust. When Andrew came home that afternoon three pickups were parked before Virginia's house. He heard hammering inside.

"Now what?" he asked Barbara.

"They're tearing the paneling out of the south bedroom. She's going to have a large window put in, which she says she'll keep open because the rest of the house is heated with gas."

"In the meantime—"

"She said the carport wasn't so bad last night."

"It was below freezing," Andrew said. "She could have done this last summer instead of planting trees and statues around the yard and hanging mirrors in the house."

"Oh. She has another suitor. An oilman from Midland. He's very good-looking."

Virginia had a knack, Andrew admitted, of getting things done quickly in a town where most people thought in terms of months, or even years, for any sort of remodeling project. Within a week she had two large sliding windows installed in the south wall, and as Andrew went to work in the morning he saw her catching the sun behind the west pane, the east one open; that afternoon, she reversed her position.

When Andrew dropped by to inspect her remodeled room, Virginia showed him a new electric space heater.

"Have you heard of Saint Lawrence?" she asked. "He was martyred on a grill. He told his tormenters to turn him over because he was done on one side. But I'm being broiled and frozen simultaneously, so I've out-martyred him."

. . . .

About once a week that winter Andrew and Barbara shared a bottle of wine with Virginia in her bedroom. The room had been stripped to the rafters and studs, only the outer shell remaining; overhead they could see shingles, which Virginia said were asphalt, still another reason for the open window. When the wind blew, the doily on her nightstand fluttered, and Andrew or Barbara often retrieved letters with foreign stamps on them which had been blown to the floor. The Corwins kept on their winter coats while Virginia sat on the edge of her bed in layers of white clothing, including heavy wool socks and a long scarf wrapped around her head and neck. She kept a cordless telephone beside her, and their conversations were occasionally interrupted by calls from Houston, New York, Mexico City, Bogotá (Rudy usually), and London.

She told them she had slept with a general in Vietnam to obtain supplies for her hospital.

"He thought he was clever to get me in bed in exchange for doing what he was supposed to anyway. I thought I was clever to get my supplies at such small cost. Besides, he was very handsome."

Barbara said, "A fair exchange."

"When they shipped me out of Vietnam I rewarded myself with a vacation in Spain and became involved with a pilot there. One day as we were leaving the Prado we met some old friends of mine from Bogotá. They asked me, 'What are you doing in Madrid?' 'Oh,' I replied"—she feigned a yawn, tapping her mouth with her fingers— "'nothing much.'"

She looked at her glass suspiciously after her double confession. "Say, what's in this wine, anyway?"

As Andrew laughed, he recalled his first meeting with Virginia the previous summer. Now, hearing of her liaisons, he thought he understood why she had kept her back to him as they talked: he had guessed her to be forty, fifty years younger, and she must have known that, must have caught something unconsciously flirtatious in his voice, must have, as she sat, ill and lonely in a bare yard in a desolate little West Texas town, imagined herself for a few minutes to be about to turn still another man's head. Remembering that he had thought her eyebrows might have been penciled on while he was fetching his toolbox, Andrew decided he had been right.

On her dresser between two wig blocks, one with a silver-blond wig on it, was a small nude figure, a slender young woman standing on a golden ball, her head thrown back and her arms flung wide to the world. Andrew pointed at the nude. "She has your spirit."

"Thank you." Virginia smiled. "That's the Heidelberg Venus. Isn't she lovely? Have you been to Heidelberg? There's an enormous wine barrel in the castle there. I saw it with a friend, a wonderful man from Switzerland. Our guide let us dance on the barrel. Afterwards my friend saw the Venus in a shop window and bought it for me."

In December, between cold fronts when the temperature dropped into the teens, Virginia had the asphalt shingles replaced with a metal roof. On New Year's Day Cabora had one of its rare snowstorms, and the temperature fell below zero three nights in succession.

"Concepción was very careless," Virginia told Andrew. "She left a cup of tea on the dresser. The tea froze and broke the cup."

In late January the lumber yard found a wall covering with no petrochemicals in it. Virginia's workers insulated the walls and ceiling with fiberglass, and the room became "nearly bearable," as Barbara put it, although Virginia still kept the window open because of the fumes from the rest of the house.

In February Virginia asked the Corwins, "Would you object if I replaced that old wooden fence along our property line? I want to build a proper wall, with a proper gate."

Andrew said, "I don't object, but I'm not sure we can afford our share right now." Barbara nodded in agreement.

"That's not what I'm asking," she said impatiently. "I want it, so I'll pay for it. I'm planning a courtyard, and I want to have it ready for the season."

"A courtyard?" Andrew chuckled. "The *season*?"

Barbara frowned at him. Virginia's back became even straighter, she flushed, and Andrew suddenly understood what the expression "looked down her nose" meant.

"And what would you call it?" she asked.

"I'm sorry," he said. "By 'season' do you mean you'll have your courtyard ready by summer? I don't know what you mean by the word."

"I suppose my vocabulary is out of date." Virginia's an-

noyance seemed to fade. "What do I mean? In a sense
you're right. Summer will be my season, because I can get
out of this miserable prison of a house. But I was thinking
of the word in a social sense: of times when we can come
to know people we want to know better, over wine or dessert or a luncheon; when we make new friends." She
winked at Barbara. "Or enemies too. Life would be dull
without a few enemies."

Andrew nodded. "A more intense period of human inter-
action. Communication."

"Is that how you say it these days?" Virginia laughed,
and it was Andrew's turn to be red-faced. "Very well:
more intensity. But I prefer 'season.'"

· · · ·

The wall was built of cinder blocks on a broad, solid
foundation. It enclosed Virginia's front and back yards and
was six feet high, with two rows of latticework blocks at
the top. A steel gate was installed in the wall on the Corwins' property line, and the warping plywood sign
announcing "Los Arcos" which Andrew had disliked was
replaced by a true arch, complete with keystone.

"I'm having my portion of the wall painted pink to
match the house," Virginia said over the telephone to Andrew; "tell me what color you want, and I'll have them do
it."

"That's all right," he said hastily; "we'll paint it ourselves."

A few days after her wall had been painted, the name
"Los Arcos" appeared on the arch, this time lettered in
crisp blue script.

In March dump trucks came with dirt and sand, and
workers soon prepared a raised, level area extending from
the carport to the front wall. A layer of concrete was
poured over that, and bundles of thick red tiles were
stacked in the yard, but they were not laid.

"I'm broke again," Virginia told the Corwins over wine. "When I run out of cash, I stop. I'll have the tile laid in April."

On the warmest evening yet of the new spring, they were celebrating the acceptance of Barbara's most recent paper by the same annual conference of the American Chemical Society at which she had read the previous fall. It was to be held in San Francisco.

"An improvement over St. Louis," Virginia said. "And I believe your acceptance came much earlier this time."

Andrew put his hand on Barbara's shoulder. "That means she's becoming a VIP."

"Don't be silly," Barbara said.

"Of course she is," Virginia said.

The wind, which had bent Virginia's slender sycamore to the southeast most of the month, had dropped for once. Andrew and Barbara had moved Virginia's lawn table onto the untiled terrace. Concepción had a sprinkler whirring in the middle of the yard, and with a nozzle that sprayed a mist so fine it looked like a cloud, she was watering flowerbeds newly dug along the far wall. Whistling, she carefully washed the gray satyr by the sycamore. Andrew noted that she had planted honeysuckle at the foot of several new trellises before the house. She had also dug flowerbeds outside the wall. Her grass was already green, and she had coaxed her rose bushes to bloom six weeks early.

Andrew said to Virginia, "For someone who told me nine months ago she'd come here to die, you seem to be doing very well."

Virginia's face had cleared of the angry splotches, and her eyes no longer watered. She had not diluted her wine. She said, "I suppose we decide to die when the effort to live seems too much. The clean air has made staying alive easier for me here, and so have my neighbors."

She leaned forward and took their hands in hers. Andrew, expecting strength, was surprised at the weakness in her long fingers. She continued, "So I've decided to live a little longer."

"Good," Barbara said.

"Isn't that hubris? Saying 'I've decided'?" Andrew asked. "You know, too much—"

"Overweening pride," Virginia said. "I know the word. No, I don't think so."

Tiny gnats flew around Virginia's head, lighting on her ears and neck. She seemed not to notice. Andrew watched them with annoyance. Remembering that Barbara had said Virginia had found a non-allergenic perfume, he concluded that something in its ingredients must be drawing them.

He said, "I mean, you can't 'decide' about chance. An earthquake could swallow us up. A plane could fall on the house."

"Earthquakes are unlikely here, so I've lessened that chance. I didn't buy a house on an airport runway. Anyway, we all ignore chance. Otherwise we'd still be in the Stone Age."

She raised her glass tipsily, and her voice rose, "So I've decided to live a little longer, and to hell with chance. *Salud!* To decisions!"

"Good decisions," Barbara added.

"Any decision! God save us from shilly-shallying."

As they were leaving Virginia gave Barbara a flat, foil-covered box with a dark red ribbon around it.

"It's a nightgown," Virginia said. "I found it when I was going through some things this morning. I bought it for myself several years ago, but it was too short. Anyway, it's nylon, so I can't wear it."

"Thank you," Barbara said.

Virginia held her hand over her mouth in comic shame. "I believe it's quite naughty."

As they got ready for bed, Andrew said, "I like Virginia's bravado about 'deciding' to live. I like her will power, or at least her pretense of how strong her will is."

"I don't think it's bravado." Barbara came from the bathroom adjusting the gown Virginia had given her over her hips. It was floor-length, black with long, puffed sleeves, and high-necked.

She said, "I think Virginia lives closer to the edge than we realized. I'm certain she has had at least two heart attacks, one of them since she's been here."

"She said so?"

"Just from things she let slip during our lessons."

"Rudy claimed she was eight-five."

"She may be. Even older, maybe."

"Then 'bravado' is the right word," Andrew said.

"I don't see why. She said she'd decided to live. If she hadn't I believe she would have died."

"You mean she would have willed herself dead?"

"Nothing that mystical, although she's very strong."

"I was surprised when she held our hands tonight. Hers are like—oh, wilted lettuce or something."

Barbara nodded. "I know. I was talking about strength of purpose. Plain stubbornness. Anyway, I believe her about 'deciding.'"

"I don't," Andrew said.

"Sometimes I wish my Spanish was better so I could talk alone with Concepción," Barbara said. "I have the feeling that we see Virginia only as she wants us to—erect and alert and all that—and when we leave she collapses. Concepción sees her other side, her weakness."

Andrew mused, "What's that saying?—'No man is a hero to his valet'?"

"I don't mean that. If she is using all her strength for her public side—I mean us and whoever else she sees—I admire her even more."

Looking at the black gown again, Andrew started to comment disparagingly about Virginia's notion of "naughty" when, as Barbara bent to turn back the bed-spread, the lamp on the nightstand caught some trick in the weave of the sheer fabric and it became transparent.

While they were making love, he felt a part of himself slipping away, back to Virginia, and he wondered about chance, and beauty, and that quality about her that made him think *regal*. Even before he had seen her portrait in the living room, the Elizabeth I-Isabella portrait, he'd been thinking that: Virginia was regal—he had felt her regal ire when he laughed at her word "season"—she had been de-sirable beyond most women, was still so perhaps, the clear vestiges of extraordinary beauty remaining because of— what? Improbably, the genes had been there for regal beau-ty, and against higher odds the mind with regal potential, and the odds against the combination factorially higher yet. The thought came to him easily of her reclining in some younger year, offering the . . . gift, yes, she would have been regally aware of that, the gift of her lips, breasts, and long legs, her generous body to her husband, husband by chance, to some fortunate lover, lover by chance. And there was that, part of what made her desirable, that male urge to possess—wasn't *possess* even used in the Bible in the sense of carnal?—to possess, subdue that regality of hers. And the joke was that she would have given herself to a man and lost nothing, afterwards would have been as whole and beautiful and regal as ever. She would have been well aware of the joke.

Chance. . . . As Barbara shifted and raised herself to him and they quickened the rhythm of their embrace, a per-verse, unwelcome memory came to him of their second trip to Europe, their one venture out of Spain. Standing on a street in Nuremberg, they had looked up to see the medi-eval statue of a merry, beautiful young woman overhead on the wall of a cathedral. Then, to his disgust, they saw from behind carved worms, toads, unspeakable creatures crawling in and out of her rotting flesh. *Frau Welt*, Barbara read in the guidebook, and went on about the allegory of the statue, the temporality of life, but to Andrew it had been another manifestation of the foreignness of a place where Barbara's Spanish had been of less use than their English, and they had gone back to Spain.

He and Barbara slowed their rhythm, ground themselves gently together as they had learned to do over the years, and crested amid low sounds of pleasure. And while the good ache of sex ran through him, Andrew felt sadness for Virginia's decline and decay, and he wondered it if wasn't merely selfish, if he grieved not for hers but his own.

6

The tiles were laid on Virginia's terrace by mid-April. A framework was built alongside the terrace with trellises that arched over to the wall. Water circulated by a hidden pump rose in a crystal plume and fell in the birdbath. A life-size statue of a girl, nude, her right arm extended upward to steady a tall, slender water pot on her shoulder, was placed in the center of the yard beside the mimosa tree, which had been trimmed to a ball shape.

"The artist was ignorant of female musculature," Virginia told Andrew. "Look at her breasts."

"They look like breasts to me."

"How unobservant," Virginia scolded. "With her arm above her head like that, the right breast should be a good two inches higher than the left."

Two larger, heavier sets of steel lawn furniture, white with garlands of decorative leaves, appeared on the terrace. Each table had a broad fringed umbrella decorated with sewn-on elephants, tigers, and camels. Hundreds of wooden beads in many shapes hung from the fringes.

On the first of May, Virginia invited the Corwins to

"port wine, coffee, and dessert." The guests included, besides Lawrence Coke and the Midland oilman, whose name was A. J. ("call me Buster") Broyles, the Corwins and the Lunsfords; the mayor of Cabora and his wife; Edward Paddock, the town's most prominent doctor, and his wife; the wife of a rancher whose name was on every cattle guard for thirty miles along the highway east of Cabora; the dean of Andrew's division at the university; Dr. Abel Cantu, a genial-looking man whom Andrew remembered as having been the head of the Spanish department at the university when he and Barbara first arrived, and his wife; and Gerald and Mindy Solomon, who, Virginia said, had been State Department employees for many years, primarily in Panama and Brazil. A small, intense-looking man of about sixty in a dark brown suit arrived late. Virginia introduced him as Reverend Marlatt.

The port was from the Texas vineyard of an old friend of Virginia's near Del Rio. Andrew had seen it at the local liquor store, steeply priced. Concepción brought the bottles to him to uncork, and she served a fruitcake for which Virginia received many compliments. The mayor's wife whispered that it came from a mail-order bakery in South Texas. The guests clustered around the two tables on the terrace, breaking off conversations when the mayor or Dr. Paddock captured everyone's attention. Broyles, who Andrew thought was in his early sixties, wore western clothes, including a string tie. A thick silver buckle with small spur-shaped inlays of gold gleamed under his hefty paunch. He spoke knowledgeably of Oman, Qatar, Bahrain, and winters on the North Sea. Virginia announced that the Cantus had just returned from an eight-week trip by car into Mexico that had taken them all the way to the Gulf of Tehuantepec. They compared notes with the Solomons and the Paddocks, who knew the area. Reverend Marlatt said little, ate a piece of the fruitcake, declined a glass of wine as well as coffee, and left early.

A full moon rose half an hour after sunset—"I arranged it with the caterer," Virginia claimed—and diffused its soft light through the honeysuckle on the trellises overhead. Virginia sat nearest the door to the carport, a tiny bell by her hand on the table. She was dressed in a sari woven of silk—raw silk, she explained when the rancher's wife questioned her—ivory in color with a heavy fringe of red and gold. Over her bosom her necklace suspended gold crescents set with, alternately, small rubies and emeralds, though some of the settings were empty. A circlet of thick, plain gold was set in her hair. She wore sandals with slender thongs of braided red leather, and she flirtatiously displayed a heavily jeweled ankle bracelet to Dr. Paddock. A Mozart symphony rose tinnily from a small white tape recorder at her feet. After the first flurry of greetings, she seldom spoke. The elderly doctor, who was tall and still extraordinarily handsome, hovered near her with what Andrew assumed must have been known as chivalry in an earlier time. Now and then, without changing expression, Virginia took a thirty-second nap.

"How does she know all those people?" Andrew asked Barbara later.

"She goes to old Dr. Paddock for her medicine, and you can see he's crazy about her. I suppose he owes her professional courtesy too. Some people got to know her because of that letter about the play. The mayor and his wife introduced themselves to her at the suggestion of some VIP in Austin who knew her there. The Solomons knew someone who knew her in Colombia. Reverend Marlatt calls her almost every day, or comes by."

"Why did she invite him? I tried to talk to him and gave it up. Surely Rudy wasn't right about him converting her."

Barbara smiled. "I don't think there's any chance of that. Out of mischief, maybe? She said something once jokingly about 'siccing Dr. Paddock' on him. She says Dr. Paddock

is an agnostic. But poor Reverend Marlatt seemed too in-
timidated to start anything."

• • • •

During the summer the Corwins met at luncheons and
"desserts" in Virginia's house a painter and an opera
singer, both women, from Mexico City; two elderly law-
yers, one male and one female, from San Antonio; a
Japanese woman from Houston who, with Concepción,
cooked a spectacular dinner; a state senator, female; the
vineyard owner from Del Rio; geologists from Odessa and
Amarillo; a screenwriter from New York; businessmen
from Antwerp and Bogotá; a member of the board of re-
gents for the university; and numerous people from the
Cabora area, including, twice, the president of the university.

And during the summer workers replaced all the paneling in the house, removed the gas lines and heaters, and
installed an electric central heating unit. A half-wall of cin-
derblocks was built around the rear and side of the
carport, large sliding windows were installed above it, the
front was enclosed with double patio doors, and the carport became Virginia's spacious, airy study. A half-bath
with an outside entrance was built behind the carport for
the convenience of guests. A hexagonal gazebo with a
raised floor and a roof of thick cedar shakes was erected in
the back yard.

"I prefer the morning sun there, and the afternoon sun
in front," Virginia explained.

Rudy visited again in early September. The Corwins
waited in vain for him to step off the eleven o'clock bus on
a Wednesday night. On Thursday night Andrew went
again, and this time Rudy was there.

"The bloody idiots lost my bags in the El Paso airport,"
he shouted as he stepped off the bus. "Took twelve hours
to find them."

"I hear she's added all kinds of rubbish to that hovel," Rudy said on the short drive home. "Foolish woman! She should be putting that money away in certificates of deposit."

"She's enjoying life," Andrew said. He was sleepy. He had met an eight o'clock class that morning.

"Poppycock! She's had her turn."

Virginia gave a party Friday evening in Rudy's honor. Within half an hour he had offended both the mayor and Dr. Paddock with remarks about Cabora's backwardness, particularly its inadequate public transportation, and the ugliness of the approaches to the town—"Tumble-down hostels and that great American institution, the ramshackle petrol station." He complained to Andrew about the State Department's lack of political finesse in South America.

"My God, what do you teach in your political science classes?" he asked. "Your ambassadors cannot speak the language of the country; they hardly speak English. They are lambs among wolves, compared to the British and the French. Or even the Russians."

Before Andrew could reply, Rudy shouted to Virginia, "Golden throat of Bogotá! Where is your guitar? Sing us a song."

Other guests drowned out Virginia's objections, which were not very vehement, Andrew thought. Concepción brought a small guitar which the Corwins had not seen before, dusting it off as she came. After a perfunctory tuning, Virginia sang a Spanish ballad which, Rudy said loudly, had "bewitched every male in Bogotá." While she sang, he whispered to Andrew that she had spent a fortune on plastic surgery.

"Otherwise," he chuckled, "she'd have wattles like a turkey's."

Virginia finished her song—her voice broke several times, but Andrew heard clearly a rich yearning that he thought might indeed have once charmed males in Bogotá,

or anywhere—to loud applause. She and Dr. Cantu, who
had a rich tenor voice, sang another Spanish song together,
and then she put the guitar aside. A few minutes later,
when she had dozed off as she sat erectly with her hand
over the bell, Concepción muttered angrily to Rudy. He
burst into laughter.

"What did she say?" Andrew asked.

"Ah." Rudy scratched his head. "It is an idiom from her
mountain people, very difficult to translate. 'The peacock
has more feathers to lose than the sparrow.' Something like
that."

Early Saturday morning, Rudy's shout startled Andrew
as he was tugging at some morning glory vines encroaching
on his tomatoes.

"Glorious day!" Rudy said. He was wearing a white suit
and a white plantation hat such as Andrew had seen only
on the covers of paperback romances. "Madame is pros-
trate after her soiree; she cannot move. But she'll be back
in the traces by noon. She must be, because she has directed me to issue luncheon invitations. Can you come?
And your lovely wife, of course."

Andrew hesitated. "We'd better pass. Barbara is revising
a paper, and I have exams to read."

"So be it. But you cannot escape so easily. Tomorrow
her highness has decreed a champagne breakfast. Ten
o'clock."

Andrew smiled and shrugged. "All right. If Barbara
agrees."

"Virginia pays dearly for these excesses," Rudy said.
"Do you know she risks a heart attack with every exer-
tion? She has had several. She will be in bed for days after
I leave. Concepción is very cross because of this."

"You couldn't persuade Virginia to entertain a little
less?" Andrew asked.

"Only death could do that."

The next morning Virginia's guests—Dr. Paddock had

apparently forgotten his annoyance with Rudy—crowded around the dining table. Mindy Solomon shrieked, Rudy shouted, and the others laughed as champagne corks exploded from the bottles and the wine overflowed. Andrew, who was opening the bottles, was reminded of children with forbidden firecrackers. Raucous cowboys and college students littered the streets of Cabora with beer cans on Saturday nights, but on Sunday mornings the parking lots of the large cathedral on the mountainside south of the railroad tracks, the equally large Baptist church north of the tracks, and the several dozen smaller Protestant churches were full. So it was, Andrew thought, the combination of circumstances—the toasts with fluted glasses of bubbling wine at an unheard-of morning hour, and Sunday morning at that when the Solomons and Lunsfords and possibly the Paddocks and Lawrence Coke too would be in church ordinarily—which filled Virginia's tiny dining room, lined with mirrors that multiplied her guests many times over, with a conspiratorial air of playing hookey.

"To freedom," Frank Lunsford said, raising his glass, "and retirement too, because it sets you free."

"That's true," agreed Mindy Solomon, a small, trim woman with short white hair who moved and spoke with brisk energy. "We're the only free Americans. We're the only ones who can say exactly what we think on Sunday morning—"

"Over champagne," Clara Lunsford interjected.

"—Over champagne, and not have to answer for it to anybody on Monday morning."

Gerald Solomon nodded. "Not a damned soul."

"Except our wives," Frank said.

"Husbands." Clara elbowed him.

Lawrence Coke bent to Virginia and said mischievously, "Bachelorhood has its amenities."

Virginia had stood for a few minutes as her guests arrived and then sat in the one easy chair in the dining room. She too raised her glass. "To the Bill of Rights, and our annuities."

"And Social Security," Frank added.

Gerald said, "Trouble is, by the time you've worked for forty years you forget how to be an iconoclast."

"Ha!" Rudy shouted. "Not so Virginia! She's been a bloody hell-raiser all her life."

"Rudy!" Virginia said.

• • • •

"I like that idea of old age and freedom," Andrew said that afternoon after a nap. The champagne had given him a headache. "I'd like to look ahead to not giving a damn what the Canutesons of the world think." He had had an unpleasant session the previous week with his department head about the content of his federal government course and about his preference for blue jeans and dislike of ties as well.

"It's sad to think one has to wait that long. I'm sure if Virginia had been feeling better she'd have disagreed with Frank and said we should live free, whatever the consequences. Rudy was right about her."

"Probably so," Andrew said. "I didn't like the mirrors today. They made that little room seem even more crowded."

Barbara paused, then nodded. "Yes. I felt that too. But maybe that's what she wants."

"The more you pack in a room, the more intense it is? The more life you get for your money?"

"Yes. Something like that."

After his class on Monday morning Andrew called to offer Virginia's guest a ride to the bus station, but Rudy declined, saying, "I need the walk, and I have plenty of time. I've said my goodbyes to Madame. She's in bed, as I predicted."

• • • •

Barbara read her paper at the conference in San Francisco in October. She went alone, Andrew pleading an accumulation of exams to be read. His real reason, which he suspected Barbara understood, was a reluctance to go with her to the conference sessions. In St. Louis he had found them incomprehensible. Barbara returned with an invitation to participate in a workshop on laboratory techniques at the University of Ohio the following March. It coincided with spring break in Cabora, and she had already accepted.

7

During the same month Virginia persuaded Barbara to walk with her twice a week to an afternoon aerobics class in the Community Building a few blocks away.

"Now don't tell me she did aerobics," Andrew said the first afternoon when Barbara came home red-faced, her sweatshirt wet under her arm-pits.

"She floats about, very slowly, with her arms out and her eyes closed. She complained about the music immediately."

"Rock and roll?"

Barbara nodded. "And its loudness. She advised the instructor to see a doctor about her hearing problem. But on the way home she told me the problem was bad taste, not hearing, and there's no cure for that."

• • • •

That winter Virginia began writing. She enrolled in a creative writing course at Cabora State, a correspondence course from the University of Texas at Austin, and, for good measure, another with the Authors' Institute in Boston. She submitted the same chapters of her autobiography to all three. Their comments ranged from "plodding and unimaginative" to "eminently publishable." Virginia read them with delight to Andrew and Barbara. The Authors' Institute, after charging her $800, awarded her a $50 prize and urged her to take an advanced course for another $800. A novelist in California agreed to critique her work for a monthly fee.

One evening in December she read aloud a piece she was submitting to a "first-person experience" contest sponsored by a woman's magazine. She held a small fan before her face.

"I had a tooth pulled today," she explained. "I will spare you the battlefield."

Her story began with an account of a nurse at the turn of the century who, knowing she had cancer, had removed her own breasts. Then it told of Virginia's own mastectomy, dwelling on her fears when she had first learned she had the small malignant growths in her breasts, which she had discovered herself, and her serious doubt that their removal was preferable to the agony of spreading cancer and the certainty of death. A woman's breasts, she wrote, are her most obvious manifestation of her femininity, her womanness, her beauty, her attractiveness to the opposite sex, and therefore of her certainty of her biological as well as social niche and importance; their removal is a shocking physical maiming, at least as psychologically damaging as amputation of a limb, probably more so. After she finally made the decision, she changed her mind a hundred times as she waited in a sterile, pitiless hospital room for the operation, the knife. Then there was the physical suffering, the unavoidable brute pain. And after that her confrontation with her mutilated body, her coming to terms with the scarred remainder of what a man might once have admired and desired to caress, of what she might have wanted a man to caress; her coming to terms with the lifeless straps and padding that substituted pathetically for the missing flesh and allure of her body; and finally her discovery not only that she could cope with her new self but that she could function in society, be attractive, be a happy woman.

"I'm sorry," Andrew said awkwardly when she finished.

As she was reading, he had been unable to look away from the full curve of her bust. "It must be a terrible experience."

"Was it convincing?" Virginia asked.

"Yes. I—"

"Wonderful." Her giggle startled the Corwins. "It's my first attempt at fiction."

After a moment Barbara said, "Fiction or not, your optimistic conclusion could give a lot of women strength."

Virginia waved her hand in dismissal. "Oh, life is just a sloughing off. That's the drabbest of commonplaces. You might as well mourn trees losing their leaves."

Barbara laughed. "Virginia—"

"Think about it: hair, teeth, breasts, limbs, uterus, testicles, even our heart and lungs; even our brains. We replace our joints with metal sockets—"

"And our skulls with silver plates," Andrew added.

"The lucky ones lose what they miss the least. And they lose it late."

Andrew resisted an impulse to touch the nickel-sized bare spot on the crown of his head. It was true, he thought: in the mirror now he could see clearly the double path of his baldness and the folding of his cheeks at the jawline which, as his father's and grandfather's had, would someday hang like dewlaps; Barbara had had a partial upper fitted during the summer, and the dentist had warned of lower molars which could not be filled again. Despite her fitness, the flesh of her inner thighs was loosening, would someday hang like flaps. That very day in class, in a tone Andrew once might have used to ask his grandfather about World War I, a student had asked him about demonstrations on the campuses during the Vietnam War.

"But how does it read?" Virginia asked. "That's what I want to know."

"It's very good. I was taken in," Andrew said.

"Does it capture you with a quick narrative hook?" She

pushed the wine bottle toward Andrew and looked coyly over her fan. "Do you think it has a chance of winning?"

In January six graceful wooden arches, warped and shaped by a local craftsman, were installed over Virginia's terrace and painted pink. And, also in January, Virginia became the terror of a local radio program.

"I dial all but the last digit of their number before the announcer starts his question," she explained; "then I dial that number as he asks it, so I'm always the first caller."

"What if you don't know the answer?" Andrew asked.

"Oh, I always know."

Andrew said with unintended rudeness, "Sounds like an exercise in vanity."

"Certainly." When she smiled, he could not tell which tooth had been replaced. "We all need that."

During a warm spell in February, a contractor moved the gazebo farther back in the yard and began laying the foundation for an additional room behind the house. It was to be adobe, Virginia said, with a generous overhang on the roof, large windows and patio doors on the south side to catch the winter sun, and its own bathroom, all free of allergy-causing materials. The room was for a woman in Houston, Dorothy LeMaster, whom Virginia had known in Bogotá.

• • • •

It was a Saturday afternoon, and Andrew and Barbara had invited Virginia to walk downtown with them for lunch. A health-food restaurant, the sort of place that came and went quickly in Cabora, had opened that winter in an old adobe house, formerly a bar, on Main Street, just four blocks from the Corwins' house. They sat at a table in the rear in what had been the previous tenant's small beer garden. It was protected by a high board fence. The day was windless, for once; their table was against the north wall of the enclosure, and the south sun shone on them so warmly that Andrew and Barbara quickly removed their coats.

"Dorothy has emphysema, among other problems," Virginia said; "she was always a heavy smoker. She also is coming here to die, but she'll be quicker about it than I've been."

Andrew asked, "Doesn't she have any family?"

"They don't want to take care of her."

Andrew chuckled. "But you can."

Virginia shrugged. "We were friends years ago. If you stop being friends, you never were."

"Shame on me," she said, and slapped her cheek lightly. "There's another epigram."

"But it makes sense," Barbara said.

Andrew nodded. It was the answer he expected from Virginia. Whether he thought her logic sound no longer made any difference; he had come to believe she was telling her truth, and that was enough.

Virginia was delighted with the open-air tables and with the food, the bean- and alfalfa-sprouts, yogurt, feta, tofu, and baked potato concoctions. She was soon talking to the owners of the restaurant, Alex Dybach, a balding man in his early thirties wearing a wide-collared shirt open halfway down his chest, and Juanita Ellison, a slender, slightly older woman, tanned and freckled, whose hair clung tightly in moist brown and silver ringlets about her head. Dybach seemed gay in every gesture to Andrew.

"I will send you many customers," Virginia promised. "Some of my friends here cannot step inside a restaurant because there is so much plastic. And if you are interested, I can give you mountains of literature about nutrition and allergies."

"We would love to have it," Juanita Ellison said, and she arranged to come to Virginia's house the following Monday morning.

"Another strand in the vast network of Virginia's acquaintances," Andrew said after he and Barbara had seen Virginia to her door.

"She gives," Barbara said, "and she asks nothing in return."

"Not always." Andrew reminded her of his trips to pick up Rudy and of various handyman jobs he had performed around Virginia's house.

"Still," Barbara said, "the balance is in her favor."

• • • •

When spring break came in March, Andrew traveled with Barbara to the workshop at the University of Ohio. While she was in seminar sessions on Monday, the first day, Andrew explored the campus. That evening they ate hurriedly at a pizza parlor near their guest quarters, and Andrew went with Barbara back to a workshop lecture by a Professor Huizinger from Florida. Andrew spent most of Tuesday and Wednesday in the library researching sources for a paper on volunteerism he had been intending to write for several years, and he declined to attend Barbara's evening lectures with her.

"Too esoteric for me," he explained.

When she returned after ten o'clock on Thursday night, Andrew was lying on the floor watching television, his head on a cushion and his feet in a chair.

"How was it?" he asked.

"They're expecting too much from us. I'm exhausted."

"But it's worth it?"

"Oh, yes. I love it."

She showered and came from the bathroom in her robe, her hair in a towel. Sitting on the arm of the chair, she watched with him for a moment.

"How's your paper coming?" she asked.

Andrew glanced up at her. The movie was one of HBO's high school farces, full of promiscuous cheerleaders and moronic adults. He said, "Meaning I could do this at home. I spent the day at the mall. How's that for intellectual?"

"Dr. Huizinger invited me to come to Miami this summer. He said he could get me some research money from a grant he has."

"And?"

"I said I'd think about it."

The next evening Andrew went with Barbara to hear a Nobel Prize winner speak at the banquet closing the workshop, and on Saturday they flew home.

• • • •

Rudy had visited Virginia while the Corwins were gone. He had raised hell, she told them, about the money she was spending on the room for Dorothy LeMaster.

"Dorothy never liked him," she laughed. "Her husband was a coffee exporter, very wealthy. She was quite beautiful in her younger days, and I believe she may have rejected Rudy's advances."

"That's an impressive ghetto blaster." Andrew pointed at the new radio-cassette player on Virginia's desk. It had several rows of chrome switches, dials, and multi-colored lights. A Mahler symphony came from its detached speakers.

"A what?"

"Ghetto blaster. Juvenile delinquents deafen you on the street with these."

"I see," Virginia said. "But not with Mahler, I assume."

They were sitting in the converted carport drinking Virginia's friend's Del Rio port. The carport was once again a bedroom, for at the same time the contractor was building the adobe room in the rear, Virginia had decided to have her bedroom enlarged, an outside entrance added to it, a recess built for a dressing table with running water and a scallop-shaped sink, and hot water pipes installed under the floor. A wicker pagoda about ten feet in diameter, lavender and useless-looking, Andrew thought, had appeared in the front yard, which was becoming quite crowded. The carport also had become something of a maze, for Virginia had added two large abstract sculptures, one carved and polished from a huge, twisted juniper root, the other an arbor-like structure of welded sheet iron in which several painted whales rested. The Corwins had seen the pieces in the university art department's winter show. And half of the patio door was blocked off by a new rowing machine with a large panel of controls and gauges.

"I was partially responsible for the breakup of Rudy's marriage," Virginia said. "He and I flew together once to Caracas. It was a coincidence, and all quite innocent; he went there on business, and I was completing my husband's obligations to a research foundation. This was after his death. We were there about three weeks. But Rudy's wife took it all wrong, and she left him shortly afterwards. Stupid woman."

She was wearing several rings, one an unwieldy framework of gold forming a cage nearly an inch high. Andrew wondered why, despite her love of jewelry, she never wore earrings. The simple answer came to him as she talked: she had no earlobes, no flesh left for earrings. We do wear away, he thought again, remembering her remark about life being a sloughing off. The bones of her hands were ridges, the flesh valleyed between them. For an instant of horror he saw her flesh eroding, shrinking against the bones, saw her as bone. Then he thought, I'm no different, and, as if that made it all right, the horror vanished.

Virginia diluted her port with water and drank. In Bogotá, she said, the wife of the Nigerian ambassador once asked her to be the ambassador's mistress. The ambassador wanted to take a mistress in the western fashion, his wife explained, and she thought Virginia was the only woman worthy of him.

"I had other obligations at the time," Virginia said. "Pity. He was quite charming."

"Why does she keep building onto the house and putting things in the yard?" Andrew asked later. "It's getting to be the town joke."

Barbara finished marking a lab report, added it to a stack papers, and put a rubber band around them before she replied. "It's a metaphor, isn't it? Look how Concepción got the grass and honeysuckle to grow in that rocky yard. Your house is alive and growing; you are your house. I suppose Concepción understands or intuits something like that about Virginia's relationship with the house."

"You mean Concepción is keeping her alive?"

"No, but if you watch her in the yard—Concepción I mean—you can't help but feel her pleasure."

"Importance, I would say."

"Yes, you're right. I think she's aware of herself as Virginia's sustainer—no, that's wrong—intermediary, maybe."

"Intermediary?"

"Between Virginia's attitude toward life—I mean being alive—and the house as the result of her attitude."

Andrew nodded. "That makes sense. And she's doing a hell of a good job of it."

"Yes."

After a moment, Andrew said, "Still, the metaphor is barely under control. What about the nude statuary? The satyr? Is that vicarious sexuality? Virginia's contribution to keeping sex alive? Or her memories of it?"

"Why not? We do what we can."

Remembering Virginia's lobeless ears, Andrew thought, but did not say: And the pink of her house and walls, is that flesh? Is that her replaced flesh? Does she desire through it, does she caress through the green of her lawn, her comfortable lawn chairs, her port, her music, Concepción's enchiladas?

Barbara mused, "Sometimes I feel as if her will keeps us all alive."

"I don't follow that."

"I mean the group she's formed, including us. We had nothing to do with each other before she came. Don't you have the feeling we're all more alive because of her? When

did we ever drink champagne in Cabora in the morning?
Or any other time, come to think of it?"

"No. I understand what you're saying, but she's not
keeping you and me alive, anyway."

"That's silly, I suppose," she said.

"We're the only ones under sixty," Andrew said. "Canuteson asked me in the office if we'd joined the AARP."

Barbara flushed angrily. "They're more interesting than
anyone on the faculty, especially John Canuteson. He
hasn't had an original thought in twenty years. You're
more likely to have an intellectual conversation at Virginia's than in the faculty lounge."

"That's true," Andrew said. "Most of them have traveled, and they read. They know what's happening in the
world."

"And they care."

"Yes." Andrew was thinking that Barbara was right
about Canuteson, and that the same could be said for a
dozen faculty members, all male, all about the same age.
And that he was one of them. We do the right things, or
some of them, he thought—meet our classes, go to our
committee meetings, belong to Lions and Rotary—but
there's no real energy in us; not like Barbara's or Virginia's. All that thrashing around in the sixties, he
wondered; did we wear ourselves out? We're all dead.

"So maybe she is keeping us alive, in a sense."

Andrew said, "Rudy says Concepción will go home to
her village when Virginia dies. I wonder if Concepción
thinks about that: about when Virginia dies, she'll leave all
this, all this planting and growing? About how it's useless,
in a way."

"I doubt it. And I don't think it's useless, either."

"It's not likely that anyone else would care for the yard
that well. Virginia's water bill must be astronomical. A
year after Virginia's gone, everything in the yard will be
dead, even the trees."

"It's the process, isn't it?" Barbara said. "Of living, I mean. If Concepción and Virginia had come here just for a month they'd have done the same things—started the grass, and so on. It's doing it that matters. They think alike in that respect. Or maybe they don't think, they just do; they don't live miserly."

8

"I have been appointed the wildflower chairperson for Cabora," Virginia told the Corwins late in March.

"Who's the appointer?" Andrew asked.

"The Deity. My mission is to blanket this desolate hamlet in bluebonnets, Indian blanket, and Indian paintbrush."

Her name was in the weekly paper in a front-page story every Thursday, and she appeared in a photograph arm in arm with the mayor and a state representative. The Corwins heard her quoted on the local newscasts. Another allergy sufferer complained in a letter to the editor that Virginia was adding to his woes, but she replied, after first establishing her credentials as an authority on the subject, that wildflowers were non-allergenic.

"The Garden Club is up in arms," Barbara told Andrew. "Virginia was picked because she's a friend of a friend of Lady Bird Johnson's. They're all but threatening bodily harm to her because she's moved in on their territory."

Andrew chuckled. "I'll bet that worries her."

"She listens to them very sympathetically, then in effect tells them to join her or get out of the way."

"As I would have guessed. Politics of the steamroller."

During the same weekend Barbara made up her mind to work in Dr. Huizinger's laboratory in Miami that summer.

When the Corwins told Virginia, she said, "Splendid! I have heard of him. Yes, you must go. Go, work hard, and come back and tell me what you've learned."

"Andrew's a good cook, so I won't worry about him," Barbara said.

"Of course not. He can fend for himself. And if he can't, too bad." Virginia frowned dramatically and growled, "It's the law of the jungle."

Virginia's adobe room was completed in May. Her friend Dorothy, a tottering, emaciated woman with large, startled eyes and caked makeup, came early in June with two trunks of clothing and two small antique tables. Juanita Ellison, the partner in the health-food restaurant, brought her from the Amtrak station to Virginia's house in a pickup equipped with heavy tires and a roll bar. Dorothy also brought a portrait of a brilliantly smiling, lovely young woman, her long hair piled high over her head in a style Andrew associated with the thirties or early forties. He thought the artist might be the same one who had done the portrait of Virginia in the living room.

"That's how she looked, more or less, in her early thirties," Virginia told the Corwins out of Dorothy's hearing. She said her guest's trunks contained clothing from her days in Colombia, old and worn out. "I remember the tables from Bogotá. Apparently that's all she has left, or what the children haven't taken from her."

The remodeling of Virginia's room, complete with a chandelier that Andrew and Virginia had to duck under, was also finished in May. Andrew and Barbara spent an evening a few days later assembling a white, precariously dainty canopy bed Virginia had ordered from Sears. Andrew had to make several trips back to their house for tools, screws, and even wire. When they finally had the bed together, the wire ribs in place above it, and the frilled canopy arranged over the ribs, they put on the mattress that Virginia's London friend had sent—it fit badly—and Virginia hung a small stuffed burro with packsaddles from the canopy.

"Just a bit of nonsense that Rudy gave me," she said; "I've carried it through a dozen countries."

Two weeks after her guest had arrived, Virginia told the

Corwins one evening at Comanche Overlook that she had made a mistake in inviting Dorothy to live with her.

"Her mind has dwindled to two themes," Virginia said. "Death, and the dangers of smoking, which caused her emphysema; in other words, death again."

"I can attest to that," Andrew agreed. He had sat next to Dorothy at one of Virginia's luncheons; her clinical description of the effects of emphysema on her lungs, and her increasingly labored breathing as she talked, had quickly taken away his appetite.

Virginia said sharply, "I've told her to stay in her apartment when I have guests, if she has nothing else to say. She is not the same woman I knew in Bogotá. That woman is dead. Literally dead."

"Still, her disease is a fact," Barbara said. "We shouldn't pretend it's not there, or that people don't die from it."

"I never deny the facts, but very few facts are important enough to dominate our lives."

In the canyon below them, a dozen javelinas ranging in size from a pair of very large boars to several young ones smaller than jackrabbits shuffled out of the cholla and dark, squat junipers in single file. Virginia and the Corwins were silent, but the dark animals heard something, or caught their scent, snorted and squealed suddenly, and raced down the slope into the brush.

"Oh, to hell with it," Virginia said.

"What was all the music about at your house last night?" Barbara asked. Around nine o'clock the Corwins had heard Mexican music coming from Virginia's yard.

Virginia smiled. "Wasn't it lively! My workmen had promised to serenade me when they finished the bedroom. Last night they kept their word. I should have called you, but they came unexpectedly."

"That's all right," Andrew said.

"I danced to a *corrida* with the contractor," Virginia said.

She stood up and looked beyond Cabora toward the mountains to the north. "Sometimes the Solomons bring me out here also. I've told them this: when I die, I want to be cremated. I want my friends to bring my ashes out here, and bring plenty of champagne. I've set aside some money for it."

She turned toward Andrew and Barbara, smiling, and flung out her arms. "Drink! Drink gallons of champagne in memory of whatever pleasant times we had together. Then, when a good breeze comes up, throw my ashes over this canyon. And don't you dare shed a tear."

"That sounds like a high-class act," Andrew said.

"It does," Barbara agreed.

Virginia leaned back, her hands on the railing, her laughter deep in her throat. "If Indira Gandhi can have her ashes scattered from an airplane over the Himalayas, surely I can have mine thrown in a canyon in the Davis Mountains."

On the first day of July Barbara left for Miami. Andrew, enmeshed in his summer workshops, was a bit ashamed that he scarcely noticed her absence except on weekends. She wrote that she had taken an efficiency—"a closet, really"—at a rate higher than a landlord would dare charge for the most luxurious apartment in Cabora. She called him occasionally to tell him about the intimidating new world she had entered—computers that, despite their compactness, zipped through statistical procedures which the mainframes of a decade earlier had balked at; a laboratory full of people of every color who spoke a dozen varieties of English and who, unlike the Corwins' Cabora colleagues, expected a great deal of her and themselves. Andrew bristled defensively when she suggested this, more so because he knew she was right. And she told of her cultural re-entry, after Cabora, into urban life—of over-crowded buses, of leaving her tiny ("Darling, you have no idea how tiny") apartment at six a.m. to reach work at eight, of losing her money and cards to a purse-snatcher, and of seeing a first-run movie and hearing Al Jarreau, whom she and Andrew both liked, in person.

"It sounds like you're having a hell of a good time," Andrew said one Sunday morning from the depths of his living room recliner. He had just returned from the kind of Texas-style breakfast—sausage hot with chiles, eggs, biscuits, grits, gravy, and several cups of coffee—that Barbara hated. She was describing a Cuban restaurant she had gone to with a group from the laboratory the previous evening.

"Yes, I am."

Late in July the workmen returned and began tearing into the outer wall of Concepción's room; Virginia had decided to double its size.

In August Virginia gave a party to which, in addition to Andrew and her elderly friends, several younger couples came.

"The moon has failed me," Virginia complained to Dr. Paddock as it rose over the mountain to the east. "It's not full."

"It's gibbous," Dr. Paddock said.

She leaned on the old man's arm. "It's pregnant."

"It's convex, and therefore gibbous."

"It's hunchbacked," Virginia said. "We scientists must always give way to the poets."

Virginia played her recorder, and than a bearded young man accompanied her on a guitar while she sang the same ballad that, Andrew remembered, she had sung at Rudy's request, but tonight she sang with a full-throated energy that Andrew could not reconcile with his recollections of the weakness in her hands, or of that other night. Dorothy, laden with costume jewelry and eerily gaunt in the moonlight, sat beside Virginia. She seemed, Andrew thought, to be absorbed in the act of breathing, in mustering the strength for it. She tasted the wine, began coughing, and returned to her room.

The Paddocks, Lunsfords, Solomons, and Cantus left early, but Virginia's younger guests stayed. As the guitar player strummed and sang, a woman in a Mexican dress clambered atop the wall and danced barefooted with easy balance along its length under the moon and the abundance of deep desert stars, the full skirt of the bright yellow dress floating out from her thighs.

Watching the dancer, Andrew thought that he understood what Barbara had said about Virginia keeping them alive. He leaned to Virginia and said, "You make things happen, don't you?" But she was asleep. One of her secrets, Andrew wondered, or the secrets of the very old? Go full tilt, then recoup with equal intensity. Or is it the secret only my generation doesn't know? We can't do anything with intensity, even rest. He remembered Barbara's speculation that Virginia probably collapsed after their evenings together, and he thought sadly that that other, hidden side of her life, her weakness, was encroaching on her public side.

Across the table, a woman he had not noticed before flashed a smile at him. Large hooped earrings, plastic, and the tight, wetly clinging brown and silver ringlets of her hair glinted in the moonlight, and Andrew recognized Juanita Ellison. He moved around the table to sit beside her. When her hand brushed his, startling him, he remembered with sudden desire how long it had been since a woman, since Barbara had touched him. By the time the party broke up around eleven, Virginia appeared to be exhausted. Andrew took one arm, Concepción the other, and they helped her into the house, Concepción grumbling and scolding at every step.

Juanita was waiting when Andrew came out. He put his hand on her waist, and she turned and fell in stride with him. They passed through the gate Virginia had installed in the fence and went in the kitchen door of the Corwins' house. They drank brandy in the living room, and then

Andrew steered Juanita (fastidiously, he thought) to the seldom-used guest room. After they had undressed with the awkwardness of strangers, they fumbled until they found a semblance of familiarity, then came a fitting together too quickly, an impatient interruption while Juanita removed her earrings, and it was over. After Andrew brought more brandy, a cool breeze dried their sweat, and they tugged a sheet up over their nakedness.

Juanita found his hand and said, "We can thank Dr. Stone for this. Isn't she a wonderful old lady?"

"We're very fond of her," Andrew answered, unaccountably irritated that she wanted to talk about Virginia, even more irritated that he had automatically included Barbara, that he had failed to be faithful for two months. He withdrew his hand.

And when the moon was dipping toward the peaks west of Cabora, Andrew shivered, barefooted and shirtless, as he watched Juanita drive away from the pink wall in her pickup with its fat tires and roll bar.

The next weekend he flew to Philadelphia to visit his mother, and then on to Miami to join Barbara. Despite her description, he was unprepared for the rumble of traffic, the sirens, the voices of people living closely together and their disconcertingly intimate thumps against the walls and ceilings, the air conditioner's whine, the claustrophobia of her apartment, which was smaller than their guest room in Cabora. Barbara arose early in the morning, before the daylight appeared in the single small, barred window. When she opened the refrigerator, Andrew could feel its cold air in the three-quarter-size bed.

"This bathroom is a casket on end," he said.

"I know." Her almost-gleeful tone contradicted her words and puzzled Andrew. "Isn't it awful?"

She took him to the Cuban restaurant, to the nightclub where she had heard Al Jarreau. He rode with her to work on the bus, listening to Spanish that was familiar, yet, in its energy and tension, not at all what he heard in Cabora. Amidst the strangeness and discomfort, despite Andrew's feeling that Barbara worked, was gone too much, they reunited, they were happy.

"I'd forgotten how much I like to kiss you," Barbara told him his third night there. They were sore from their lovemaking the first two nights; they had made love before dinner that evening, and were about to do so again.

"It's the basis of our marriage."

"Not a bad basis," she said, her breath rich with wine and food.

She worked in Dr. Huizinger's laboratory until three days before the fall semester began in Cabora, and they returned together. On her last day Huizinger offered another fellowship for the next summer, and a full-time research position for the following autumn.

"I have until March to decide about the fall position," Barbara said.

"How can you turn it down?" Andrew asked. She had been offered double her salary in Cabora.

"It's not so much, if you think about how expensive Miami is."

By summer's end, although Virginia had failed to arouse interest in her project among most of Cabora's homeowners, the mayor had proclaimed "Wildflower Day," the city workers had planted wildflowers in the islands where the highways divided at the four entrances to the town, and the merchants had flowers growing in every cranny along Main Street.

Dorothy died in October in a Midland hospital, where Dr. Paddock had sent her a week earlier. Her daughter, Virginia said, came one morning, picked up a hair dryer and the two antique tables, collected her jewelry—all worthless, according to Virginia—in a paper bag and took the empty trunks, leaving the room for Concepción to clean up.

"She was in a good deal of pain, which Dr. Paddock says she took stoically," Virginia told the Corwins. "Still, she didn't die well."

"Why not?" Andrew asked.

"She whined constantly for this or that and was a nuisance to Concepción and me, particularly Concepción; what nonsense to make such a fuss about dying. So good riddance."

At Christmas Andrew and Barbara flew to London. For three days they followed the tourist route to Westminster Abbey, St. Paul's, Parliament, the Tower of London, the stores on Oxford Street. They spent their fourth day in the British Museum, and, while Barbara returned there the next day, Andrew went back to Parliament. They traveled to Oxford by bus and went to the Camera, the Bodleian, and some of the great colleges: Christ Church, Magdalen, Balliol, and Queen's. They took a bus one morning to Hampton Court.

Sitting on the upper deck of a red bus back in London that night, both of them tipsy from drinking warm English beer, Barbara said, "I have one complaint. I want to stay two years instead of two weeks."

"Righto," Andrew replied, and kissed her. But after that things went wrong for him. It started with the shopkeeper who snapped "Damned Americans throwing their money around" and refused to change a hundred-pound note for him. The next morning he couldn't face the kippered herring Barbara ordered for breakfast. Suddenly it was all unreasonable, the stingy, indifferently uttered "Sorry" that was no apology at all, the cars on the wrong side of the road, the sunless sky, the homely taxis, the restaurants that were never open when they should be. He wanted to go home.

"We should have gone back to Spain," he said.

"Do you think I don't understand why you like Spain?" Barbara asked. "It's because you can dump everything in my lap there. You don't understand a word, so you can just tag along with your mind turned off."

She took a bus to Salisbury and Stonehenge. Andrew remained in the hotel with a book, and when he became bored with that he poked around the area near the hotel, looking in shop windows. He thought that what Barbara had said about his liking Spain was probably right.

9

The morning after they returned to Cabora, Mindy Solomon and Clara Lunsford brought the news that Virginia had suffered a stroke and was in an El Paso hospital.

"Apparently it's her second since she's been here," Mindy said; "the first happened about a year ago, but only Dr. Paddock knew. This one was much more severe."

She had been in intensive care for over a week. Her left side was paralyzed.

Clara said, "Rudy is with her. He arrived several days ago from Bogotá and got in some sort of trouble with immigration at the airport, but it's all right now."

"Can Virginia take phone calls?" Andrew asked.

"Yes, but they're supposed to be short." Clara smiled. "You may find her a bit abrupt."

"I've had a philosophy lesson," Virginia said to Andrew when he called, before he could offer his sympathy. Her voice seemed strong, but halting as he remembered it from two and a half years earlier. "There's a garrulous man here who cleans the bedpans for five dollars an hour. He says the job has taught him something important about life: no matter whose shit it is, it stinks."

Andrew laughed, then asked, "When can you come home?"

"Rudy and Dr. Paddock are bringing me tomorrow evening. This time it really is to die, and I expect my friends to help me do it."

Andrew laughed again and said, "What kind of talk is that?"

"I believe it's called straight talk." The receiver banged in his ear.

The next morning the Corwins, Lunsfords, Solomons, and Concepción helped Dr. Paddock's nurse push the canopy bed against the wall and set up a hospital bed in the middle of Virginia's remodeled bedroom. As Andrew and Barbara went back to their house, Andrew noticed that large stone urns had been placed at ten-foot intervals on the top of Virginia's wall during their absence. They had been painted white.

That evening Rudy and Dr. Paddock arrived in Dr. Paddock's Lincoln with Virginia in the back seat, reclining on pillows and breathing heavily as if she had been running. They had driven with the windows open over two hundred miles in the crisp January air. Virginia was not wearing her wig, and her sparse gray-brown hair did not conceal her mottled scalp. Andrew was shocked at her thinness.

"I can move my right arm and leg," she said. "Remember that, so you'll know what works and what just hangs."

Andrew and Rudy got their arms under her and lifted her awkwardly out of the car with Barbara and Clara Lunsford's help.

"The orderly who carried me out to Dr. Paddock's car in El Paso was a giant," Virginia said to Mindy Solomon, who walked beside her holding her arm as the men carried her into the house.

"A Hercules," Rudy said. "Virginia wanted him to run off to Mexico with her."

"Or anywhere. My last fling."

Concepción held the door open for them as they entered the house, speaking rapidly and angrily while Rudy and Virginia laughed.

"Concepción says I've let people starve me," Virginia said as they laid her on the hospital bed. "She says I'm so stupid I don't even eat without her around." The strength he thought he'd heard in her voice, Andrew decided, was not so much strength as a new, harsh tone, impatient and nearly rude.

Concepción tucked and re-tucked the covers around her. Virginia insisted on the stuffed burro being moved from the canopy and re-hung from the chandelier over the hospital bed. While Gerald Solomon and Frank carried in a heavy wooden box of materials in manila folders from the carport, she had Andrew set a small table with the cordless telephone and a notebook on the right side of the bed. She sent Concepción to pour wine and ordered Lawrence Coke to bring the glasses to her guests.

When everyone had a small glass of the dark port, the Corwins, Solomons, Lunsfords, and Dr. Coke stood in sudden, awkward silence on one side of the bed, Rudy and Dr. Paddock on the other.

"*Salud!*" Virginia looked at them slowly, moving her eyes but not her head. She said without smiling, "Now I'm ready for the Roman way."

"You're not in Rome," Dr. Coke said. He tried to hit a joking tone, Andrew thought, but the reply fell flat.

"One is always in Rome." Virginia looked at Mindy. "Don't forget: scatter my ashes from Comanche Overlook."

"Oh, Virginia."

"And don't 'Oh, Virginia' me."

Andrew pointed at the statue of the nude on the dresser and said, "You'll be back in form in a few days, just like your hedonist spirit."

"She's already begun therapy." Dr. Paddock pulled the covers back from her left foot. "See here: try moving it, Virginia."

Her foot moved, barely perceptibly, to a chorus of en-

couragement, but Virginia frowned and passed her right
hand down her left side. "This is as close to vegetable as I
plan to get."

Later, while Dr. Paddock drank a second glass of wine
with the Corwins, Clara, and Rudy in the living room, he
told them, "Virginia is suffering from post-recovery depres-
sion, and I believe she is serious at the moment about
taking her life. I don't know what access she may have to
something that she could harm herself with, so we must all
watch her closely."

As Dr. Paddock finished and turned away, Rudy grinned
at the Corwins and stage-whispered, "We'll have to watch
the old lady like an eagle! She's tricky!"

• • • •

"Do you agree with what Dr. Paddock said about Virginia committing suicide?" Andrew asked Barbara as they
got ready for bed.

"Yes."

"I don't. Virginia likes to live too much,"

"That's the point," Barbara said. "If she can't function
fully it wouldn't be like living, to her."

Andrew shook his head. "The only times I ever heard
her bring up the subject of death were when she first came
here, except when she was involved with Dorothy."

"Hasn't it been in the air ever since we've known her?"
Barbara asked. "You reminded her yourself that she'd said
she came here to die, that time before her terrace was
tiled."

"I was joking," Andrew said. But he thought she was
right, that something in him had been suspended since the
day he'd heard the old woman playing her recorder in the
yard, had looked over the fence and seen . . . what? What
he'd thought for a few minutes was a very beautiful young
woman, he'd been sure of that, he now admitted, and then,
even as she aged before his eyes, but grew no less beautiful,

she'd said, "I came here to die," and he'd never been able to accept it, and he still could not.

"And don't forget what she said at Comanche Overlook last spring," Barbara said.

"All right, and there. But for the most part death has been the last thing on her mind for two years."

"Of course," Barbara said impatiently. "That's what I meant. That's the whole point."

After they turned the lights out, Andrew asked, "What do you mean, 'function fully'? She could barely walk when she came here, and she couldn't see. I wouldn't call that functioning fully."

"But her mind was all right."

"It still is."

Barbara said, "You heard what she said about being a vegetable; maybe she thinks the odds are getting too high."

• • • •

Rudy was at the Corwins' house before breakfast the next morning. "Constitutional!" he shouted as Andrew opened the door. "Join me for a walk."

"How's Virginia?" Barbara asked over Andrew's shoulder.

"Busy as bloody hell. She made calls half the night to four continents. Her telephone bill will be astronomic. Called a dozen old boyfriends to say her good-byes. Two had died she didn't know about."

"Here are the circumstances," Rudy said as soon as they had rounded the corner of the house. Walking between Andrew and Barbara, he steered them by their elbows toward the middle of the empty street. "The old girl will be ready to go in three or four days. She's making sure all the legal work is done so Concepción will have some cash immediately, say forty or fifty thousand, and an income for life. Concepción will go home and live like royalty, believe me, until she's cheated out of it."

"Let's hope she's not," Andrew said.

"Certainly. Let us hope not. I will inherit the rest: whatever money is left, securities, and the house. What do you suppose the house is worth, with the improvements Virginia has made?"

"Oh, I don't know; forty, maybe fifty thousand; there's not much of a market here," Andrew said. He pulled loose from Rudy's grasp. "I don't feel right talking about this."

Rudy grinned. "Because she's not dead. But she will be, believe me. It's a pity she was so stupid in Bogotá and lost that apartment building. You two would have been $50,000 richer yourselves, my friends; Virginia would have seen to it."

"I told you before, we're not interested in her money."

He grinned again. "Good. Good to have scruples. Good, because you're not getting any. Now, to the problem: when Virginia finishes her business, she wants to take potassium cyanide, because she has no desire to become a brain in a useless body. She has enough cyanide on hand to kill half the population of Texas, but she has carried it with her for twenty years, and she's afraid it may have lost its efficacy. I have told her that is nonsense."

"Yes," Barbara nodded.

"She has no faith in my knowledge of these matters, however, so when she called me in Colombia, she instructed me to bring a fresh supply. I attempted to do so, but there was an alert of some sort in the El Paso airport, and the drug agents were inspecting very carefully. I had to get rid of it. Never mind how."

"That's risky business," Andrew said.

"Yes. Problem number two is that, efficacious or not, the cyanide is not in capsules; Virginia has the capsules, but they must be filled. Concepción is not stupid or blind, she knows Virginia extremely well, she does not trust me, and she's a strict Catholic; she'll sound the alarm if she sees me filling them. So—new cyanide or old—may I fill them in your house?"

"No," Andrew said.

"As I thought. So much for your friendship with Virginia."

"Now wait—" Barbara began.

"I told her so two years ago, that she could not depend on you. When Virginia's husband learned he had cancer, at his request my father supplied him with cyanide, then caught a plane out of Colombia and stayed away for three months. Virginia knew this, and she was deeply grateful to my father. Later, it was his turn, and she did the same for him. Four hours after her plane left for Buenos Aires, he took the stuff."

"I *am* her friend," Andrew said. "We are. Where the hell were you the first winter she was here? You have no idea how much she suffered then."

"Not enough to ask for my help, which she knew she could have. You Americans confuse suffering with discomfort."

Barbara said, "We've spent a lot of time with Virginia."

Rudy waved his hand in dismissal. "Now we come to the true test, when a friend doesn't want to spend time with us. Our friend wants to die. She knows what's ahead for her—nothing pleasant—and so she wants to die. She needs our help."

"You're asking us to be accessories to what could be construed as murder," Andrew said.

"Who is killing her? If I give you the keys to my car, you could drive it into a tree at a hundred kilometers an hour and kill yourself. Would that make me a murderer?"

"Not per se," Barbara said.

Andrew said, "Some people would think so, if I had been talking about suicide."

"All right." Rudy held up his hands in surrender. "I'll

fill the capsules somehow. Another problem: the American police are more diligent than the gendarmerie in my part of the world. Since I will inherit Virginia's house and therefore will be the prime suspect if the police think it was not suicide, I must be out of the country before she does it. Will you drive me to the El Paso airport?"

"I suppose we could." Barbara looked at Andrew.

Andrew shook his head. "We can't risk it."

"Risk?" Rudy laughed loudly. "What risk? Think of the risk Virginia is taking. She may have only a few days. Hours, perhaps."

"We can't do it," Andrew said.

"So I must take care of that by myself too," Rudy said. "God spare me from such scrupulous friends."

Andrew stopped and faced him. "You know, I'm not even sure I agree with her decision to do it."

"But you agree it is her decision, not yours." Rudy watched him closely.

Andrew hesitated, then resumed walking. "I suppose."

But later as Andrew drove to work past the pink house and returned for lunch, glimpsing through the arched gate the half-crouched satyr near the leafless sycamore, the frivolous wicker pagoda, the girl with the water pot, he could not believe what Rudy had told them, could not believe Virginia, who, like the nude on her dresser, raced toward life with open arms, would consider giving death a minute, a single extra minute, of her portion. But what if he was wrong? He thought briefly of telling Dr. Paddock what Rudy had said, or even the police, and knew he would not. Whatever Virginia meant to do, she would have the strength for it, and the strength to keep well-meaning, meddling friends at bay.

Barbara went to see Virginia that afternoon and again that evening, returning soon each time because, she said, Virginia was making and receiving telephone calls, and the house was full of people—the Solomons, the Paddocks, the

Cantus, the mayor and his wife, Lawrence Coke, Buster Broyles, Reverend Marlatt, Clara Lunsford, Juanita Ellison, the contractor who had built the adobe room, and several others Barbara didn't know.

"Virginia called Dr. Paddock an idiot today," Barbara laughed as they went to bed.

"What brought that on?"

"Not to his face. He was working with her, getting her to wriggle her toes. After he left, she said, 'What an idiot.'"

"Meaning she's still depressed, as he put it?"

"I don't think she's depressed at all. She's a little bad-tempered because she's trying to do a lot of things—make sure Concepción's taken care of, tell old friends goodbye—"

"Set her house in order."

"Yes. And she thinks she doesn't have much time,"

"She's not afraid at all, is she?"

"She's afraid of the next stroke."

"What about the cyanide business?" Andrew asked. "Do you think she really has some?"

"Of course."

"Was Rudy right about it not mattering if it's old or not?"

Barbara nodded. "It would work just as well."

"How does it work?"

"It causes the blood to be unable to pick up oxygen. In effect, it causes suffocation."

"What does it look like?"

"About the same as table salt."

"Is it fast?"

"Very."

Andrew said, "If she really went through with it, and if she had Rudy out looking for a new supply of the stuff, she'd be putting him in jeopardy."

"Yes," Barbara agreed, "but she's stubborn. If she wants

it, she'll get it. And besides—don't you suppose she's taken risks for friends? From her point of view, the chances Rudy is taking are small compared to the danger she's in."

"You're repeating Rudy's argument."

Barbara flushed. "Because he's got a point."

The following afternoon Virginia called Andrew. "Come over here," she said in the harsh tone he had noted on the day of her return. "I want to give you the Heidelberg Venus."

"The Venus?"

"Don't you want it? You've always said you liked it."

"Sure I want it. But—"

"Then don't 'but' me; I'm fed up with people who 'but' me instead of doing what I want them to do. Come over and get it."

"She wants to give me that little nude on the dresser," he said to Barbara.

"Oh, that's sweet."

"Want to come? You haven't been over there today."

She shook her head and picked up another lab report. "I don't feel like it today."

Andrew turned to go, then stopped. "You know what? This is goddamned morbid. I feel like a vulture on the highway."

He wasn't prepared for the dark flush and sudden twist of Barbara's mouth. She said, "Jesus Christ, that's the stupidest thing I've ever heard you say."

Andrew arrived at Virginia's at the same time as Reverend Marlatt. Concepción, looking tired and not overjoyed to see them, opened the door, gestured toward Virginia's bedroom and let them find their own way.

"A minister and a political scientist!" Rudy, who had been sitting on Virginia's canopy bed, stood up to shake their hands.

Reverend Marlatt began, "Dr. Stone—"

"A formidable combination!" Rudy sat down again.

The change, Andrew thought, was that Virginia had stopped preparing herself to please, or charm, or delude the world, stopped arranging herself in that regal combination of jewelry, cosmetics, perfect—even if borrowed— hair, and posture. She lay on the tilted hospital bed, her gown carelessly open; the regality was left in the rawness of her commands. For an instant Andrew did not comprehend the meaning of the thick scar tissue over her chest; then he realized that her story about the mastectomy had not been fiction after all.

"Dr. Stone," Reverend Marlatt said again.

"There she is," Virginia said to Andrew. She pointed at the little statue on the dresser. "Take her, and may she give you as much pleasure as she has me."

"Thank you."

"You bet." Virginia said to Rudy, "'You bet' is West Texan for 'You're welcome'; also for 'yes,' and whatever else you want it to mean."

"Dr. Stone," Reverend Marlatt began once more, "this morning you were so busy—"

"Yes, I've many chores to finish," Virginia said. "We can't have any more of our discussions."

"We were going to talk about life everlasting."

"I know nothing about immortality, but I lived many years among scientists, and I learned a good deal about infinity. That's where my remains—a few grams of ashes— will be scattered very shortly. To infinity."

The preacher said gently, "But your soul—"

"Oh, the soul." She laughed, and Rudy stood up as if he had been given a signal. She said, "Mr. Marlatt, I must ask you to leave, and not to come back."

Rudy silently let him out at Virginia's bedroom entrance. Reverend Marlatt said nothing. Andrew thought his lips were trembling.

"Madame Heartless!" Rudy grinned after he closed the door.

"I should have done that months ago," Virginia said. "Sometimes a little heartlessness is merciful."

Andrew looked down, not sure what to say after Virginia's rudeness and the sudden tension and release in the room.

"Are you shocked?" Virginia asked him. "You shouldn't be. I've tried to keep the edges of my life cleanly trimmed, but sometimes I get careless. Then I have to use the shears."

"Then the fleece flies," Rudy said.

"I'm not shocked," Andrew answered, knowing that wasn't quite the truth.

Virginia said, "You need to keep your edges trimmed also. Choosing something from the menu of a health-food restaurant is too easy. Make up your own menu."

"Talking in riddles!" Rudy said.

"Perhaps you're right." Andrew remembered the full-throated strength in Virginia's song the night he and Juanita Ellison had gone to his house. He wondered if she was guessing, or if, despite her exhaustion, she had watched them from her darkened window, wondered what she might have felt—envy, approval, vicarious pleasure, nostalgia for some assignation of her own half a century ago?—as he and Juanita, whom he hadn't seen since, had passed through the gate.

He turned the plaster nude in his hands. The young woman's russet hair was cut in the style of another age, pageboy he thought it might be called, an age when Virginia herself might have worn her hair cut like that, might have posed, gladly, for a statue like that. The figure was not in the plump classical mold, not like the girl with the water pitcher in the yard, but taller, brittler, greyhound-lean, with reddened lips and rouged cheeks; she was running, coming down on her left foot, her right kicked back, running toward the sunrise of the universe, Andrew thought, freedom, beauty; her outflung arms raised and tautened her breasts; her slender torso drew the eye to the juncture of her thighs, then back to her arms and outward, to what they welcomed, what they would embrace.

Andrew said, "I still have one more 'but' to—"

The telephone rang, and Rudy handed it to Virginia. "Donald!" she began.

She waved an unmistakable farewell to Andrew, and for good measure Rudy escorted him out of the room. Although his exit was more congenial than Reverend Marlatt's, it was no less final. As he saw himself and Rudy passing the full-length mirrors of the hallway and dining room, it occurred to Andrew to be outraged, or at least indignant, that whatever he had meant to say—he wasn't sure it would have been a farewell address, since he still wasn't sure he believed Rudy, just as he hadn't believed Rudy's story about the highway patrolman and the chewing gum—that whatever he had meant to say had been so unceremoniously cut off.

"All ready," Rudy whispered, grinning as he let Andrew out of the house. "The timetable is in order."

They were standing on the porch under the trellises. Andrew turned to answer him, the back and thighs of the statuette silky in his hand. He could think of nothing to say.

10

When the Corwins returned from the university the following afternoon, Clara Lunsford and Mindy Solomon met them in their driveway with the news that Virginia was dead.

"She did it as she said she would, with Rudy's help." Grimly, Clara pointed westward in the general direction of El Paso, two hundred miles away. "He left for El Paso at six o'clock this morning on the bus, and she did it about three o'clock. But they may catch him yet; the sheriff has found out his flight isn't until six. Apparently Virginia got impatient and didn't wait to take the poison as long as she was supposed to."

"Poison?" Barbara gripped Andrew's arm.

"He left cyanide in that little burro hanging from the chandelier, in the packsaddles," Mindy said.

"Potassium cyanide," Clara added importantly. "Virginia left a note saying she arranged it all herself, but the police think she had to have help."

"How's Concepción?" Barbara asked.

"She's very upset, naturally," Mindy said, "but even more so because she argued with Virginia this morning. Apparently she became suspicious when Rudy left so suddenly. She believes that Virginia took the cyanide because she was angry at her."

"Oh, that's not right," Barbara said.

"Of course not," Mindy agreed. "We told her. She was talking to Virginia. Virginia sent her to the carport for something—a diary, I think—and when she came back Virginia was gasping for breath."

Clara said, "Dr. Paddock was there within ten minutes, but it was too late."

"So she couldn't have suffered much," Barbara said.

"Not very long, that's certain."

Frank Lunsford joined them, shaking his head. "The sheriff just got a call from El Paso. Rudy pulled a fast one. Instead of going to the El Paso airport he crossed straight into Juarez about one o'clock and caught a plane right out. He must've suspected Virginia would jump the gun. He's probably in Colombia by now."

That evening the Corwins had wine and fruitcake with the Lunsfords, Solomons, Paddocks, Cantus, Lawrence Coke, and Buster Broyles in Virginia's dining room. They were there at Concepción's insistence—she was acting on Virginia's orders, Barbara said—and at Mindy Solomon's also.

"We're under orders to drink the last of her Del Rio port," Mindy said.

The police had questioned Concepción, the Lunsfords, the Solomons, and Dr. Paddock, who had instantly recognized the bitter almond smell of cyanide. Not one but two notes from Virginia had been found, in both of which she said she had carried the poison with her for years in anticipation of the time she would need it, and no one else was in any way responsible for what she had done. Her will, however, named Rudy as the beneficiary, after a sum of money and a trust fund had been arranged for Concepción, and so the police wanted to talk to Rudy. But it was clear that he was gone and had no intention of returning.

As Andrew and Barbara left, Concepción clung to each of them, crying steadily. The Solomons were to spend the night with her.

• • • •

"Well," Andrew said as he emerged from the bathroom after his shower, buttoning his pajamas, "At least that's one thing Rudy didn't bungle."

Barbara was sitting on the edge of the bed, her hands clasped in her lap. She said without looking up, "Maybe he had some help."

"Some help?" Andrew continued getting ready for bed silently, a queer flutter in his stomach. He brought his bathrobe from the bathroom, then took it back. He kicked off his bedroom slippers, put them on again, and sat on the far corner of the bed.

"She insisted on a fresh batch," Barbara said.

Andrew held his breath, released it. "And you had it in the lab."

"Of course." She had not moved. "I even put it in capsules. She didn't trust Rudy."

"How did you arrange it with him?"

"I called after we talked to Rudy that morning. Actually, I talked to Virginia, not Rudy."

"That's why you didn't go over there yesterday," Andrew said. "You'd already taken the cyanide to Rudy, so you had to stay clear."

"Yes."

Andrew went over the notes for his lecture the next morning, then switched off his reading lamp. Barbara read the *Smithsonian* for another half hour before she turned out her light. She pulled the covers up and lay with her back to Andrew.

Andrew asked, "Why did you do it?"

"Because she wanted it done, and because I loved her."

"Why didn't you tell me?"

"Because you loved her too. If that makes any sense."

"What did she say to you?"

"She said thank you. That's all."

After another long silence, Andrew said, "We're not very much alike, are we?"

"No, we're not," Barbara answered.

During the night the shaking of the bed awoke Andrew, and for more than an hour he listened to Barbara's nearly silent weeping. And envied her.

• • • •

After some difficulties, the Lunsfords and Solomons arranged for Virginia's body to be sent to San Angelo for cremation. Meanwhile, Concepción and the Cantus had many telephone conversations with Rudy, some of them heated on Concepción's and Rudy's parts, regarding what Concepción could or could not have of Virginia's possessions. A week after Virginia's death, her ashes were returned. By then the Cantus had driven Concepción and a veritable truckload of her trunks and boxes to the El Paso Airport, and they had seen her off to Colombia. After Concepción's departure, the Solomons and Lunsfords called Andrew and Barbara to come over and take some memento of Virginia's from the house. Andrew refused, saying he had the Heidelberg Venus, but Barbara returned carrying half a dozen of Virginia's heavy wineglasses.

"I suppose she owed you something," Andrew said.

"We can have the champagne glasses too, after they're used at the overlook," she said.

On a chilly evening in late January, half a dozen cars parked at Comanche Overlook, and Andrew, clad in a parka and heavy wool pants, found himself once again opening bottles of champagne. A brisk wind was blowing out of the northwest, and Gerald Solomon noted that Virginia would have been displeased, since her ashes would probably be carried up out of the canyon.

"I suppose you can't have everything," he said, and Buster Broyles agreed. Mindy Solomon read a Chinese poem which she said had been Virginia's favorite, and then Clara Lunsford opened the white stone bottle containing Virginia's ashes and swirled it over the railing.

"*Salud!*" Frank Lunsford shouted. "Remember, Virginia said no tears!"

"Sometimes she asked too much," Barbara said.

They watched the gray ash quickly disperse, much of it sailing upward as Gerald had predicted. In the silence after it disappeared, Barbara, her face flushed from the wine and the cold air, held out her glass to Andrew. When he had refilled it she held it high at the railing and said, "To Virginia! A good life!"

"A good life!" Mindy and Clara echoed.

Barbara drank off the glass. She turned to look at the others. Her eyes found Andrew, and she smiled at him. Her face was wet with tears. "A good life!" she said again, and she threw the glass into the canyon.

Mindy and Clara hesitated a moment, surprised, then followed suit, and one after another, the rest threw their glasses also. Andrew too hesitated, watching the others at the railing but not seeing them, thinking of their pride in their possession of Virginia in some formless but real sense, and that was part of her uniqueness, you could possess her and yet accept that she belonged to others also. Remembering Rudy's gossip about how many lovers she had had, he thought, I hope she did; I hope she had as many as he said, and more, and I hope their pleasure and her pleasure was great. And then he hurled his glass far out over the canyon.

A few days later, Rudy called Andrew from Bogotá. "What am I to do with that bloody house?" he asked. "I dare not return there to take care of it. Do you want to buy it? I will sell it to you more cheaply than anyone else."

"Sorry," Andrew said. "But I'll help you list it with a real estate agent, if you like."

"At the moment I don't like," Rudy said. "Perhaps later."

. . . .

In early February Barbara accepted Professor Huizinger's offer of another fellowship for the summer. Two weeks after that she told Andrew she was going to take the job in Miami that fall.

"You should find a decent place to live this time, if you're going to stay," he said carefully.

"Yes, I should," she answered just as carefully, and they said no more.

At dinner one evening in March, just as Andrew had been thinking that a year ago Concepción had been coaxing a few early blooms on her roses, Barbara said abruptly, "Should we sell the house? Or do you want to buy my share?"

"Sell it, I suppose," Andrew replied, surprised not at the question but that he—and perhaps Barbara too—had kept the idea submerged for so long. They went to a lawyer, Laura Spoolman, to set the machinery in motion for a divorce. She told them they would have to live apart for sixty days. That seemed inconvenient to both Andrew and Barbara, so they agreed to wait until sometime after Barbara had gone to Florida.

On their way home, Andrew said, "Here's another marriage Virginia broke up."

Barbara said, "She didn't change anything; actually, she probably slowed up the process. She made me think more about my options. Options and risks."

"That sounds like a textbook, or a stockbroker," Andrew said.

"It does, doesn't it? What's a better way to put it?"

He said, "That was a stupid remark I made. She didn't break us up. You had already found yourself when she came along. And I was already stuck."

"You're not stuck here. I think you could—"

"In myself I mean. Sleepwalking."

"That's true." She sounded surprised. "You have been for a long time. That's why you're not even angry about us."

They listed the house, but there were no buyers. By mid-April the spring weather had become summery, and as he set his tomato plants Andrew glanced more than once at the brown grass that remained brown inside the pink wall next door; it had neither rained nor snowed that winter, and spring was always dry in Cabora. Occasionally he pushed the hose over the wall and let the water run around the sycamore, for he was sure it would die otherwise.

In mid-May Barbara left by car for Florida. One of her colleagues in Miami had found an unfurnished apartment for her, and she took some furniture with her—her desk, a favorite armchair, and the guest room bedroom set—in a U-Haul trailer. Andrew flew to Philadelphia for a week and returned. Next door, he noted, the honeysuckle was holding its own, although it was mottled yellow. The roses had never bloomed; a bit of green was showing under the brown grass, but the dandelions were all that was really alive. The satyr had been overturned, probably by children running through the yard.

A few days before the first summer sessions started, Andrew tried to call Juanita Ellison, but he got a "disconnected" message. The restaurant, he discovered, was closed, and had been closed, he was told at his office, for several months. The same agent who was handling his house had placed a "For Sale" sign on the front steps.

Near the end of June a buyer suddenly took the Corwins' house.

"One of those things that happen here sometimes," the pleased agent told Andrew over the telephone. "They're retired, they've got the cash, and you've got what they want. Are you ready to settle?"

"Settle it," Andrew said, and he didn't realize until that evening as he was absent-mindedly tending the tomato plants he would not harvest that he had to find a place to move to, and quickly.

When the solution appeared, its seeming inevitability startled him so much that he almost rejected the idea. He was watering his tomatoes. He glanced over at the satyr in the dead grass under the sycamore, and remembered wondering how Concepción felt about, or if she ever thought of, the transience, the futility of coaxing forth that spot of green and life, her employer Virginia's little interlude that would soon be brown and dead again. A sudden belligerence at the whole idea, the trivial notion of transience flew over him, and then, through no physical change or opening of gates that he could remember, he had set the gray satyr upright and washed it off, he was watering the brown grass. At nightfall he went back to the house and began trying to call Rudy; at eleven o'clock he reached him, and within sixty seconds they had settled on the monthly rent.

"You will find her diaries and a photocopy of her autobiography in that large box she kept beside her during her last days," Rudy said. "They are under the manila folders. You have my permission to read them if you wish. Perhaps you will write a book about her."

"I'm not a writer."

"Nevertheless, you may read them if you so desire."

• • • •

Two weeks later Barbara called from Miami. "I received this huge check in the mail today," she said in a pleased voice. "Are you sure it's all mine? I've never had so much in my life."

"It's your share," Andrew said.

"What should I do with it?"

"Whatever you want. Buy a Porsche. Put it in a CD. By the way, do you want me to have Laura Spoolman file our divorce papers now? We have our sixty days in."

"Oh. I don't know. What do you think?"

"I'm in no hurry."

"Then let's wait," she said. "So what are you going to do? How long do you have before the new owners take possession?"

"I've already moved out. And taken my telephone with me, obviously."

"Are you in an apartment?"

"I'm living in a pink house with a pink wall around it and statues in the yard."

"My god. I should have guessed."

"The grass is greening up again. The first water bill will bankrupt me when it comes in."

She was silent for a moment. Finally she said, "Have you turned it into a shrine?"

Andrew was sitting in the adobe room Virginia had built for her friend Dorothy. It was always cool, he had discovered; cool, he wondered as he thought about Barbara's question, like a grave? He had arranged the carport as his study and used it daily, but he had scarcely entered Virginia's and Concepción's bedrooms. Someone had set the large wooden box containing Virginia's files on the canopy bed. Beneath the folders, now layered with dust, would be neatly packed books, one a larger manuscript, thick, which would be Virginia's autobiography. On the cover of each of the smaller books, in crisp characters, would be printed, "Diary of Virginia Stone, M. D.; 19— to 19—."

He said, "Not a shrine, no. And you didn't have to say that."

"Sorry." After a silence, she said, "So what's the gossip at school? I suppose they're saying I'm insane for walking out of a tenured job."

"Probably. This is West Texas, you know; I'd be the last to hear."

"Speaking of insanity. I may not be in Miami this fall. I have a chance to work in a fantastic experimental lab in Frankfurt. In Germany."

"Germany? Fat lot of good your Spanish will do you there."

"I'll manage."

He said, "Yes, I suppose so. Virginia would have been pleased."

"Odd that you say that," Barbara answered. "I was just thinking, if there's any serious shrine-building going on, I'm doing it."

"I understand." Andrew remembered—and was guiltily relieved—that he hadn't mentioned inviting over the Lunsfords, Solomons, Cantus, and Paddocks that Friday night. Four bottles of white wine were already chilled in the refrigerator, and there was a bottle of port on the kitchen counter.

He said, "Out of curiosity, and to consider your movements from another view, are you trying to get as far away from me as you can?"

"Not at all. It's just where the opportunity is."

"One of the good options you learned to think about."

"Yes." After a moment Barbara said, "You know, you have enough from selling the house to take off for a year, or even two if you skimped a little. Why don't you? Maybe you'll find you have a book to write—"

"Come to Frankfurt and write it?"

"Maybe, maybe not. Why limit yourself? Maybe you'll find you have a life to live."

Andrew thought about John Canuteson and Maury
Harper sneering over a poster announcing travel grants to
Third World countries a few days earlier. Canuteson had
said, "I'll stick to Colorado, thanks just the same." Andrew wondered if the poster was still up.

"I might experience resurrection," he said.

"You might."

· · · ·

He had placed the little Heidelberg Venus on a shelf by
the patio door. Her arms flung out, she welcomed something approaching, something vast and good—or perhaps
simply unknown and unpredictable—descending from the
ceiling of the adobe room. In the hallway, the mirrors that
reflected and re-reflected many versions of him as he
passed were scattering shafts of orange light from the
evening sun. He paused at the door to Virginia's room and
stared at the large wooden box on her bed. Most people
wanted to coast, Barbara had said, to be safe.

And what was wrong with that?

Everything, she would answer.

Virginia's diaries and her autobiography were in the box,
he supposed. They could teach him, but would he learn?
Virginia's ghost was not in her bedroom, in this house.
Barbara was right once again: she was more likely to en-
counter it in Frankfurt. He closed the door to the bedroom
and went outside.

A half-moon rose like a serving of cottage cheese over
the mountain to the east of Cabora. It would be a gibbous
moon by Friday, Andrew thought, remembering Virginia's
flirtatious argument with Dr. Paddock.

He had meant to water the grass. Instead he stood by
the gate with its arch and looked at the pink house within
its pink walls. As darkness grayed the walls, he thought of
the notion he'd once had about Virginia's pink walls being
her surrogate flesh, and shook his head.

He had also meant to turn the nozzle onto the patio and

its white lawn furniture to wash away the layer of dust. Instead he sat down in one of the chairs and drew his finger along the fine gray coating of dust on the arm. It reminded him of the gray ash Clara Lunsford had flung into the air at Comanche Overlook. Suddenly the need to wash the dust away pulled at him so strongly that he shuddered. He gripped the arms of the chair until the urgency passed. Then, from nowhere, grief came upon him. He bent in the chair and wept, shaking as Barbara had in their bed.

Night fell, the desert chill settled in, and still he wept. Finally he sat up and wiped his dusty hands on his pants. Then he arose and went into the house to call the Solomons, the Lunsfords, and the others to tell them the party was off.

9 | » The Other Pond

W HEN the fish stopped biting, Gramps said he had some chores to do at the barn before we went back to town. Then Dad pointed at the ridge that started above Ed's Pond and said, "We could walk across on the ridge and meet Gramps at the road when he's finished." We thought Mom would say no, but she didn't.

Liz and I just looked at each other like Now what? We all—Liz was fourteen, Denny was nine, and I was in the middle, getting blamed for everything—we all used to groan when Mom drove around the mall three times just to park closer to Dillard's. She walked all the time, but she'd say, "I don't like the idea of walking just to get somewhere." Dad said that didn't make any sense. I didn't think so either.

"Say, that's a good idea," Gramps said. He liked anything that kept us on the farm a little longer.

"Let's go!" Denny yelled.

Liz and I just looked at each other. We still knew pretty much what the other was thinking, even though we'd stopped talking much, except to fight, after she got in junior high and started living on the telephone. We'd wondered Now what? yesterday too, when Mom gave in to Dad about coming out to Haskins to Granny and Gramps' with us. Last night she'd sat over on the couch reading one of her economics books while the rest of us played Monopoly. She'd got a job teaching a class at the college that spring, and she was all the time studying for it, or her courses. You'd think she would want to play Monopoly, if she studied economics. Denny kept asking her to play even after the game had started and she couldn't, unless we started over. He's always doing that, trying to get her to play catch with him and Dad, or Dad to help them put sprinkles on something in the kitchen. Some dumb thing.

Then Mom said she would go fishing with us at the farm, and Liz and I wondered again. I heard Dad say once when they were arguing that Mom used to like the farm, but if she did it was before I could remember, or even Liz. I thought maybe she'd rather go to the farm than talk to Granny. Granny talks a lot about clubs and relatives but not about things Mom's interested in.

So we got up before daylight, and Mom drank coffee while Granny fed the rest of us eggs and sausage. Liz drank coffee too, showing off.

"Let's take Gramps' pickup," I said after breakfast. "Liz and Denny and I can ride in the back."

"Yeh!" Denny said.

"No. That's too dangerous. We'll go in the van," Mom said.

"Can we, please?" Liz leaned against Dad, blinked her eyes, and pulled *please* out like you stretch a balloon.

"Your mother's right," Dad said, and hunched his shoulders. Once at a football game I got this funny feeling like I saw somebody I ought to know. What it was, was the players in the huddle did that like Dad—hunched their shoulders—to straighten their pads.

"The point is not that I'm right," Mom said. "The point is I said no."

"We never get to do nothing." Denny started snuffling.

"Whinny-whiny Denny," I sang.

"Bud." Dad tapped me on the shoulder. We knew we

couldn't ride in the back of the pickup, and Liz didn't even want to, but you need a no to get a yes later. It evens out.

The sun was up by the time we got to the farm and drove back into the pasture to Ed's Pond. That was Dad's name, Ed, but it wasn't really his pond; Gramps and Granny just called it that because he always fished there.

Denny and I started casting our Zebcos right away before Dad got his float harness rigged up. I started on the left side of the pier, where it was too mossy to fish, and Denny tagged along behind me.

"I'm taking this side," I said.

"It's my side."

"I was here first."

"You tangled my line up with Liz's so you could beat me." He started snuffling again.

"Bud, let him have that side," Dad said. It worked every time.

I wanted to tell Denny how I'd faked him out, but I just whispered, "The snapping turtles'll bite your weenie off."

Gramps took his cane pole to the deep water by the dam. He used grasshoppers for bait. Liz had on her swimsuit and was casting from the end of the pier. It wasn't really a pier, just a few planks Dad and Gramps had put on some poles.

After it warmed up a little Mom put on her bathing suit and read in a lawn chair beside the van. Sometimes she looked out over her sunglasses when Denny yelled at Dad to see if there were any turtles around him. Dad had killed a big snapping turtle at the pond once. Its jaws were smooth, and Dad said it could take a three-cornered bite out of a fish clean as you could cut it with a knife. It had a tail like an alligator's.

Liz fished for half an hour, then hauled out her sunbathing stuff—her towel with the Coors ad on it, her sunglasses, lotions, jam box and tapes, and a can of Coke— and lugged them to the pier. She was a real pain. She used the phone so much Dad said his clients couldn't call at night, so he put in a phone just for her. Then sometimes she'd use both phones at once.

"Dad," she called, "tell the boys to fish at the other end with Gramps. I want to take my top off."

"No."

"Moth–er! Please tell Dad—"

"No," Mom said.

"Oh, *God!*" Liz groaned. Then she flopped down and started smearing suntan gunk all over herself.

As I passed the pier to get a drink, I said, "You wouldn't go topless if you were the only one for a million miles."

She turned the big mirrors of her sunglasses toward me and showed her teeth. "Gretchen and I sunbathed totally nude last Saturday."

"You liar," I said.

She kept smiling. I hated that about older kids. They'd tell you something, and you were pretty sure it was a lie, but they knew you weren't quite sure. Like when Liz told me Mom had told Misty Carpenter's mother she was going to make Dad move out. I said I was going to ask Mom, but Liz said, "If you do I'll never tell you anything again as long as I live, and I know something about Dad, too." So I didn't, but I still thought she was lying. And she didn't tell me what she knew about Dad, either.

"How come you came out here, if you're just going to read?" I asked Mom at the van. "You could read in San Antonio."

"Can't I be with you without doing everything you do?" She put her book in her lap. "Come let me give you a hug."

She just did that to embarrass me, but I let her put her arm around me. I said, "You don't usually come to Haskins, let alone the farm."

"You're a suspicious lot, aren't you? I wonder why?" She took off her sunglasses and watched me. I looked

away, trying to spot a killdeer screeching down at the
pond.

"How come you came out here?" I asked again. "How
come you came to Haskins?"

"For old times' sake, Buddy," she said. She squeezed me
and let me go. "How's that?"

"Whose old times' sake?"

She put her glasses back on and picked up her book.
"Go fish now. Did you know I love you?"

Dad waded out of the water twice to get a drink at the
van, which meant he wasn't serious about fishing. When he
comes to fish he fishes. I could tell he was talking to Mom,
and maybe she was answering, but she didn't look up from
her book. He'd stand there and then hunch his shoulders
and go back in the water. We kids always thought Dad
was good-looking. He'd played football in college, and
with pads on he must've looked like Mr. America. He was
an insurance agent and dressed in sharp suits just like the
newspaper ads.

We didn't think about Mom like that. Once I heard her
tell her friend Glenda Storrs, that she rides to college with,
"I'm a cheerleader who didn't realize she had brains till she
was thirty-five." That really surprised me, the cheerleader
part I mean.

About mid-morning, after Mom moved back into the
van out of the sun, Gramps shouted at Dad, "I believe
they've stopped biting."

"I'm ready to quit," Dad said. He had four good bass on
his stringer, and I'd caught two small ones. Gramps had
caught some perch. Denny was sulking at the van; after
he'd lost two spinners in the moss, Dad wouldn't give him
any more.

That's when Dad suggested our hike, and everybody, out
of surprise because Mom had said okay, agreed to it. Even
Liz, who thinks she's too good to do anything with the rest
of us.

"You should wear your jeans," Mom told Liz.

"Naturally, just when the sun gets perfect," Liz said. She looked at Dad. He didn't say anything, which she decided meant she didn't have to wear them.

"Take your time," Gramps told us as he started the van. Denny was already halfway up the ridge. "I've got quite a few chores to do."

"Maybe we'll see a rattlesnake!" Denny said when we caught up with him. He grabbed both Mom and Dad's hands and walked between them.

Dad said to Mom, "Glad to have another hiker." They pulled loose from Denny at the same time.

"It's better than sitting in the van while Gramps feeds his cows."

Liz remembered that the grass on the farm was full of chiggers, and she started griping that she'd have red spots all over her legs.

"Walk on the cowpaths, and don't brush against the grass," Dad told her.

Denny and I were zigzagging from one side of the ridge to the other, looking for arrowheads. A cottontail jumped up right at our feet, and a buzzard swooped up over the ridge. It was so close we could see its raw red head.

Dad pointed at a tree with a twisted trunk. "That cedar isn't any taller now than it was thirty years ago. I remember—"

"You know every square foot of the farm. I've heard that," Mom said.

"If I have chiggers next Friday, I'm not going to Gretchen's party," Liz said.

I ran back and fell on my knees. "Oh please come to our party, Liz! Even if you're covered with gobs of green pus!"

She gave me a shove. "Nobody would ask you to a party."

"Bud." Dad pointed at me. It's always me. He said, "I

restocked the Canyon Pond up here after that big rain three or four years ago."

"Where's the Canyon Pond, Dad?" Denny asked.

"Straight ahead. It's the deepest pond on the farm."

"I want to see it. Can we see it?"

"Can't miss it."

Down to our right a little farther on, in a canyon that cut into the ridge, we saw a small clear pond without a single ripple on it, even though there was a breeze up on the ridge. There wasn't any mud around it, like most ponds; the grass ran right to the water. The dam was lined with green willows that leaned over the water, and there was a huge cottonwood at the upper end. The breeze was ruffling its leaves, and you could see them reflected in the water. They looked like big green snowflakes. There was moss around the edge of the pond, like a black hedge someone had planted.

"It's lovely," Mom said. The way she said it made Liz and me look at her. She was standing on the edge of the ridge, her hand on Denny's shoulder, and smiling—I mean like happy smiling, not just smiling the way people do. But sad too. It was a funny time for me to think this, because I wanted to run down to the pond, but for a second she was beautiful, to me. She was wearing jeans, but she hadn't put on a shirt over her swimsuit, so except for the straps her shoulders were bare, and they were square and graceful-like, and her face was healthy looking, like she'd just scrubbed with soap and water, even though we'd been at the farm all morning. She had some wrinkles, but it was a nice face, and she had eyes that looked like she knew things that were important to know.

Denny said, "How come you're crying, Mom?"

"I'm not crying," she answered, but she brushed under her eyes with her thumb.

Our eyes met for just a flicker that said Now what?

again. Dad had been looking at the pond all that time too, but he was frowning. A bass jumped clear out of the water down there, a really big one, you could tell that from where we were. It rolled and shone in the sunlight like a big tin can and landed with a tremendous splash.

Dad grinned. "Told you I'd stocked it."

"Let's swim in it," Mom said.

"All *right*!" Denny yelled, and he want scrambling and falling down the slope through the brush and the bunch-grass.

"Denny, you wait for us. That pond is deep," Dad called.

I was going to beat Denny down to the pond, but then I remembered something. I stopped and looked at Mom. "You can't swim."

"Of course I can. Why do you say that?"

I felt stupid. "Because I've never seen you."

"That's ridiculous. You certainly have."

"No he hasn't," Liz said. "I haven't either."

Dad was looking at Mom too now. She began, "Oh, that's impossible—" and stopped. Her face was red. Then she said as she started climbing down, "Well, I can, anyway, and I want to swim here."

Denny would have beaten me into the pond except he tried to pull his jeans off over his shoes wrong side out and got stuck in them. I ran up beside him, kicked off my shoes, took off my jeans, and said, "Last one in the water."

"My god, check the size of them," Dad said. Big bass were swimming right up to the edge to look at us. The bottom of the pond was brown, and the bass looked thick and black from above until they turned and the sunlight caught them, and then they were bright green above the black stripe along their sides, like colored tinfoil, and silvery white below.

"They're curious," Mom said.

"How come they're not afraid of us?" Liz asked. She waded into the water slowly, watching the fish. That surprised me too; she'd stopped swimming—I mean really swimming—about the time she started worrying about a tan. All she did was lie around hoping boys were looking at her.

"Because nobody's fished here," Dad answered. "But that doesn't make any sense. People fish here all the time." He was looking around like he couldn't figure something out.

"It doesn't look deep to me," Mom said. I was in the pond and diving by then. It was barely cool, just about perfect. It was like a little golden world, so different all at once I was almost scared. Underwater the moss was green, not black, brighter green than any grass. The bottom was covered with brown and yellow leaves from the cottonwood and willows. I floated up for air and dived again. A big bass swam toward me, slow but steady. Its mouth was closed tight, like a bulldog's. I was a little scared, but I kept my arms at my sides, and it came right up to me until I felt, and heard it too, the hard edge of its mouth scrape against my nose like a file. Then it turned away.

I shot up out of the water, yelling, "I bumped noses with one! I bumped noses!"

"So did I!" Denny said. I didn't even think to call him a liar.

"They're so tame you can practically pet them," Mom said. She waded in until the water was up to her chest— that was as deep as it got—and turned around real slow, watching the fish. Her arms were long and green-gold in the water. The fish circled her and even brushed against her legs.

Denny yelled, "Will the snapping turtles bite me, Dad?"

"There aren't any turtles here."

I followed a little channel to the shallow end. Some bass swam right along with me. There as a big low limb on the cottonwood, and I tried diving from it but smacked into the mud. The bass swam away in a hurry when I did that. Then I tried the steep bank at the end of the dam. It worked better, and Denny and I began diving from it.

Mom and Liz swam underwater too, and they came up blowing water and laughing, their hair tight around their heads. Mom even let Dad lift her half out of the water once, holding her at the waist, and her hands were on his. Then Liz started doing cannonballs with Denny and me from the high bank.

Pretty soon—I hadn't noticed it happening—the whole pond was muddied up so we couldn't see the fish any more. Mom got out and stood in the sun to dry before she put her jeans on. Dad climbed up on the dam and walked from one end to the other, looking at the sides of the canyon. Liz stopped diving and went over to stand by Mom, but Denny and I kept jumping off the steep bank till Dad called us.

"Those fish are living on borrowed time," Dad said when we were back on the ridge and Liz, was who slapping at deer flies, had finished griping about chiggers again, and mud in her hair; "That pond will dry up this summer."

"I thought you said it was deep," Mom said.

"I don't see how it could silt in that much. Don't remember all those trees, either."

A little farther on Dad stopped and pointed off the ridge to our right. At first all I saw was a thick line of sumac bushes growing across another canyon. "*There's* the Canyon Pond," he said.

It was a lot bigger, with steep sides. You could tell it was deep.

"I stocked the wrong pond," Dad said. "That's why—"

"Oh, please," Mom said. She laughed, kind of, and started walking again. Liz looked at her funny and hurried to catch up.

"What?" Dad asked. When Mom didn't answer, he said to Denny and me, "That's why the fish weren't afraid of us. I'll bet Gramps doesn't know that other pond is there. Even the cattle don't know it is; they haven't muddied up the edge."

After we caught up with Mom and Liz, Denny said, "Dad! Let's take our rods back and catch those big bass."

"No," Mom said.

Dad kept his eyes on the ground and said, "Might as well, after the water clears. When the pond dries up this summer the coons will get them."

I elbowed Liz. "Even you could catch one, they're so dumb."

"Gunch." She stuck her nose in the air.

"They're not dumb." Mom bent to touch one of those dark-red little flowers that were shaped like thimbles, what Gramps called a buffalo rose. "They're special."

"They're fish," Dad said.

"They're in a state of innocence. If that makes any sense to you," Mom said. She went real red-faced all of a sudden, like she'd said more than she meant to but wasn't taking it back.

On the way back to town, Gramps said the other pond had been dug before Dad was born.

"Soil Conservation people made a mistake," he said. "It's been dry for forty years, but the rains the last three years must have been enough to keep the fish alive. I'd forgotten about it."

"They're not just alive," Dad said. He was driving and Gramps was in the other front seat of the van. "The big ones will go six pounds."

"Fish in new water," Mom said.

"What?" Dad glanced in the rearview mirror. Denny had flopped in Dad's float-tube and was dozing off. I had my nose in a comic book, and Liz was rubbing on stuff for chiggers.

"Fish in new water," Mom answered. "They're supposed to grow faster." Dad hunched his shoulders.

After lunch Gramps and Dad took naps, and when they woke up we played dominoes while Mom read some more. Then we didn't talk much about going back to the pond, we just got ready to do it. Dad said the water would be clear by evening, and if we sneaked up real easy just before dark we might catch the big ones before they figured out what was happening. I got mad when Liz said she was going. She was just doing it because they'd be easy to catch, and she could brag on it. Then Mom said she was going too, and that she wanted a rod and reel.

"Why not?" She smiled at Dad in a way you don't smile back to and said, "They're just fish. We might as will sack 'em up." Liz rolled her eyes at me like Who knows?

Denny spoiled it all when we got to the pond. Dad drove the van along the ridge part of the way, and then we walked. Denny and I were ahead of the others, but I was going to wait to sneak up, like Dad said. But when Denny saw the water, he ran ahead waving his rod, ready to cast. So I ran too and caught up with him where the path went between clumps of skunkbrush, and I hipped him into the brush. I reached the pond first, Denny crying and yelling behind me, but I cast too hard and my spinner went into one of the willow branches over the water. By the time I shook it loose Denny had cast his line, and he got one just like that. It wasn't big, but Denny was so excited he forgot to crank his reel and just backed away from the water, yelling, until he pulled it out.

Liz ran up on the high bank we had dived from, and she—she's always dumb lucky—hooked a big one on her first cast. It went clear across the pond with the line hissing through the water, then jumped way up in the air. Liz's rod bent double, and the drag on her reel sounded like a chicken squawking. She started screaming, so Gramps dropped his pole—he hadn't even baited up yet—and grabbed her line, but that was a mistake because the bass could run against it solid then, and the line went *twang!* and broke.

"Goddammit to hell!" Liz yelled. Gramps was so surprised he just stood there with the slack line in his hand. Dad and I both hooked big ones then. He pulled his in right away, but mine went into some moss in the shallow water. I was sure he was still hooked, but I couldn't get him out.

"Don't muddy the water!" Dad said when he saw me taking off my jeans.

"I've got a big one caught in the moss," I said. He didn't answer, so I waded in. The water hadn't really cleared up from that morning, and a muddy cloud swirled around me. I followed my line to the moss, reeling to keep it tight the way Dad had taught me. Where the line went underwater, I felt along it into the moss as far as I could. The water seemed a lot colder than that morning, maybe because it was almost dark. The moss was black now instead of green. It stung my arm, like it had needles or maybe bugs in it.

I could feel the fish jerking down in the moss, so I closed my eyes and ducked underwater to reach farther. Denny was yelling, Liz was swearing because no one would fix her line, and Dad was telling her to shut up. I heard all that, but underwater I could hear other things too, kind of low drum sounds, and the moss was in my face, and stinging. The jerking on the line felt strong as I got closer. I edged forward and reached out, but still not far enough. The jerking got stronger, and then I felt something hard like the shell of a big turtle, and I jumped back.

I stood up for air. Dad had said there weren't any turtles, but I didn't know if I believed him. Gramps had said the pond had been dry, and now there were fish and moss, but Dad had said the coons would kill the fish, and I thought, How can they be so sure of things if they didn't even know the pond was here? In the moss and muddy water there could be anything. I ducked under again, but I couldn't make my hand go down the line. I backed away toward the bank, shivering and ashamed. Nobody was watching me, so I jerked the rod hard and broke the line. Then the fish stopped biting. The pond had muddied up a lot worse than in the morning. Gramps and Liz hadn't caught anything. Dad's big one was barely four pounds, not six. He had caught another one about like Denny's.

Gramps said, "Sorry I let your fish get away, Lizzie."

"It doesn't matter," Liz said, but you could tell she was still mad.

We all must have thought about Mom at the same time. She was sitting up the slope a ways from the pond, her rod and reel on the ground beside her. She hadn't even cast it once. She was bent over, hugging her knees, and all at once I shivered again, because she was crying. Not so you could hear, but crying anyway.

"Sarah, there's no need of that." Dad had strung Denny's bass with his, and he was still carrying the stringer. He went over to put his arm around Mom, kind of awkward because his hands were wet and smelling of fish.

Mom stood up and moved away from him. She pointed at the stringer and said, "Wasn't it a lovely pond?"

We stared at the bass. Fish on a stringer never look like they do in the water. Just glazed-eyed and dying looking. Gramps shuffled his feet and cleared his throat. Liz was scratching her ankles, but she was listening close.

Denny took the stringer from Dad and held out the fish to Mom. He said, "You want to carry them?"

She backed away and said, more like she was talking to herself than to Dad, "We must have a knack for ruining ponds."

She started up the slope toward the van. Dad hunched his shoulders, and then just slumped. Liz and I looked at each other, and what we were thinking instead of Now

what? was We know what. But really we didn't. At least I
didn't. Liz climbed after Mom. I looked at Dad and then at
them. It was lighter up on the ridge and I could see the van
clearly, but all at once everything seemed dark everywhere,
darker than the black moss down in the muddy pond, and
full of jaws as sharp as knives.

10 | »
Duty
and the
Civic Beast

THE girl appeared several days in a row
between the CPA Building and Skeen's Cafe-
teria before Jerry Weaver became aware of
her. This happened just after LaVonne had
asked for maternity leave beginning March 1. Her family
additions always coincided with the tax rush. Jerry was
scowling along, shoulders hunched, head and pipe thrust
forward, seeing nothing, not even—having walked the
same route to lunch several thousand times—not even the
acquaintances he spoke to. Scowling along when something—the girl's hips filling and emptying space in a vigor-
ous bump and grind, or the clinging black skirt and inordi-
nate splashes of lipstick and eye shadow—something finally
snapped her into focus, and he saw precariously high heels,
a lavender, un-office-like blouse, earrings tiered like wedding cakes, flaring orange-reddish hair, so *much* he saw—
and then, clearly meant for him, a smile.

Jerry managed three steps before he turned to stare at
the . . . *wriggle* of her, writhing from heels to flaming hair.

She looked back at him and smirked.

What was that song? "I was looking back to see—?" He
hummed, couldn't remember. Wednesday was tomato aspic
day at Skeen's, but for once his stomach didn't somersault
as he passed it. He glanced at the cottage cheese, took pork
chops instead; lunged at a wedge of lemon pie drifted high
with meringue; then he passed the long table where he usu-

ally sat with the other CPAs and went to a table by the window in case she came back by. Thinking, *I could hire her.*

She wouldn't understand depreciation schedules. But neither did LaVonne. Closing his eyes, he saw her, breasts quarter-mooned over a typewriter. Slit skirt. A. J. Mac-Dowell ogling from the hallway.

Anyway, she was gone. For a moment Jerry felt that universal male ache for all the ripe, ready girls who have wriggled on around the corner. Then he ate his meringue.

She was there Thursday, and again on Friday, when he fiddled with his pipe until he saw her coming.

"Hello," Jerry said. His chest thudded.

"Hello," she smirked. An extra wave billowed through the black skirt, the lavender blouse. Her lips glistened.

On Monday she didn't appear.

He waited half an hour, enduring the gibes of his building mates.

"Heavy date?" Roy Cranston of Cranston and Murphy.

"I'm ready now, sweetheart." A. J. MacDowell, of Walter and Sons.

And so on.

The baked potatoes were finished at Skeen's. He took cottage cheese, lime Jell-O, iced tea. And there she was at the table by the window.

"Mind if I join you?" he asked, sitting down. "You work around here, I guess."

"No." She took a cigarette from a gold-colored case and waited. He fumbled in his pockets, found to his surprise a matchbook, and, as he held the match, felt the edges of her nails, nearly the same color as her blouse, steadying his hand. He was acutely aware of the men finishing lunch at the long table. The colored bits of her earrings shivered like the Jell-O.

Her name was Violet Riley, and she had—he decided later, although she certainly had not said so—some kind of

secretarial experience. At any rate, he offered her a job for
two months starting on the first, the following Monday.
She could at least answer the telephone and tell clients to
have a seat, and, after all, that was about all LaVonne did.

She accepted.

How disguise the spring in the step, lilt in the whistle?
Jerry was sure Midge would sense something—the way he
slapped the cards down and kidded Mary Beth at the
Bloodgoods Thursday night, took off with a juvenile squeal
of the Electra's tires, breezed through his side-straddle-
hops. She seemed not to notice anything.

On Friday morning LaVonne, folding her arms over her
swollen bosom, asked if he had found someone to fill in.
He had.

"Isn't she coming in to be shown around before I
leave?"

"Won't be necessary."

He met her again at Skeen's, his neck and the horseshoe
of baldness above it burning from the stares at the long
table. He liked the way she gazed out the window, chin on
palm, cigarette poised, a little smile-smirk playing that said,
"I know what you're thinking." Crunching an ice cube, he
wondered how George Crane or A. J. would face up to
that, and grinned. Scared to death.

"Are you married?" he asked.

"Divorced."

Her eyes were green. He shifted, accidentally moved his
knee against hers. "You're pretty young to be divorced."

"How old do you think I am?"

"Ahh—twenty-four, five?"

"Twenty."

I have children older than that, he did not say.

She had a child, a son. Her mother—on social security—
kept him. Something about unpaid child support, going to
court. Jerry frowned sternly. His knee was snugly against
hers. His eyes smarted from her perfume; it reminded him

of heat waves on a summer road, of the wild optimism coursing his veins one night at a carnival, decades ago.

His colleagues caught up with him Saturday at the golf course.

"What *is* that you cornered?" Roy Cranston said. "You're too old for that kind of thing."

Jerry whipped the cart over a narrow bridge and fishtailed to a stop. "Needed a fill-in for LaVonne. She's got some experience."

"Experience," A. J. said. "That's pretty clear, all right."

Roy sighed as he set his tee. "Old tomcat's at it again."

On Monday Violet was there promptly at eight, breasts quarter-mooned over the typewriter, slit skirt. She looked uncertainly at the keyboard. Patting her shoulder, Jerry said, "The main thing is to answer the phone and keep people from barging into my office." He explained which callers were to be put straight through—George Crane or anyone else from Barberry Oil Company, Allen Hosinger at Pace Realty, some oil-lease dealers, a couple of big farmers—and that the income tax rush would keep him, and her, in the office at lunchtime. And about night work. To all of which she smiled that knowing smile that made him feel his collar was aglow, smiled again at his encircling arm the first time he called her to his desk.

There were a few comments.

"Fine specimen," George Crane said, closing Jerry's office door.

"Pretty efficient."

"Could tell the way she was filing her fingernails."

Jerry grinned. The heat of his collar warmed his shoulder blades.

And when Ray Stark put the suitcase full of his year's records on Jerry's desk, he growled, "It must be tough, being an accountant."

"Hazards of the profession," Jerry sighed.

They had lunch on the divan in Jerry's office, scattering

Whataburgers or Church's chicken and biscuits on the coffee table. Wednesday Violet went to court about child support and was late, but when she came she set a radio by her typewriter, and at noon Jerry's knee twitched to rock music while he pulled apart a quarter of fried chicken.

On Thursday morning he told Midge he'd have to skip the Bloodgoods. That night, while he compiled Ray Stark's Schedule A, Violet played the radio at her desk, smoking, chewing bubble gum. She had brought an old typewriter manual, and she pecked sporadically at the keyboard.

When Jerry took her home, he pulled her over in the car seat and kissed her, enjoying the waxiness of her lipstick, the heavy aura of her perfume, her passivity; but when his hand began to travel, she opened the door, twisted out, and hurried across the patchy grass to where a light gleamed above a concrete step.

He had showered by the time Midge got home.

"How was it?" he asked. Shirley MacDowell, A. J.'s wife, had taken his place.

"Good."

"I got Stark's Dairy ready to go," he said.

Midge adjusted the study lamp on her side of the bed and opened a book. She was taking a history course by correspondence. "Mary Beth bids better when you're not there trying to play footsie with her."

Monday he worked late on the Barberry production records. After an hour or so, he took two beers from the office refrigerator, called Violet in to join him, and that night she said, "Don't" in a this-is-not-nice voice that took him back to his teenage days, as did the ache in his groin when he gave up and drove her home, and he felt so good he ran a red light, got a ticket, and had to talk fast to get out of a Breathalyzer test. On Wednesday night he brought a bottle of rosé and made no pretense of work. She became a little tipsy. She said she had not graduated from high school; pregnancy and marriage had stopped that. She had a boyfriend, Bryan Suddeth, an assistant manager at a small store in Southside Mall.

"What about you?" she asked.

"What?" Jerry grinned. His feet were crossed on the coffee table, his hand at the nape of her neck, leaning her toward him. He heard someone else working late, maybe A. J., call a goodnight down the hallway.

"Why don't you stay home and drink with your wife?"

"Druther be here." He refilled her paper cup.

She turned the music up. "Why?"

Jerry snapped his fingers, his pipe bobbing in time. "Why? I don't know. Maybe I love you."

She smirked and emptied her cup. "That's a joke." Then, so suddenly Jerry was astonished, there were no more don'ts.

The boys were rough on him Saturday morning.

"Look at you," A. J. said; "bags in the bags under your eyes."

"Somebody else partner him," George Crane said. "I don't want to carry his clubs."

"It's carrying him I'm worried about," Roy Cranston grumbled.

To which Jerry retorted, "You girls want to play golf or chitchat?"

At lunch he said, "Got to go back and work on Barney Diehl's return. Maybe get it out this weekend."

"Aren't you running later than usual?" Midge asked.

"Got a girl taking LaVonne's place. Take some time for her to—"

"So I heard," Midge said.

At the office he slept soundly on the divan for three hours, got up stiffly, made coffee, and dug into Barney Diehl's complicated travel expenses. He worked steadily until after eight o'clock, but then he began to remember odd things about Violet that pleased him—her leaving her earrings on with their tinkling circles of pink, green, and blue glass; the surprising slackness of her flesh, less resilient than Midge's; afterwards the nonchalant bubble blown from her carefully preserved gum. He dialed her number.

She was out, her mother said. Wouldn't be back until late. A child shouted in the background.

Jerry tasted the bile of jealousy. Where, he wondered, did they go, her and her little assistant manager? To a movie? Dark little nightclub somewhere—he saw her earrings flash as she leaned over the table, smirking, and shut that off. What kind of car did he drive? A ten-year-old Mustang; a beat-up Plymouth.

He worked until midnight, finishing Barney's Form 2106 and Schedules E and F. At home he found ham, cheese, and potato chips, and was into his third sandwich when Midge, in robe and gown, padded in from the den.

"What are you doing up?" he asked, startled.

She sat down at the bar, pushing the chips away. "Something good on channel thirteen,"

He opened another beer and picked up his pipe. "Finish Barney Diehl tomorrow, for sure." He was glad Midge was up to observe: no lingering perfume, no lipstick smudges, just a tired accountant with a clear conscience.

"That pipe has, over the years, deformed your face."

"You've told me that before. At least I don't smoke it."

"Which makes it even more unreasonable. Gerald and Robby called. Gerald has some extra lab fees. Robby has to get something taken care of on the car. Something about the steering."

"Maybe I should go back to school," Jerry said. "Have the whole family in college."

Midge smiled and stood up. "I don't think school could stand the shock. I'm going to bed." She was tall, graceful; she made no attempt to hide the gray hair over her forehead. She had, A. J. and Roy often told him, gotten better-looking over the years. Probably they were right.

During the night they were awakened by the howl,

growl, baby's cry—all of that in its thick, mournful lust—
of a cat under their window.

"Damn it," Midge said, and when Jerry tugged half-
heartedly at her hip, "Oh, go to sleep." His mind wandered. He thought about Barney Diehl's shaky Schedule A
deductions. About cats. What was it Roy Cranston said a
veterinarian had told him about cats?—"It's barbed . . .
species survival insurance . . . ?" The cat yowled again,
around the patio. Jerry wondered where Violet was.

When the Spurs had lost Sunday afternoon, he went to
the office and called Violet. She said after an exchange of
muffled voices, "Someone will bring me." He lurked for
three-quarters of an hour in the lobby, half-hidden by a
pillar, before a car stopped at the curb, an Electra the same
model as his and almost the same color, and Violet, in
jeans and a gray jacket, got out. Jerry let her in, locked the
door behind her, and as soon as they were out of sight in
the hallway, kissed her fiercely.

"Not now—"

"Now." Afterwards he fell back on the divan, panting.
She covered herself with her jacket and watched him, her
head on the armrest.

"Well," he said, "have a good time last night?"

She tucked her legs under the jacket. "Are you jealous?
Why should you be jealous when you have a wife at
home?"

He went to the refrigerator, thinking it was the first time
he'd ever walked across his office in only his stocking feet.
If A. J. or Roy—! He wished Violet had left the jacket on
the floor.

"Just a civil question." He set two beers on the coffee
table.

"Yes, I had a good time."

"What'd you do?" Her hair seemed softer; it was drawn
back in a ponytail. And something else—what?

"Went dancing." She smiled sleepily. "We danced for hours."

No makeup, he realized. "You go to bed with him?"

"It's none of your business, is it? Why should I tell you?"

"We can tell each other things like that," Jerry said. "That's what we're supposed to be able to do. Why not? You want to know the last time Midge and I made love? I'll tell you. A week ago last night. Last Saturday night. You go to bed with him?"

"Yes."

He tipped his can up and drank. Her face seemed less pale without all the eye gunk, lipstick, and rouge. *Wholesome* crossed his mind. He asked, "How was it?"

She smiled, derision pulling at the corner of her mouth. "Perfect."

Crumpling his beer can, he snatched her jacket away with a harsh, thick snarl, wanting to impale himself like a weapon upon her. "Perfect. Aren't you lucky."

It was dark when he drove her home, the window open to the cold air, his arm on the sill. He felt good, the good drained feeling. He covered her hand on the seat and said, "We're two of a kind, you and I."

She pulled away. "No, Jerry. We're not anything alike at all."

"Sure we are. We—"

"No!" she said, and he lost the thread of what he was going to say.

He stayed late every night that week, keeping Violet back Tuesday and Thursday, but working until after nine before he called her in. As he opened a beer on Thursday night, she held out a neatly typed 1040 form for Arch Winstead, an oil-lease buyer. Jerry had penciled it in the day before.

"It looks good," he nodded, frowning; "looks just fine."

She held it up to the light. "You can only see where I made mistakes in two places."

Jerry sank down on the divan. "Get the radio."

At home he collapsed in bed without showering, and when he awoke to Midge's call for breakfast the smell of Violet's perfume was strong on him and the bedsheets. He folded the covers back, hoping they would air out, showered quickly before Midge could stop him, and went in apprehensively to cold eggs.

"We're going out tonight," Midge said.

"Can't. Got to—"

"Tonight you can. You forget every year. George's birthday."

So they went to the Shrubbery with the Cranes, Jerry suggesting Whataburger instead, and Ruth Crane telling him he'd said that every March twenty-sixth for the last fifteen years. They had a bottle of champagne and then another, and just before or after Ruth had viciously spiked his ankle he noticed through the ferns a young couple, the man in a dark blazer, woman in a dark suit with ruffled blouse, dining quietly at a table for two under a jade plant. Something familiar—he couldn't place them.

"I'm fagged out," Jerry said wearily while Midge and Ruth were gone to the little girls' room.

"How're you coming on those Garfield totals?" George asked.

"A little behind, but you'll get them; this burning the candle—"

"We need them by the middle of the week," George said. Then he began grumbling about the Spurs' inability to fast-break.

The golfers took up the complaint the next morning, and no one seemed to notice that Jerry didn't insist on driving the cart. George mentioned the Garfield totals again, and Allen Hosinger asked if he had worked up some depreciation schedules for Pace Realty.

"I'm fagged out—" Jerry began.

"We need them Thursday," Allen said.

Midge was pulling the sheets from the bed when he got home. He saw a lipstick smudge on one of his shirts in the laundry basket and fancied he could still smell the perfumed sheet.

"Going back this afternoon?" Midge asked, setting grilled cheese sandwiches on the table.

"Got to."

"Why don't you take a nap first? The bed here's better than that divan. You'll get some real rest."

"Who says I'm going to take a nap?"

"Oh, come on, Jerry," Midge smiled, but he jammed his pipe in his mouth and drove to the office, where he looked longingly at the divan, then plunged into Barberry's Garfield file.

At seven o'clock he called Violet. She was going out, but she agreed to come in Sunday afternoon. He went home to find a note on the bar: "Casserole in the oven. Gone to Town & Gown with Shirley and A. J. He's not so dedicated."

When he picked Violet up Sunday, she asked, "Did you like your ribs?"

"What?" She was wearing, he noted with satisfaction, the low, wide-necked blouse in which he had first seen her.

"Friday night at the Shrubbery. We were straight across from you. You kept looking right at us."

The dark blazer. He glanced at the blouse, at her hair, fluffed nearly pink in the afternoon sun, tried to fit her face with the dark-suited woman's severe bun. He grinned, shook his head, and reached in the top of her blouse. "You don't give him much of a view, do you? First time you've been there?"

"No, but Bryan says we're not going back. Too many loud drunks."

"Drunks? There?"

"Yes. You."

She typed slowly but accurately, Jerry noted, on Pace Realty's depreciation schedules. When he was nearly finished with the Garfield file, he asked for more ledger sheets from the storage cabinet.

"What's this?" she asked, holding up a paperback. "*Carnal Capers?*"

"Got it in an airport," Jerry said. "Something to read."

She put it back. "It's filth."

"Not much different between that and us."

"They shouldn't print things like that."

They were on the divan later when A. J. called from the outer office.

"Jesus!" Jerry grabbed his shirt; "didn't you lock that door?"

She backed behind the storage cabinet. "You shut it."

"Jerry! Wake up!" A. J. shouted.

"Coming! Just a minute." Jerry swore, trying to keep his balance.

When Jerry put his head through the narrowly opened door, A. J. said, "We're out of Schedule Cs. You got any to spare?"

"Just a minute," Jerry mumbled. The radio was booming; Violet had dropped a shoe in plain sight of the doorway; Jerry's shirt was buttoned wrong, tail out on one side. He turned off the radio, got the forms from the cabinet, and handed them out to A. J.

"Many thanks," A. J. said. "Hell of a time to run out."

"Yeah," said Jerry, "hell of a—" But A. J. was gone.

"This is ridiculous." Violet retrieved her shoe.

Jerry watched her pull her skirt around straight. He began to laugh.

"Jeez, did we panic!"

"There's nothing funny about it."

"Look at my damned shirt." He sat down and laughed

in shrill locker-room hoots till he had to wipe the tears away. "Never live it down."

The next morning he and A. J. parked at the same time.

"Hell of a note," Jerry said, grinning; "your timing—"

"I don't know what's going on with those Schedule Cs," A. J. said. "There aren't any more in town. You better hang on to what you have."

"Hell of a note," Jerry began again, but Roy Cranston drove up, and A. J. turned back to ask him about Schedule Cs.

On Thursday night he again fell into bed reeking of Violet's perfume, but at breakfast all Midge said was, "Don't forget about the dinner-dance on the twelfth. We're hosts, with the Cranes and the MacDowells."

"What do I have to do?" Jerry muttered.

"Just be there. I know it's a bad time. Are you going to have to ask for an extension for anybody?"

"I don't know. I know I can't do everything."

"That's true. Nobody can do everything."

On Sunday Violet let him bring her to the office, but she pushed his hand away in the car. "Bryan and I are getting married next month," she said. "They're going to make him manager."

Jerry gunned past a pickup. "That mean you're quitting?"

"I'll work until after the fifteenth. *Work*."

Her hair, dully auburn, was brushed down flatly. She wasn't wearing earrings, and she had on almost no makeup.

"What's the difference?" Jerry asked. "Between you and me. What difference does it make if you're getting married?"

"I don't need you now. The child support is coming, too. That's the difference."

The girl in the chase, the tawdry lure, gartered, writhing,

ready-thighed—and forever slipping away, unmarked, seemingly untouched. Jerry parked in the CPA lot, his arms heavy, the power steering sluggish. "So where does this leave me?"

"Where you've always been."

He looked at her tightly buttoned blouse, colorless lips: so prim, so . . . ordinary. He shouted, "No! You've changed!"

"Nothing has changed," Violet said. "I'm the same. You're the same. You'll always be the same. We all do what we have to."

That night he confessed his infidelity to Midge.

"She pulled herself in front of me like a spinner in front of a bass, I guess," he said.

Midge smiled. "You're not a bass, Jerry; you're a cat-fish."

"That's not so," he said futilely.

"Why are you telling me? Do you want a divorce?"

"Well, no; of course I don't. I just—"

"Robby called," she said. "The car needs a new muf-fler."

They were late getting to the dinner-dance Saturday night, but the Cranstons and the MacDowells had every-thing under control and were ensconced at the bar.

A. J. slapped Jerry on the back. "You look like your best hound dog died."

"Cheer him up, A. J.," Midge said as she left to check the place names. "Please. He's been pulling that long face all week. He thinks he's not appreciated."

"Sit down and tell me your symptoms." A. J. pushed a beer to Jerry as he eased onto a broad, padded bar stool next to Ruth Crane.

"Nothing much," Jerry said. "Sometimes you get to feel-ing worthless. Like what have I done? What am I doing?"

A. J. said, "What the hell are you talking about? Every-body knows you and Midge keep us going. You give a hundred and ten percent. I don't see how you do it. So what the hell are you talking about?"

Ruth was wearing chorus-girl hose, patterned in huge black diamonds. Her foot rested on the bar railing a few inches from his.

A. J. lowered his voice. "You old tomcat. Damned music banging away, shirt buttoned wrong, shirttail half out; I'll bet your pants were on backwards, too."

They exchanged rueful looks and shook with silent, belly-deep laughter. Jerry's shoe duck-walked along the railing toward Ruth's. "Well," he grumbled, "somebody's got to do it."

Ground
Rules

IVA was talking about her relatives back in
Kansas, mixing childhood memories with
present comedy and misfortune. Wesley uh-
huhhed at the proper intervals. Sometimes
she laughed, her fingers touching her blouse above her
faintly defined breasts. Her good strong laugh, infectious;
but a disconcerting high note along its edge made Wesley
think of hysteria.

"Gary always got the Free Parking money," Iva said.
"And Boardwalk and Park Place, naturally. I even hated
his token. The tall beige one. He would lie there reading a
comic book and acting bored. We all had our favorite to-
kens. If I landed on Boardwalk after he put a hotel on it
I'd shriek at the top of my lungs while he took my money.
I was sure that was how my life would be. Now he's just
been fired as a stocker at Safeway, and he has five kids and
they're on food stamps."

Wesley asked, "Want to split a beer?" This was ritual:
their Friday hike down the riverwalk to the deli, his al-
ways-broken promise not to order corned beef, their
careful maneuvering to get the corner table with obsceni-
ties carved in its top; Iva's excursions (much embroidered,
Wesley thought) into her childhood.

"You'll get us fired." This too was ritual, the pretended
shared danger, the conspiracy. Haskell-Fisher's manage-
ment was legendary for its puritanism, but by mid-morning

Fridays the various Powers were on their way to the Gulf or the lakes. There was no danger.

Iva shifted from relatives to her upstairs neighbor, who, she was sure, was making nuisance calls to her. "I count his steps from the kitchen door. One two three four. I know where his phone is. Pause. Five seconds. My phone rings."

One small matter regarding Iva tugged absurdly at Wesley's conscience, a bit of blabbing at the airport six years ago. Absurdly, but he was a fastidious man. They had gone through Haskell-Fisher's tough training program together, and when they finished, the survivors—nineteen of thirty—threw a party, crowding into Ed Archer's trailer. Most of them were living in by-the-week efficiencies, but Ed had a big trailer. Wesley called Barbara in Denver, told her they were in the money and headed for Chicago. Then he went to the party. He had been stalking Linda Gammage, trim, calculating, the acknowledged star of the group, and she seemed receptive. But she got a phone call and left without a backward glance. He found himself dancing with Iva, both of them high, and later, at his suggestion, they were in one of the bedrooms of the trailer, Wesley caressing the low swelling of Iva's breasts, Iva talking, talking about a Michael who wanted to marry her, but he worshipped his three lovely children, and perhaps he would go back to his wife because of the children, even though their relationship—his and Iva's—was, physically and every other way, perfect, the most perfect thing possible. She gripped Wesley's hands fiercely when they went beyond the Free Zone. The other celebrants left. Ed burst through the door, drunk, and ripped his shirt open, growling, ready to join the orgy, while Iva laughed and screamed and held her blouse to herself. Wesley convinced Ed that a threesome was not wanted and got him out of the bedroom.

And that was all. But as they left the trailer, rearranged and nearly sober, Iva said to Wesley, "We didn't do anything, did we? We didn't do what you wanted to at all, did we?"

He had complained about that to Ed over beer in the airport bar two days later while they waited for the plane that would take Ed to Kansas City and Wesley to Chicago. Wesley made no false claims of conquest; he was too exacting for that. It was Iva's triumphant assertion that smarted.

"What did she win?" he asked. "Nothing. There was no contest. I know when I'm too drunk to get laid."

"Huh, huh," Ed rumbled. Wesley did not tell him he had called Iva the next afternoon, suggesting a more private celebration. He had gotten her out of the shower, she said; she was freezing. Michael had called; maybe he wouldn't go back to his wife. She turned Wesley down.

Six years later, Wesley still regretted his remarks to Ed. No whining, no gloating: one loses privately and wins the same way. He tipped the shared beer glass and finished it, alerted by an altered note in Iva's voice. Her eyes roved over the big glass jars on the display case, the customers leaving the deli. Wesley looked at her long arms and face, her squarish jaw, short brown hair. Before that night in Ed's trailer, he had scarcely noticed her, other than her tall awkwardness, her tendency to laugh too loudly too easily. A spinster, he thought, waiting for a spinster's body, waiting for the thickening that leaves waist, hip, and torso stern and undelineated. She had been one of the marginal ones, like Ed Archer. A year ago, however, she had landed back in Haskell-Fisher's headquarters, two promotions behind Wesley. Ed had been fired long ago in Kansas City. Linda Gammage had quit, formed her own company, and was a millionaire, Wesley had heard, or bankrupt.

Iva was in Chatterjee's section down the hall. Wesley had his own section. She had walked into his office one morning, her laugh still too loud, had shaken his hand and invited him to lunch. With good timing: after the division chief's briefing of section heads, after the section conferences, before Wesley had settled down to his computer screen and telephone. Openly, briskly. Wesley had approved. She knew Haskell-Fisher.

From that their Friday lunches had evolved. Or rather from Ed's trailer, from an hour of thwarted groping, his chivalry in removing Ed, her imagined victory, even from her shivering refusal the next afternoon, which, Wesley suspected, she also regarded as a victory. A conspiracy. He had told her, when she asked, that Barbara did not know about their lunches and had never heard of her. Neither statement was true.

"I talked to my old graduate school friend last night," Iva said. "Carol. The one who knows someone who knows Michael."

"Um."

"He's still living with his wife. But they have trouble all the time."

A legacy of Ed's trailer also. The continuing saga of Michael. Wesley asked, "Would you go back to him?"

"No. Not now." She traced the rude letters in the table, then looked up at him. "Do you want to split another beer? Is anything happening in your office that another beer would mess up?"

"Nothing."

When Wesley returned with the beer, Iva was dabbing at her eyes with a tissue. She said, "Do you remember that I didn't come back on time from my vacation? I'll tell you why. I went to St. Louis and stayed a week with Carol and George. George started kidding me a lot. He never used to. I mean so handsy Carol got mad at him."

At the edge of her voice, Wesley caught the flutter of hysteria that went with her laugh. Her face had reddened, and her eyes had a watery brightness. She spilled a little beer as she set the glass down. "The morning I left, he took me to the airport as he went to work. On the way, he turned off an a side road and parked and raped me."

Wesley opened his mouth and closed it. She had pushed herself back in the chair. Her arms were straight and stiff, her hands gripping the table edge, her voice breathless.

"He just pushed me down in the seat. I scratched his face. I kept saying, 'What about Carol?' but he just did it. He didn't say anything. Afterwards he stopped at the departure gate and said, 'Get out.' Three hours later I was meeting my mother at the airport in Wichita."

"Jesus. The son of a bitch," Wesley said. Anger thickened in him, and perplexity; he tried to imagine a cramped car seat, her long legs and torso, and failed. He watched her tensed fingers, remembering their fanatic strength in Ed's trailer. "He must be big, this George."

She shook her head. "No. His face was bloody. I wonder what he told Carol that night? But she's never said a word about it."

"You didn't tell her?"

"How do you tell your best friend her husband raped you? I thought she would know from the scratches. I thought she would call me that night in Wichita, but she didn't. She called after a month, and we just started writing and calling again as usual."

"I'm sorry," Wesley said.

"This is the first time I've said anything about it to anyone. I watched TV around the clock at Mother's. She thought I was sick. I was. Do you know how long it's been? Eight months." She breathed deeply, released her grip on the table, and moved her chair closer. "Can we drink another beer? Oh: do you know what I did after he drove off? I screamed. Standing there with my bags by the automatic doors."

Wesley pushed away from the table, incredulous at the idea of her screaming. "What happened then?"

"People just walked around me. A policeman took me inside. I wonder why I didn't before? George parked close to some houses. When he did it I mean. Why didn't I scream then?"

Wesley stroked her hand. "You can't figure stress reactions." He was in control now, had in place her story of the struggle in the car, her defeat, his hatred for this George, his anger at her.

Iva smiled. "Can we have another beer? I'm beginning to relax. Eight months is a long time to keep something like that locked up."

Wesley looked at his watch and frowned. "Pushing our luck a little. If we hurry."

"Let's do."

As he poured the beer, she said, "I'm feeling so *good.* I'm feeling *crazy.*" Her cheeks were flushed again.

"Crazy?"

"Maybe I won't go back this afternoon." Her eyes, still bright with wetness, followed his. "Maybe I'll just go home and take a nap."

Their lunches were a simple thing. They always met down on the street, swinging into step. She hadn't been in his office in a month; even then no more than a minute. Their calls—"Can you make it? Yes, no?"—lasted fifteen, twenty seconds. She knew Haskell-Fisher. Victory, Wesley thought, desire and satisfaction surging in him, feeds on patience. And defeat on its own image, its own story. And suppose the story were true, even the screaming? After all, she'd been on vacation.

Wesley asked, "Would you like for me to join you?"

Her eyes had not left his face. She smiled. "All right."

"I should go back first," he said. "Clear up a few things."

She nodded. "Give me an hour. My apartment's a mess."

There was nothing to do at the office, other than be seen. He knocked on her door fifteen minutes early.

"We said an hour." She was irritated, he saw, or hurt. She had changed into a sort of jumpsuit, shiny, tight-fitting, with a zipper than ran diagonally from shoulder to hip. And glittery earrings, a little tawdry. The apartment was indeed a mess: books scattered on chairs, unwashed dishes, shoes by the television.

"I couldn't wait." He pulled her to him, feeling the flimsy material of the jumpsuit along her back, and kissed her lightly on the lips, kissed her for the first time in six years. "You can't blame me for that."

Iva held him at arm's-length for a moment, then hugged him tightly, her face against his neck. "No, I couldn't blame you for that."

Michael was still with them, Wesley discovered. Iva ruffled his hair and smoothed it, saying, "I've been wanting to do that for a long time. It was the first thing I noticed about Michael." And later, when Wesley nudged her for a caress, "Michael liked that too."

They slept briefly, Iva's long back pressed against him. When he had showered and dressed, she had coffee ready.

"I don't drink it," she said. "I don't know if it's good or not."

"It's terrible." Wesley set the cup down, grimacing, and Iva giggled. He made it back to the office half an hour before quitting time.

On Monday, Wesley got into an argument with Chatterjee during the division chief's briefing. They were still at it when they returned to his office and found Iva waiting, her eyes sparkling with conspiracy. She was half-sitting, half-leaning on the corner of his desk, her long arms bracing her.

Chatterjee paused at the door, but Wesley said, "Come on in." And to Iva, "How's my girl? Would you excuse us, please?" That's all right, Wesley thought as Iva left the office, her face reddening; a minor lapse. He said to Chatterjee, "Where were we?"

Then Iva turned in the doorway and began to scream.

12 | »
A Drive
in the
Country

DAN Springer passed through Foley's and crossed the inner mall. In Penney's a glassware display caught his eye, and he bought a pair of large goblets. He watched from Penney's outside entrance while Helen Lininger parked nearby. When she had moved to the passenger side, he scanned the parking lot. Then he put on his sunglasses, walked quickly to the car, and off they sped toward the expressway, a little breathless, Dan checking the rear-view mirror. He said sternly, "Today we watch the time."

Helen touched his hand on the steering wheel. "What did you buy?"

"Surprise."

Just outside the city, just after they had both sighed audibly, a large Oldsmobile caught up with them, horn honking. Dan stiffened in the seat, sure he would see Bryan Lininger's heavy jaw and black-framed glasses, but when the car drew even he didn't recognize the driver.

Dan looked at Helen. "Do you know him?"

"No." Smiling, she watched the Oldsmobile pull rapidly away, pass a pickup, another car.

Some notion of déjà vu about the gradually climbing highway was worrying Dan. The steep hill ahead confirmed his feeling so positively that he nodded, then checked himself irritably: geologist's eyes, noting unbidden the lay of the land, strata in the highway cuts, even cow-paths in the pastures.

"Let's have a beer." Helen got up on her knees and reached into the back seat.

"Barely nine o'clock." Dan passed his hand down her thigh.

"Look." She turned around, pushing his hand away, and held up a green bottle with bits of ice on it. "Ringnes."

It was sharp and strong, was good. He stretched against the seat and put his dark glasses in his pocket. Then he asked, "Things all right at the house?" *House*: their language. They never said "home," whether they meant his or hers.

"Laurie decided she was sick this morning. Her temperature was normal, so I sent her to school. Allison's dating a boy on the golf team. And yours?"

"Danny's still lobbying for a computer. He's wearing me down."

Dan relaxed even more, now that the obligatory questions which meant "Does Bryan suspect? Does Sandra suspect?" were past.

At the Harper intersection Helen said, "Let's take the river road."

"I thought we were going to Parsons."

"It's not far out of the way, is it?"

If they took the river road they had to make a pilgrimage to their river bend. Dan parked the car under a leaning blackjack oak, and Helen quickly found the path hidden in the wall of tamarack. Dan opened another beer and followed her through the blooming, heavily scented tamarack down to a slough, its surface cracking into curls of drying mud.

"River's been up," Dan said. They went around the mud. When they reached the fine gray sand on the other side, Helen kicked her shoes off. Skirt flying, she ran ahead to a long, silvery log at the water's edge.

"Feel it," she said. "It's silky."

Dan stroked the wood and pressed his thumbnail into its softness. "Cottonwood. Look how smooth the river has worn it."

She put her hand on his as if to keep him from talking and looked across the river at the steep bluffs. He set the beer on the log, and they kissed in the warm morning sun. When they drew apart, he opened her blouse and held her breasts for a moment.

"Let's walk." Helen took his hand. "Why don't you take your shoes off? It's ridiculous to walk in this lovely sand with your shoes on."

"We won't be here that long." Dan tipped up the beer and drank, then handed it to Helen. The heat reflected from the sand and the coldness of the grainy beer spun his head a bit.

Helen took long strides at the river's edge, her tracks filling with water. Dan asked, "How would you have explained it if someone in that car had known us?"

"I was going to Harper and you needed a ride. Why should I have to explain anything?"

This was the first source of his love for her, this idealism, Dan thought, her insistence on her untouchableness, like an undiscovered layer of oil sand, in a vigilant and, after all, very small community. It was also the source of much of his own fear.

Dan heard a car coming on the road. Helen said as they started back, "I read a story in one of Allison's books about a woman and her lover. They say things like 'This Situation Is Impossible' and 'Things Can't Go On Like This.' In capital letters."

Ice wedged under Dan's ribs, the same ice he felt as he entered his house after these outings with Helen. They turned at the log. At the slough Helen put her hand on his shoulder to steady herself while she brushed her feet off and put her shoes on. Dan wasn't sure if the car he had heard had gone on; the blackjacks and tamaracks muffled sounds.

"Did you lock your door?"

"Yes." She walked ahead of him.

"So what are you saying?"

She looked back as she entered the tamaracks. "About what?"

"The story and our situation. Are you saying it can't go on?"

"Oh. So there were steps. The next step was to tell the husband, and after that to get a divorce."

Suddenly a tall boy in shorts appeared on the path ahead of Helen, and she screamed as they bumped into each other. A girl in a bathing suit stopped behind the boy.

"Mrs. Lininger!" the boy said.

"Oh—Gary, is that you? I thought you were in school." Helen pulled her blouse together.

"I got exempt from my finals."

They were all silent. Dan dropped the beer bottle in the tamaracks and put on his glasses.

Helen began to edge past them. "It's beautiful here, isn't it? Do you come here often?"

The boy nodded. "It's nice."

"Nice to see you," Helen said. The girl mumbled agreement, and then they were past each other.

"Christ!" Helen flung herself into the car and slammed the door.

"Who was that?" Dan resisted the urge to gun the car away in a shower of gravel.

"One of Allison's friends."

"Maybe we ought to go back."

"Oh, stop it." Her giggle, and the scorn in it, startled him. She turned to get a beer, scuffing the dash with her muddy shoes.

Her face, Dan saw, was beginning to flush, her nose reddening; a grin tugged at one corner of her mouth. She caressed his thigh under the steering wheel and said, "Tell me about this Parsons."

"I went to junior high and high school there."

"Do you go back often?" she asked.

"No. My parents moved after I graduated. I haven't been back in nine or ten years, except to drive through."

They were silent at the stoplight in Fairfield while a Safeway truck backed up twice before it could negotiate the turn. Dan noted the faces on the sidewalk, glad he had not removed his glasses after they left the river. Helen laughed as they picked up speed again. "My god. Gary Dodson. Can you believe it? A path through the brush, and there he is."

"Do you think it will get back to Allison?"

"Who knows?"

They passed through Eunice, Cedar Springs, and Cheyenne. A few miles beyond Cheyenne, Dan saw a low-gabled, pink-streaked building on a hill ahead of them. He chuckled. "There's Parsons. See that? It's been a dancehall at least three different times, and a church twice."

A sign indicated that it had last been the Pizza Paradise. Dan said as they topped the hill, "It was also a genuine whorehouse for two weeks once, till the churches got wind of it."

"Were you a client?"

"Too young."

Weedy lots along the highway were filled with rusting pipes and oilfield machinery. Dan looked sharply into the rear-view mirror as the car coasted into town, saw nothing. "There was oil play when I lived here. It didn't last long, but there were more bars and more fights. Some pretty rough kids in school."

"Did you work in the oilfield? Is that how you got interested in geology?"

"I roughnecked one summer."

Turning onto the main and only business street of the

town, he pointed at a gray building, its front boarded up. "My first job. Chandler's Feed Store. Used to sneak smokes with Johnny Chandler on the dock out back."

He slowed before a brick building that had been partially demolished. "That was Bink's Supermarket. They lived next door to us. He had a great day when I was a junior. The bank foreclosed on him in the morning, and his wife left him at noon."

Helen said nothing.

"I'll be damned." Dan made a U-turn around a flagless flagpole in the center of an intersection. "See that barbershop? The barber there was convicted of bootlegging. He—"

"Show me where you lived," Helen said.

Turning off the main street, Dan drove up a steep hill past a small, unkempt park. "Kids used to park here if they were short of time and couldn't go to the country."

"You too?" He knew she was watching him closely.

"Well. . . ."

"Oh, don't play coy." She looked out her window. "So is there anything else besides Lover's Lane?"

"Our house." Dan turned right, then stopped abruptly. Trailer houses lined both sides of the street. "What the hell?"

"Are you on the right street?"

He backed the car into the intersection and looked at the frame houses on each side. "Sure. There's Salaskas', the only two-story on the block. There's Martins'. That was my first date. Jennifer Martin." He looked down the side street again. "There were six or eight houses down here. We all had huge back yards. Ours was about where that brown trailer is."

"Darling, I've had enough of Parsons."

On the highway again, Dan said after Helen had opened a beer, "The Grant County park's about fifteen miles from here. It has a little lake. We could have lunch there."

Helen rested her head against his shoulder. "That sounds nice."

The Parsons visit hadn't gone as he'd imagined, but not because of the disappearance of the old house, its replacement by trailer houses. He had assumed, not consciously, but assumed a sharing—no, a giving—of an earlier version of himself when things had more time and room to seem important. A gift to Helen, but she had refused it.

Helen touched his arm. "Strawberries. Let's buy some."

The roadside stand was just a bench with bunches of radishes and asparagus and strawberries in paper bags on it. Four stripped saplings held up a low brush roof. Behind the stand in the shade of some blackjacks was a small trailer house. Chickens clucked in a nearby pen.

"They're beautiful." Helen showed Dan a handful of strawberries. "They're small, not like those huge tasteless ones in the stores."

A short, heavy woman came out of the trailer and walked laboriously to them, smiling and nodding. She was about sixty, Dan thought, her dark hair in a tight bun, forehead discolored, several front teeth missing.

"Allo." She smiled again. "Good. Good. Fifty cents."

Slavic, maybe; Dan couldn't tell. He asked Helen, "One bag?"

"Two. I can take the extra home."

The woman's hands were heavily calloused, fingernails clogged with dirt. Dan gave her a dollar, half expecting a contrite look from Helen for saying *home*.

But she had stepped behind the brush arbor. "Dan, look. Is that her garden?"

Dan saw a stepped mound like a pyramid, its foliage and blooms so bright he squinted. The woman turned to see where Helen was pointing, then smiled even more broadly and broke into her own tongue, motioning them to follow her.

It had been built up layer upon layer, higher than his

head, all sand and flat thick shale, except where things grew, and there it was dark loam. Plants—radishes, tomatoes, corn, carrots, okra he recognized, and more, flowers too, and ferns under the overhanging ledges—seemed to grow everywhere. A maze-like path which reached every plot had been built with the shale, as well as a drainage system.

"Where did she get the shale?" He held up a small piece to the woman. She laughed and pointed down the hill.

"It's beautiful." Helen opened her long arms toward the garden, bent to the older woman, and said slowly, "It is very beautiful."

"She doesn't have running water." Dan picked up one of two large galvanized buckets near the strawberry patch. "She must carry it from a creek." He held up the bucket to her questioningly. She pointed down the hill again, then to a carved, oddly curved stick on the ground.

"What is it?" Dan picked up the stick. Shaking with laughter, the woman took it from him and put it across his shoulders.

"A yoke," Helen said.

"Those are five-gallon buckets. I don't believe it." Dan held them up to the woman. "You?"

"Na, na." She waved at the highway and made a steering motion with her hands.

"Her husband," Helen said.

"I want to try it." Dan picked up the buckets. "Like this?" The woman nodded, speaking rapidly.

"Come on." Dan took Helen's hand. "Let's find the creek."

They half-ran down the path, buckets rattling, the woman's laughter behind them. At the creek they found a pool that had been lined with the shale, which was everywhere in the creekbed. Dan filled the buckets and knelt to get under the yoke.

Helen said, "They're too heavy."

"It's not bad. This thing balances the weight."

He was sweating when he set the buckets down at the garden. The woman said something approvingly, and then she picked up one of the buckets easily and climbed to the top of the garden.

"The shale gutters it," Dan said as she began to pour. "She doesn't waste a drop."

Helen lifted a fern to watch the water flow by and spread into a plot of leaf lettuce. "It's lovely." She turned away abruptly.

The woman followed them to the car and tried to give their dollar back, but they refused. Smiling her missing-toothed smile, she leaned in Helen's window, grasped their hands with her strong rough ones, and joined them. Then she backed away, waving.

"Why did she do that?" Dan asked as the car picked up speed.

"Lovers." Helen brushed off the sand that had fallen from the woman's hands onto her skirt. "She knew."

The lake at the Grant County Park was empty, its bottom a network of enormous cracks.

Dan pointed at a gap in the dam. "They blew it up. See how it's silted in? They can dredge it after it dries out, and it'll be good as new." His voice trailed off; he knew he was trying to disguise his own disappointment as much as smooth over Helen's.

Looking away from the lake bed, Helen brightened. "The trees are huge. Hickories; sycamores. Even pines."

On a circle drive hidden from the main road, they found a table under a massive cottonwood. When Dan unwrapped the goblets, he frowned at their squat, thick stems. "Iced tea glasses."

"Good. Peasant glasses. I hate the mean little wineglasses people use." Helen handed him a bottle of dark red wine and a corkscrew.

She spread a large red bandanna on the table. She had

brought rye bread, butter, a thick slab of Muenster, a summer sausage, radishes. After Dan had cut the heavy, hard-crusted bread—badly—she buttered it while he sliced the cheese and sausage. They ate their clumsy sandwiches leaning back against the concrete table, looking into the woods. An audience of ground squirrels formed, fleeing when Helen tossed bits of bread, returning ever more bravely. Farther away, a red squirrel scolded from a persimmon, and in a clearing a grackle swung his boat-tail importantly.

"Strutting, over-decorated males." Helen drank from the wide bowl of her glass. The wine left small purple arcs at the corners of her mouth.

"Except in humans." Dan had finished his sandwich, and now he drew her to himself lazily, the wine rich on his tongue. The vee between her breasts deepened to a dark line. He lifted her breast to curve the line. "In humans, the female is brightly colored. She's the one who postures and—"

She touched his mouth with her fingers. "Stick to geology." They kissed hungrily, sharing the strong tastes of their food and drink. The grackle's black, puffed chest and pompous tail triggered an image in Dan's mind, some long-ago strutting of his own: a tuxedo—that was the connection, the shiny blackness—and a fraternity dance with Sandra, when he had thought her beautiful, and rightly so, when they were in love. He wondered that his desire for Helen was mingled with regret.

She pulled away. "Do you ever think of Sandra when we do this?"

"No. Do you think of Bryan?" He hoped his lie and the defensive question hadn't come too quickly in his surprise at having his mind read.

She watched him alertly. Her face was deeply flushed with the day's drinking, and Dan realized—he had learned to recognize the moment, but not to anticipate it—that they were on the verge of a quarrel. He touched the wine stain on her lips. "We're close to the Interstate. There's a motel there."

Helen said, "When I came in late the last time, Bryan said he was going to hire a private detective."

Dan bent as coldness lanced across his stomach. "Why didn't you tell me?"

She touched the surface of her wine with her forefinger, then drew it along the lip of her glass, making a small, shrill sound. "You wouldn't have gone today."

Dan asked, "Do you think he would?"

"He was joking. He's too much an egotist."

"Egotist?"

"To think I could be unfaithful to him."

Dan scarcely heard her. Her face swam in his realization of his vulnerability and a sudden conviction that she might be misjudging Bryan, that Bryan's threat had pleased her. The table and the huge cottonwood seemed like parts of a trap, but instead of voicing his fears, he said loudly, "Because he's great—in bed and elsewhere? Is that what he thinks? Or you're saying?"

"No." She stood up. "Let's go to the motel."

A car roared down the main road toward them. As if they were miming themselves, they turned slowly toward the sound. Dan grasped the corner of the table, knocking his glass onto the concrete slab and breaking it. He imagined Bryan's white-knuckled fists on the steering wheel, the lenses of his black-framed glasses opaque between them.

The car hurtled past the entrance to the circle drive, leaving dust to settle on them. They listened until they could no longer hear it.

"God damn it! Scared like naughty children!" Helen threw her glass at the slab by Dan's feet. It missed and landed in the grass without breaking. She picked it up as if to hurl it again, but instead she collapsed against the table in laughter.

"All right." Dan's anger was gone. "It's all right now."

Dan put the pieces of broken glass in a trash barrel while Helen cleared the table. She poured wine in her glass and left it on the bandanna in the center of the clean table.

"For the gods," she said.

At the motel Helen refused to believe Dan had signed in as R. M. Nixon until he flourished the receipt as proof. She drank wine from the bottle, let it trickle from her mouth into his, and said, "Pelicans." And later, pulling a blanket up from the floor to cover the damp sheets, they slept.

Dan's mouth was parched from the wine and the beer when he awoke. He looked quickly at his watch, relaxed. But he tensed with each muffled voice outside, each door closing. He envied Helen's steady breathing.

When he came out of the shower toweling himself, Helen was lying on her side, her hair tousled. Smoothing her hair down, he said, "We're in good time today."

While she showered he dressed and inspected his clothing for stray hairs, peeked outside through the curtains, checked his watch. After the shower stopped, the knob on the bathroom door rattled.

"Dan, I can't open the door."

He tried the knob, pushed. "Hold the knob so it can't turn while you twist the button."

"I did."

He watched the slight movements of the knob, glancing at his watch. The coldness in his stomach pressed up into his chest.

"Damn it," she said. "It turns, but it won't come out."

He tried the knob again, noting the two screws holding the lockset to the door, remembering that he had no screwdriver. He pushed tentatively at the door; if he thrust hard with his shoulder, he wondered, if he smashed the door open? The motel might trace them. He remembered the name he had given, R. M. Nixon, and a false license plate number too. Wasn't that a felony?

"You'd better call someone," Helen said.

"You had to lock it, didn't you?"

"That won't help now."

He twisted savagely on the knob. "God damn it!"

"*Call*."

He stared at the knob, clenching his fists. Then, as he turned to go to the telephone, the door opened and Helen stepped out, glistening with sweat.

"Jesus Christ."

"It just opened." She smiled. "Suddenly it opened."

Dan tried to hide his panting. He kissed her on the forehead. "We'll have to hurry."

The trick was to get back inside the city before the five o'clock traffic slowed them down and unblurred their faces, before the parking lot at the mall filled with people who knew them. Dan put on his sunglasses and checked the time. With luck—and they were due some, he thought—they would make it.

He pressed Helen's hand to his side, needing her warmth. "I love you," he said. Suddenly he knew what the road away from the city and the steep hill had reminded him of: the same hill, the same grade leaving Parsons. He could not separate their images. He thought, *leaving home.*

"I love you too." Helen turned to him. "That woman at the garden. Did you notice her shoes? She had taped the cracks in them. Can't you imagine her in her trailer drinking coffee from a small white cup? Good strong coffee with real cream."

She put her hand on his thigh. "That was perfect when she joined our hands."

Dan remembered the garden's slate guttering, the tiny maze-path. He hunched his shoulders, trying to forget the curved bite of the yoke, trying not to think about what Helen was saying.

She removed her hand from Dan's thigh as the car entered expressway traffic. "Do you want to know what happened in the story? The lovers told the husband, and the woman got a divorce. Then she was snubbed by all their mutual friends, hers and her husband's."

Her color was back to normal, but her eyes were bloodshot. Dan said, "You have a bit of wine stain at the corners of your mouth."

While she rubbed at the stain with her moistened fingers, he asked, "Why are you telling me about this story? You think it will happen to us?"

"No," she said. "You'd be willing to go through that, wouldn't you?"

"Yes." He remembered that he had promised his son a trip to the mall to look at computers, and he couldn't keep the bitterness out of his voice. "Yes, I would."

He felt the grin tugging at the corners of her mouth. After a moment, she said, "My god. Locked in the bathroom."

As he turned the car into the mall parking lot, he said futilely, "That old woman at the garden was ugly as sin."

"Oh, no," she said. Dan flinched under her accusing stare. "We forgot to eat the strawberries."

» Afterword
by
Robert Flynn

I HAD just finished reading Roland Sodowsky's *Interim in the Desert* and was
knee-deep in a discussion of what it meant
to me when I was astonished by a man who
said he didn't want or need stories; all he wanted and
needed was information. Before you snicker, let me hasten
to add that he was a dean, at a prestigious university, of
one of those fundamentalist faculties devoted to virgin-
born information immaculately conceived without
parentage of rude process.

The good dean thought he was arguing for "academic"
information, data that can be passed from the professor's
notebooks to the students' heads so that the students will
be informed. But in order to assimilate and use that information, the students must first have a story. There is no
information about life, life properties or life experiences
without process—"a systematic series of actions directed to
some end." Even algebraic formulas are rudimentary narratives and numbers without stories are shapes without
meaning. It is the process of adding or subtracting or mul-
tiplying—narrative—that gives meaning to what are
otherwise unrelated symbols.

The very definitions give themselves away. Biology—the
science of living matter with reference to origin, growth,
reproduction, structure and so on. Chemistry—the science
that deals with or investigates the composition, properties,

and changes of properties of substances and various elementary forms of matter. Physics—the science that deals with matter and energy in terms of motion and force. The definitions presuppose narrative—a story of events, experiences, or the like, whether true or fictitious.

What could the good dean have been thinking? Perhaps he meant he wanted pristine facts without uncertainty, that hobgoblin of fundamentalists, because stories, particularly fiction, do bring uncertainty and ambiguity. Stories suggest other possible ways of seeing or knowing or relating the information. What are the facts of the birth of Jesus? Or the death of Lincoln? It is impossible to be "informed" about those events without "story," or more exactly, "stories." The more knowledgeable one becomes about the facts, the less certain one is. It may be distressing to an engineer to know that there is more than one way of looking at a bridge.

I think what the dean must have meant was that he didn't want or need any legends or myths or fictions about creation or birth, or death, or reproduction, or changes of properties, or matter and energy in terms of motion and force. "Just the facts, ma'am." As though stories were smoke and facts were stone, whereas exactly the opposite is true. The legends and myths and stories remain and yesterday's facts are today's superstitions.

Another academic said he didn't read fiction because he could make up his own stories. I would suggest that he does and should make up his own stories. He also makes up his own philosophy, religion, physics, history, music and recipes. We personalize experience, turning philosophy into opinion, religion into belief, history into biography, physics into plumbing. But first we study formal philosophy, religion, physics, history, music. We experiment with other recipes. We continually test our philosophy and religion and music against not only prevailing thought but the weight of traditional thinking.

Certainly everyone makes up his own stories, narratives with character and plot. In order for experience to make sense we must give shape and form and pattern to it. We must create our own stories to discover our own identity; to clarify and understand the life processes of birth, growth, reproduction, death, properties and changes of properties; to build our bridges over inarticulate, inchoate, insentient subsistence. Before we can relate experience, or information, to others we must select the pertinent, eliminate the superfluous, and organize it so that it leads to the point we wish to make. The tradition of literature is as ancient and exacting as that of religion, the prevailing thought as pervasive and provocative.

We are born into a story, we live our life learning stories, telling stories, hearing stories, assimilating stories, and our death is a story that survives us. How then can we not need stories? How can we make our stories without studying the history and forms of stories, without testing our stories against the traditional and the contemporary? We read literature not only to define and identify ourselves, our roles, our world, but also to learn how to assimilate our own "life-story" into meaning. The "examined" life requires it.

Not every story is efficacious, however; not every definition is useful. We must continually ask ourselves, "Why this story?" Hawthorne tells us something about love and birth and death and human beings caught up in contradictions that romance fiction cannot. Tolstoy tells us something about war and peace and how individuals deal with the world that confronts them in a way that action fiction does not.

One thing we look for is authenticity, valid information about time and place, community life and individual experience, the customs, traditions, rituals of a people, and the imprint of history, philosophy, and religion on those people both individually and as a community. A good story will clarify our own experience. It will help us sort through and understand our own emotions, our society, the way our world performs. A good story will construct the past selectively, show purposeful communication between individuals, tell us who we are and what life expects of us. It will do more than merely inform, it will touch some moral and spiritual core, enriching us in ways we do not understand.

A good story should also give us new ways of seeing and using our language, of communicating our thoughts. It should alter our world view. It should transform our lives. It should create for us characters who become part of that bridge lifting us out of inchoate subsistence, that cloud of witnesses that shows us how to respond to victory and disaster, to love and disappointment, freedom and bondage, obsession and defamation—characters like Hester Prynne, Captain Ahab, Lemuel Gulliver, Roskolnikov, Don Quixote.

That's why I was reading; that's why I was discussing *Interim in the Desert* with the dean. These stories, these people, these communities are authentic. My family stopped at the "Knox" store on the Saturday trip to town. My parents bought over-priced, gilt-edged and be-ribboned Bibles from neighbors down on their luck, embarrassed both by their own weakness and their neighbor's need. I watched the Orielle Bastemeyers of this world unwittingly accept the honors and favors I could not earn with all my graceless effort. I knelt in the dust and listened to heroes talk about war and death and killing, and thought I had learned what it meant to be a man.

I never really believed Tom Sawyer's fence or that I would paint it, but I believed Nineswander's fence because I have painted it. The stories of adolescents in *Interim in the Desert* allowed me to revisit my youth, to understand some things I wish I had understood then, to laugh at embarrassments I wish I had been able to laugh away at the time.

For that reason the adult stories are more poignant and piquant, more uncertain and ambiguous. I see myself and others not as we were and not as we wish to be, but as we sometimes are, adults stuck in adolescent dreams and failures. I stood with Andrew and Barbara and the others, trying in dutiful ceremony to express grief for a dead friend, and failing to do that any better than we had expressed love while she was alive. With Bud's Mom and Dad I discovered a pond in a state of innocence, and with them I discovered in myself a knack for ruining ponds.

Like Jerry Weaver, I have felt worthless and unappreciated, and I waited with him for someone to express love. The adult stories not only help me clarify my experience and sort through my emotions, but help me to see my failures and to find my way to a more meaningful life.

Those are some of the people, some of the stories, and communities, and fences you find in *Interim in the Desert*. Although each of these stories is an island entire of itself, they are also part of an archipelago, the whole being more than a sum of the parts. The first third of the book is composed of stories of confused adolescents trying to find their way in a baffling and unreliable adult world, of discovering by pain and error the rules of a game they are just beginning to play, of yearning for commitment, the permanence of relationships, friends that will be true forever, love that will endure, communities that will never die.

In "KNOXless" an adolescent boy enters the adult world of faith and deception, of trust and betrayal, and discovers that the heart was not made for such distinctions.

"World War II" is a story of kindness and cruelty, courage and fear, the prosperity that tragedy buys, the glory purchased by blood, and the enigma of what passes as the truth upon which we must frame our lives.

"Talking at a Slant" is a story of confused values in a community where everyone attempts to be better than someone else, inciting malice in children, prejudice in adults, and lack of communication between children and parents. With wonderful indirection the author tells us what parents and children talk about when they talk about sex.

In "On the Wing" a boy turns away from his mother in his effort to find himself in the rough, direct, competitive world of men who do not grumble at discomfort, cry at failure, or cringe before force.

"Orielle Bastemeyer, Where Are You?" is a funny yet deadly serious story of a boy who dreams of love in an indifferent universe and struggles to be something and someone special in a world that saves its rewards for those favored of the gods, those who perform without training or practice, who succeed without effort, who are born with force and accuracy.

In "Nineswander's Fence" an adolescent confronts the confusing values of an adult world where adults still play children's games but are in charge of the rules, and learns something of pride in work and individual expression even when the rules turn that work and expression to the advantage of another.

In "Tearing the House Down" three generations face the impermanence of things that seem so important and eternal, families and communities that fall apart like deserted houses. They come to an accommodation with change and understand the blind instinct that calls them home.

At the center and heart of the book is the novella, "Interim in the Desert." Adults in this work come to terms with the adult world, discovering their own impermanence, the transience of human relationships and institutions, and the immutability of the human spirit.

In the last third of the book, stories show adults still groping for those identities that the young so easily believe their elders have already achieved—what it means to be a man or woman, a husband or wife. They live out, repeat, the same patterns that failed them before, blind to the empty, deserted communities that surround them.

"The Other Pond" is a story of the fragility of innocence and the ease with which we muddy clear water and leave our footprints on untrammeled ponds.

In "Duty and the Civic Beast" the dream of youth for friends that are true and love that lasts forever becomes a nightmare as Jerry Weaver discovers not only his own lack of commitment to relationships, business and community, but that no one really cares about him.

"Ground Rules" is another story of grown-up adolescents who once believed they would someday play by the rules they devised, only to stumble later over the rules they only half comprehend themselves.

In "A Drive in the Country" the story comes full circle as adults wish that little things mattered the way they once did "When things had more time and room to seem important." Futilely they try to recapture that importance in secret languages, passageways, and understandings only to realize they have forgotten to eat the strawberries.

That is another reason we need and want stories. We redefine ourselves in terms of others; we learn to see our world in new ways; we discover other strategies for devising our own stories. Yet the strawberries remain, like a good story, to be enjoyed again and again.